Jessica Sorensen lives in Wyoming with her husband
and three children. She is the author of numerous
romance novels. All of her New Adult novels have
been *New York Times* and ebook bestsellers.

Keep in contact with Jessica:

jessicasorensensblog.blogspot.co.uk
Facebook/Jessica Sorensen
@jessFallenStar

Praise for Jessica Sorensen

The Destiny of Violet & Luke

'Gripping and heartbreaking . . . You will be hooked, and you won't be able to not come back'

ReviewingRomance.com

'Sorensen's intense and realistic stories never cease to amaze me and entice my interest. She is an incredible writer as she captures the raw imperfections of the beautiful and the damned'

TheCelebrityCafe.com

The Redemption of Callie & Kayden

'I couldn't put it down. This was just as dark, beautiful, and compelling as the first [book] . . . Nothing short of amazing . . . Never have I read such emotional characters where everything that has happened to them seems so real'

OhMyShelves.com

'A love story that will overflow your heart with hope. This series is not to be missed'

UndertheCoversBookblog.com

Breaking Nova

'*Breaking Nova* is one of those books that just sticks with you. I was thinking about it when I wasn't reading it, wondering what was going to happen with Nova . . . an all-consuming, heartbreaking story'
BooksLiveForever.com

'Heartbreaking, soul-shattering, touching, and unforgettable . . . Jessica Sorenson is an amazingly talented author'
ABookishEscape.com

The Temptation of Lila & Ethan

'Sorensen has true talent to capture your attention with each word written. She is creatively talented . . . Through the mist of demons that consume the characters' souls she manages to find beauty in their broken lives'
TheCelebrityCafe.com

'An emotional, romantic, and really great contemporary romance . . . Lila and Ethan's story is emotionally raw, devastating, and heart wrenching'
AlwaysYAatHeart.com

The Certainty of
Violet & Luke

JESSICA SORENSEN

sphere

SPHERE

First published in Great Britain in 2015 by Sphere

2 4 6 8 10 9 7 5 3 1

A CIP catalogue record for this book
is available from the British Library.

ISBN 978-0-7515-5882-1

Typeset in Adobe Garamond by
Palimpsest Book Production Limited, Falkirk, Stirlingshire
Printed and bound in Great Britain by Clays Ltd, St Ives plc

Papers used by Sphere are from well-managed forests
and other responsible sources.

MIX
Paper from
responsible sources
FSC® C104740

Sphere
An imprint of
Little, Brown Book Group
100 Victoria Embankment
London EC4Y 0DY

An Hachette UK Company
www.hachette.co.uk
www.littlebrown.co.uk

The Certainty of Violet & Luke

Chapter 1

Violet

Falling.

Falling.

Falling.

I'm falling into obliviousness, unsure where, when, and if I'll ever land – for all I know there may be no bottom. But right now I don't care. Because right now I'm completely and utterly losing my mind. Some might argue that happened quite a long time ago, back when I decided to run out in front of that car for the first time, just so I could calm down and focus on some emotions other than the ones connected to my parents' deaths. Maybe that's an accurate argument. That I did lose it a long time ago and now I'm just going off the deep end even more, falling, falling, falling, with no way of returning. I kind of don't want to at the moment, either. Right now I'm feeling pretty good, which doesn't happen that often, if ever. And lately . . . well, lately things have been crumbling around me.

Take school, something I used to be so good at, but not anymore. A few days ago, I got a call from the school advisor wanting to discuss my attendance, or lack of it. I'd known the call was coming, but it was still a kick in the stomach I still won't acknowledge. 'Violet Hayes, we're concerned about you and your lack of attendance.' The advisor had given me the *look*, the one everyone gives me when they've discovered my gory past and start to pity me. The *look* used to be rare, since I never told anyone about my past, but with the case being reopened, it's being plastered all over the headlines and sometimes the news.

Then there are the calls from Detective Stephner, always loaded with bad news about my parents' murder case and my stalker. It's always the same: 'We haven't found Mira Price'. Mira Price is Luke Price's (my boyfriend's) mother and the woman who was allegedly at my house that night singing that fucked up song. 'And there's still no sign of Danny Huntersonly', the detective always adds. Danny is the man I refer to as Preston, my once foster father who I used to think was the closest thing to a parent I'd ever had. But not only did he encourage me to sell drugs for him in exchange for food and a roof over my head, he also made me do sexual favors for him. I used to believe that I owed him, but now I can see more clearly. Although that clearly isn't much better, it just makes me feel sick about myself and the stuff I did.

Sick.

Sick.

Sick.

Preston might also have had something to do with my parents' murders, but that has yet to be determined. A 'fifty-fifty chance'. Either Preston is a murderer, or some sick freak with an obsession and photos of me from when I was a child, who knew my mother back when she did drugs. However this plays out it's sickening and makes me hate myself for doing the stuff I did with him, stuff I can't erase no matter how much I hurt myself. Nothing can be erased in life. Life is permanent, from the breath we take to the decisions we make. And I've made some pretty shitty ones.

'Are you sure you want to stay?' Luke asks me for the umpteenth time, interrupting my disturbing, depressing thoughts and my drunken dance moves. Music is blaring around me, the bass vibrating the

3

floor, and I have a cup in my hand full of some sort of alcohol, blurry vision, and a numbed soul.

I have to squint just to see Luke's face, even though he's standing right in front of me. Luke is probably the one decision in my life that didn't turn out shitty, but that's coming from my point of view not his. He's the one who has been taking care of me for these last few weeks. Right now, he looks concerned, his worry lines setting in. Despite the permanent frown he's been sporting, though, he still looks deliciously sexy. Short brown hair I could run my fingers through, a scruffy jawline, his lean muscles visible through a grey t-shirt that fits him just right and faded jeans that sit just low enough on his hips that if I lifted up the bottom of his shirt, I'd get an eye full. Hell, maybe I will if he'll let me later. Scratch that. I know he will. Ever since the thing about Preston was revealed, Luke hasn't said no to me, which I'm finding both good and bad. Sure, it's great having a guy give you whatever you want, but at the same time I miss the bantering between us and the epic challenges that attracted me to him in the first place. It makes life interesting, gives it a little curve, sidetracks me from what's really going on in my life, the things I have yet to accept. But we can't seem to get it back, go back to that place again.

God, I wish I could go back in time.

'Violet, are you listening to me?' Luke asks, his worry increasing as he leans closer to examine my face. I shake my head and he sighs. 'Are you sure you want to stay here?'

'Yeah, I'm positive.' I throw back the rest of my beer from the plastic orange cup with pumpkins on it. Halloween is a few weeks away and everything seems to be about orange, pumpkins, and scary at the moment. I've lost count of how many of these pumpkin decorated cups I've drunk. 'I'm not ready to go home yet . . .' I scan the living room that belongs to the guy hosting the party, looking for God knows what – something that will get me into trouble probably. It's littered with beer bottles and trash, the air laced with cigarette smoke, music throbbing from the speakers, people dancing, flirting, making out in corners. A couple of months ago, I'd probably have been here dealing for Preston.

Fucking Preston.

Dammit, why can't I just get over it and move on! Just let something go for once!

'It's just that we have class tomorrow,' Luke reminds me, bringing my attention back to him, his brown eyes so full of concern as if he's afraid I'm going to break apart right here in front of him. But I won't. After the incident in his truck where I had a meltdown, and then again at his father's house, I promised myself never again would I break apart again like that. 'And we're both still trying to get caught up from those two weeks we took off.'

We've been back at Laramie and the University of Wyoming for almost two weeks since we took off to Vegas then to his father's house. The amount of school-work we returned to is overwhelming and I should be back at the apartment, studying hardcore for the Chemistry exam I have on Friday, which I should plan on attending, considering I've been warned about my attendance. But I can't study right now, I'm too rest-less, my mind in overdrive as I keep thinking about the same sequence of things over and over again.

Preston.

My parents.

Luke's mom.

Preston.

Who am I anymore?

This broken girl?

Confused.

Lost.

Seeking something she probably won't find.

'How about you head back,' I tell Luke, crushing the empty cup and then tossing it onto a nearby coffee table. 'And I'll come home with Seth.'

His frown deepens. 'Yeah, that sounds like a disaster in the making.'

I feign being offended. 'Hey, we've been getting along better,' I say, then start dancing again because sitting still is impossible. What I said is true, too. Ever since we've gotten back, Seth, one of my roommates who I've had a rocky history with – probably because he thought I was a hooker at one point – has been nicer to me. I think it's more pity than anything else. Pity because my parents were murdered. Pity because Luke's mother played a part in their deaths. Pity because the only true father figure I had turned out to be a creeper who has been stalking me since I was younger. Everyone seems to feel sorry for me, and in their own ways are trying to help me heal. But I'm healing in silence, at least that's what I tell myself. During the rare times, though, that I admit the truth to myself, I know that I'm just shutting down and avoiding everything. But I can't seem to do anything else, otherwise it feels like I'm going to break, and when I feel like I'm going to break I push myself dangerously to the edge and test potentially irreversible boundaries.

Although, it's kind of hard to do anything when I'm constantly being watched. At night there's a cop car that parks in front of my apartment, thanks to Detective Stephner. During the day I'm supposed to be with someone. And Luke, it seems, has taken on being that someone because he hasn't left my side since that conversation at his father's house. I feel bad. I mean, he had a life before he met me and I feel like I've taken that away from him. As sad as this story's going to be – the story of us – I know that eventually all this shit is going to wear him down and he's going to send me flying away, just like everyone else in my life. I used to be fine with that; used to be able to flip my middle finger at them and soar away with my wings spanned wide. But now I'm like a bird with a broken wing who's going to crash, which kind of makes me hate myself because I'm so vulnerable and weak. I miss being the strong, badass Violet, but I don't know how to bring her back.

Luke puts his hands on my hips, stopping me from moving. I realize I've drifted more into the center of the crowd and am surrounded by sweaty people dry humping each other as they grind to the beat of the song. Luke and I did that once, but that was back in the past.

'Whether you've been getting along or not,' Luke lets go of me and scratches at the back of his neck tensely as he glances around the chaos of the room, 'I'm not leaving you here alone.'

'But I wouldn't be alone,' I point out, shrinking back when his gaze fully fastens on me. The intensity pouring off him is intimidating, even for me. 'Seth's here.'

'Seth needs a babysitter just as much as you,' he states firmly. 'So that's an invalid point.'

I pout my bottom lip, tripping over my feet as I try to turn back toward the drink-serving area. 'You're a party pooper.'

'And you're drunk.' Sighing heavily, he places a hand on my arm to steady me. 'Please, can we just go?'

'Is it because of the alcohol?' I wonder, leaning into his embrace. 'Is that why you want to leave so badly?'

He shakes his head. 'I just want to go home,' he says then presses. 'With. You.'

Luke, the king of drinking, has been sober for just a little over a month now and it's been strange, but good to watch him heal himself. After a very intense week's detox, he just stopped doing it. I know it's been hard for him, even though he won't talk about it with me. He's more serious and responsible than in the past and he does look a ton healthier. He even has a job at the diner Greyson and I work at. And that's how he spends each day: work, class, comes home and hangs out with me – babysits me pretty much. He seems perfectly content doing it and it baffles me no end because people are not supposed to be content when they're with me, especially when they know so much about me.

Seeming torn about something, Luke extends his hand for me to take. 'Baby, please just come home with me.'

The words 'baby ' and 'home' flash like a lighthouse through my head and it gives me both a good and bad shiver. Emotions battle their way to the surface. I care for Luke. He gives me comfort. Security. And he could easily take it away from me. Again, another weakness I've developed. Dependability.

I'd be flipping out right now, but the alcohol makes it harder for me to feel, so maybe that's why I want to stay, to numb myself into an emotionless state.

'You've been calling me that a lot,' I say through my own drunken stupidity – sober, I'd probably ignore the comment.

I detect the slightest quirk of his lips, the first sign of humor I've seen in a while. 'Calling you what?'

There's a bit of lightness to his tone as he pretends to have no clue what I'm talking about.

'You know what.' I move to put my hands on my hips, but the room starts to twirl round and round and I end up clutching onto his shoulders for support.

He slants toward me and places his lips beside my ear, his hands finding my hips, fingers digging into the fabric of my dress and my flesh. 'Baby,' he whispers, his breath hot against my neck.

With a shiver, I nod. 'Yeah, that . . . what's up with that . . . why do you . . . keep calling me that?'

Amusement dances in his eyes as he leans back. 'Does it bother you that I do?'

I hesitate and then shrug. 'I'm not sure.'

'Do you want me to stop?'

'I . . . Again, I'm not sure . . . It's just that I don't know what it means.' Again, the truth falls out. Damn alcohol. It's like freakin' truth serum or something.

His smile cracks through. 'Well, the word itself has a few meanings, but in my case I'm using it as a term of endearment.'

'I know what the word means.' I gesture back and forth between the two of us very sloppily and end up accidentally slapping myself in the face. 'But I don't know what it means for us.' I rub the spot on my face where I hit while Luke chuckles at my lack of coordination.

Then suddenly, as he takes in the full extent of what I said, a strange look of panic and confusion crosses his face and then I start to go into anxiety mode.

Luke must notice this too because he quickly averts the subject elsewhere. 'I'll tell you what,' he says, his fingers gently folding into my skin as he reels me closer to him, our bodies aligning, chests so close I swear I can feel his heart racing, or maybe it's mine. He smells like cologne mixed with cigarettes – totally and completely Luke. 'Come home with me and we can do whatever you want when we get there,' he says.

'I thought you said you needed to catch up on school work?'

'I'm more concerned with just getting you home safely . . . and without doing anything irrational.' He tucks a strand of my red and black hair behind my ear.

I'm not sure if he means it the way that I take it. Luke knows my dirty little secret, that I push the boundaries of life, seeking adrenaline over emotion. Fear over pain.

'I'm okay, Luke, I promise.' I'm trying to let him off the hook. Take a break from babysitting me but he seems unwilling to take it.

He shakes his head and pulls me toward him until I can feel the heat of his breath on my face and almost taste his lips. 'I said I'm not leaving without you.' Then he kisses me, just a quick feather light kiss, but enough to make me zone out of reality. 'Now please just quit being a pain in the ass and come home with me.'

I'm about to give in to him, but then I see his expression. The way he's looking at me, like I'm everything to him, and it makes me want to run. Away from him. From this place.

Run.

Run.

Run.

Because I know that once I go home and the silence sets in, everything will set in.

And I hate myself for it, but in the end, I'll do *anything* to feel nothing.

Chapter 2

Luke

It's really fucking late and all I want to do is go home. I thought I had Violet with the whole baby remark, but then something I said made her panic and suddenly she's headed to get more drinks. It's killing me to watch her drown her pain in alcohol – I understand the need way too well. Watching her go through this has made staying sober easier, though, because I have to have a clear head for her. It's not a fucking cakewalk, though. My mind still does drift toward the blissful taste of alcohol whenever I'm near it. But what gets me through it, stops me from taking a sip, is reminding myself that I care for Violet; that I owe her everything after what my mother took from her.

I've been keeping an eye on her for most of the

party. It's kind of become a routine for the last couple of weeks. She gets drunk and I'm there to take care of her. But I messed up tonight when I got sidetracked by a conversation with Drey Filtphermen about this year's season and how we're going to 'kick ass'.

I nod as, half listening, I scan the crowd for Violet. 'Yeah, we should do good.' The last thing on my mind right now is football.

Drey nods and then throws back a shot. 'What? You not drinking tonight?'

I shake my head. 'Nah, I'm DD.' *Huh. Never thought that sentence would ever come out of my mouth.*

He looks at me like I just said gravity doesn't exist or something. 'Really?'

I shrug. I don't blame him for wondering what's up. I'm infamous for my ability to get trashed and scare. But I don't do that anymore, and I wish people would stop defining me as the intense, angry, manwhore drinker. 'I gotta find someone,' I say, barely paying attention when Drey yells out something else. I maneuver my way through the crowd of people smelling a lot like tequila shots, sweat and need, and finally find Seth chatting it up with Greyson in the corner of the room.

'Hey, have you seen Violet?' I interrupt their

conversation, but I know them well enough that it doesn't matter. Seth and Greyson are Violet and my roommates and both are people I consider friends. They know what's going on in Violet's life enough to understand that not being able to find her is probably not the best thing.

Seth points toward the hallway. 'The last time I saw her she was going to the bathroom.'

I head in that direction while Greyson calls out, 'Everything okay?'

I glance over my shoulder and nod, but it feels like I'm the biggest fucking liar in the world. 'Yeah, just need to find her. That's all.'

'Well, if you need any help, just let me know,' he says, taking a swig from his bottle of water.

I nod then hurry down the hallway to the bathroom area. There's a line forming outside it and I get a lot of curses thrown at me as I walk right up to the bathroom door and knock on it. 'Violet, are you in there?'

There's a pause and then I hear a muffled, 'Yeah.'

Relief washes over me. I didn't even realize how nervous I'd been for losing track of her until now. I try the doorknob, but it's locked, so I knock again and call out, but this time she doesn't respond. Thankfully the lock's fairly simple and I'm able to unlock it with a quarter. I get yelled at by some guy as I step inside the bathroom, but when I give the culprit my *go fuck yourself* look, he cowers back and I slam the door shut behind me. The bathroom is small, so I shouldn't have trouble finding her, but at first glance I can't see her in there anywhere.

'Violet?' I step past the sink area toward the bathtub. 'Are you in here?'

'In here.' Her voice is small and sounds like it's coming from the shower/tub area.

I pull back the curtain and there she is in the bathtub, her knees pulled to her chest, hugging herself so tight it looks like she's trying to curl into herself. I crouch down beside her, cup her chin in my hand, angling her face back so I can see how drunk she is. Her enlarged pupils and inability to focus on anything lets me know it's time to get her out of here.

'I'm ready to go.' Her speech is slurred and tears start slipping out of her eyes. This has happened many times so I know exactly what to do. I scoop her up and carry her out of the house, taking her home like she asked.

It's two o'clock in the morning when I pull up to our apartment complex, in a decent area of town and walking distance to the university when it's warm enough. Violet passed out in the truck on the way home after puking in the bushes so I have to carry her upstairs, something I don't mind doing. She's never been a big drinker and it shows every time she attempts to drink. I hate that it does. I want *my* Violet back.

My Violet? What the hell? Like she belongs to me. She doesn't. Although, looking down at her, her green eyes shut, full lips slightly parted, black and red wavy hair hanging over my arm, her body curled up against me, trusting me to carry her inside, she feels like she's mine.

'If she fucking heard what you were thinking, she'd fucking castrate you,' I mutter to myself. Violet has never been the kind of girl who likes to be owned by anyone. She's always strong willed and independent and that is part of the reason why I fell in love with her. I've done the whole needy women thing and it bugs the shit out of me, hooking up with women who not only want direction but also want to cling to me. I didn't hate it at the time. I loved having the control – needed it after spending most of my childhood being controlled by my overbearing, psychotic mother. But once I met Violet Hayes and saw a different side, felt the challenge, the connection, the desire to actually want someone on a more passionate level, I knew there was no going back. And I don't ever want to go back to my life before Violet. I just wish we were on more stable ground; wish she could get over the thing with my mother, that my mother was in prison so Violet had a reason to try and heal herself; wish I could help her bring that wild, independent, strength back out. I don't blame her for being angry, or for struggling, for being confused. She has every right and all I can do is help her until she's ready to move on.

As I'm reaching the top of the stairway, I give a wave to the black car with tinted windows that I know is the police car. It's here every night, parked near the curb, watching the place, thanks to Preston and his need to continuously taunt Violet with his texts and threats to kill her. This put the police on high alert since Preston is now a suspect for Violet's parents' murders.

As I arrive at our apartment door, I'm struggling to take out my keys without putting Violet down, when I notice a box in front of the door. At first I think it's part of the mail, but then I lean down and notice that it's addressed to Violet Hayes with no postage stamp, no return address, or even our address. I immediately get an uneasy feeling about it. Glancing around at the doors around us and then at the parking lot below, I hurry and get the door unlocked and us inside. After carefully setting Violet down on the sofa I make my way back to the box, deciding what to do. Pick it up and open it? Honestly, I just want to throw it away and never see what's inside, because I know it has to be bad, that whatever is in there is going to just add to the shittiness going on right now. But at the same time, not knowing could end up being bad too. With great hesitancy, I step outside and bend down to carefully tear the tape of the box, noting how light it feels. When I open it up, I can see why. All that's in there is a single photo, of Violet. My jaw instantly tightens and my fingers itch to ram my fist through the wall. In the picture, Violet is only wearing a bra and panties. She's holding the short black dress that she's wearing right now, ready to put it on, which means it was taken before we went to the party. From the angle, it looks like the picture was taken from somewhere across the street, either on the balcony of the restaurant round the corner from us, or from the two-story home that's been for sale for the last month. It doesn't say who took it, but I know who it's from. The same guy who had a room full of pictures of Violet, who sends her the threatening texts – Preston.

I flip it over and read the sentence on the back. 'Look how easy it was to get by them.'

My hands begin to tremble with rage. I'm assuming the 'them' is the police car.

'Fuck.' This is a new one for him, coming straight up to the door. I want to beat the shit out of the bastard, but it's complicated when the bastard's hiding. I think about going across the street and scoping out the house and restaurant, although I doubt he's still there. But the police can probably already see me and I'm sure they'd wonder what the hell I was doing, which would be fine if they didn't know who my mother was. They're suspicious of me, like I might know where my mother is and I'm protecting her – that's been made clear.

After locking the door, I jog down the stairs and across the parking lot to the police car parked in front of the curb of the home for sale on the opposite side of the street. When I rap on the window the driver rolls it down, looking wary.

'Can I help you?' He's probably in his late thirties, wearing civilian clothes, in his normal sedan, attempting to blend in, but clearly the disguise isn't working very well.

'I'm Luke . . . Violet's boyfriend . . .' I clear my

throat, realizing we've never even discussed what we are yet, but it feels right to say it. 'This was left on the doorstep of our apartment.' I give him the photo and the box.

The policeman looks the photo over then glances at his partner, a female officer, probably in her forties, wearing jeans and a collar shirt.

'When did it arrive?' he asks me, which is annoying as fuck. He should know this if he was actually watching the place like he was supposed to, since they were already here when we left for the party, and the box had to have arrived sometime between then and now.

'You tell me,' I say, irritated, stuffing my hands in my pockets as I glance around, looking for something out of the ordinary. 'You're the ones who are supposed to be watching the place.'

He gives me a stern look as he reaches for his coffee in the console. 'Don't give me crap about how to do my job, kid.'

'I wouldn't have to if you were doing your job.' My gaze travels over to the house on the other side of the car. 'It looks like it could have been taken from there.' I point down at the sleepy looking restaurant. 'Or there, which means it was close.' I pause, my eyes narrowing at the policeman. 'Which means *he* was close.'

The cop gives me a dirty look. 'There's no proof who left it yet.'

'It's kind of a given,' I say. 'Considering she has only one stalker.'

He tosses the box and photo to his partner. 'Thanks for the input,' he says. 'But leave the police work to the professionals.'

He starts to roll up his window as I mutter, 'Fucking douche', before walking away. I should have just waited until morning and taken it to Detective Stephner. He's more a professional and he cares more about solving this case, cares more about Violet's wellbeing.

I go back to the apartment and lock the door behind me. Violet is still sleeping on the sofa, sprawled out on her back, her arm draped over her head, her breathing soft. It's the most peaceful I've seen her look in a long time, which is sad since she's passed out drunk.

Deciding that it's best to take her back to our room instead of trying to squish on the sofa beside her, I pick her up and carry her to the bed. I lay her down, slip off her shoes, then shuck out of my shirt and jeans and climb into bed with her, pulling the blanket over us. She instantly slides closer to me until her face is nuzzled against my chest. I slip an arm around her and kiss her forehead, pretending that everything's okay. That in the morning we'll wake up like a normal couple, with the sunlight peeking through the window in the silence of our home. But deep down I know that I'll wake up probably before the sun even makes it in. And the house will be anything but silent. It'll be filled with Violet's screams.

Chapter 3

Violet

I feel so small, hiding in the dark in the basement, listening to the sounds of voices that I'm sure belong to monsters. I know if I dare look, I won't see faces and bodies but strange shapes covered in thorns or needles or something else sharp, the kind of skin monsters are supposed to have. I'll see pointy fangs instead of teeth, claws instead of fingers, soulless eyes that will reflect my horror back to me.

So I try to stay concealed in my hiding spot behind boxes and toys. I try to remain as still as possible, holding my breath. I tell myself that eventually they'll leave and when it's all over I'll go upstairs and climb into bed with my mom and dad who will tell me it was just a nightmare. Because that's what they do. They're good parents

who know how to comfort me when the world is grey, covered in shadows, when sunlight doesn't seem like it exists anymore and every bad thing in the world has come out.

I try to tell myself that the monsters didn't hurt them.

There's a lady singing like crazy. I think she actually might be crazy. And the man, his voice is so low, so calm, so very un-monster like. Maybe I was wrong. Maybe he wasn't a monster. Maybe I'm just making things up.

Then the lady stops singing and I tell myself that it's okay to look, just a peek. Turning around, I peer around the boxes. Light flows in from the windows and makes me able to see just a bit. At first the room looks empty, but then my eyes adjust and I see them. Two figures, perfectly still. In fact, the world seems still at that moment.

But then just as still as everything was, it starts moving again, faster, faster, faster, as the man steps from the shadows and shows himself to me. Tall, with brown hair, familiar facial features, wearing a plaid coat and holey jeans.

'I-I know you,' I stammer as I rise from out of my hiding spot, my bare feet shuffling across the floor.

He takes a step toward me and I freeze in my tracks as the figure in front of me shifts into a monster like I originally thought.

'Preston,' I breathe.

His lips curve into a pleased smile and I open my mouth and scream.

I wake up gasping for air and scream into the nearest thing I can get a hold of. When I was younger, I used to grab a pillow or turn into the mattress to muffle my cries, but nowadays it's usually Luke's chest, so I end up burying my face against his warm skin. I wish I could get the nightmares to stop, wish I could get rid of this helpless feeling. It's not always the same nightmare that does this to me. Sometimes it's of Preston, appearing that night in the basement, my worried brain placing him there that night even though I never actually saw him. Sometimes it's painful memories of my parents that I'd thought were long-forgotten. Sometimes it's of Luke leaving me. I've never been one to worry about people leaving me – they always have. And because of that, I'd made myself remain detached enough so as not to emotionally connect with anyone I'd worry about losing. But I messed up with Luke, got attached – way, way too attached – and now I fear both him letting go and me never being able to let go.

Every night after I wake up panicking and hyperventilating, Luke lies still, rubbing my back and whispering that it's going to be okay in my ear. After I settle down I scoot away from him, wipe the sweat from my forehead and roll onto my back. I stare up at the ceiling, trying to forget the nightmare and attempting to remember what the fuck happened last night at the party. It's still late outside, the sun not yet up. I glance at the clock on the nightstand. 5:12 in the morning. Shit. It's too early to be awake.

After a minute or two, Luke asks tentatively, 'What was it about this time?'

'Falling off a cliff,' I lie, hating that I am, but unable to tell him the truth. But it's like I'm five years old again and too afraid to speak the truth because then I'll have to accept it. Like when my parents died. It took me forever to say it aloud, which made it unbearably real.

'You seem to have that dream a lot.' There's speculation in his voice. He doesn't believe that my dream was about that, knows that I'm lying, but doesn't call me out on it.

'Guess my mind is super good at repetition.' My eyes are fixed on the ceiling, even though I can feel him watching me, trying to figure out what's going on in my head for real. If he really knew, he'd probably run though, like I wish I could.

'You know I'm here.' He rotates on his side and props up on his arm. 'If you need to talk.'

Luke's turned into such a great guy. I don't even know how the hell that happened, with him being with me so much, a festering toxin, polluting his life. And he wants to help me. I really wish he could, wish there was this button inside that he could find that would shut off my insane messed-up-ness that lives inside me. But if there is, neither he nor I have found it yet.

'You should try to get some sleep,' he whispers. His firm arm slides across my stomach, fingers finding my side, then he urges me closer to him. 'It's still really early.'

'It's hard to fall asleep after a nightmare,' I admit in the darkness of our room. 'It makes me . . .' I bite down on my lip, not ready to talk about my feelings either.

'I'll stay up until you fall asleep. Nothing will happen to you. I promise.' His face inches closer to my cheek and he brushes his soft lips against my skin. 'I'm always here for you.'

'Always is a strong word,' I whisper, squeezing my eyes shut, fighting the urge to surrender into him. 'Things might change, you know. One day . . . you might not want the responsibility of taking care of me . . . or stuff might happen that'll make you want to stay away from me.'

'That'll never happen,' he promises. 'There's nothing that'd ever make me want to stay away from you.'

It feels like I should say something back to his powerful words, but I can't find them in the darkness of my head. I open my eyes and am greeted by his intense gaze, 'What about your mom?' I ask.

His entire body tenses as a ripple of panic waves through him. 'What about her?'

I want to shut my eyes but force myself to keep them open. 'What happens when . . . if she gets arrested? I mean, that's a lot to take in and it'd be my fault she's there.'

'She fucking put herself there.' His tone is harsh, angry, eyes burning with rage.

'I might have to testify against her,' I point out, something the detective and I have talked about if they ever find her. How I have to try and remember what she looks like, to identify her from that night, which would play a part in getting her sentenced.

Luke huffs out several breaths, his face anxiety-stricken. 'Can we just stop talking about this, please? You and I, we'll be together as long as you want us to

. . . Forever, if . . .' He trails off at the end, either wanting to retract his words or fearing them and I feel my own heart slam against my chest. They're packed with a lot of emotion, a lot of meaning, a lot of relationship stuff we haven't talked about. Luke and I have so many challenges ahead of us that we haven't discussed yet. Like what happens when the police finally catch his mother? What if I have to testify against her? What if they discover she was the one that actually killed my parents? Will it affect how I feel? How he feels? Will it ruin us?

So many questions, ones that I should say aloud so we can finally talk about them. But I'm not ready to let go of Luke, my security blanket, my . . .

There are so many words that flow through my head which I can barely process, so instead I seek a distraction. My favorite distraction.

'Kiss me please.' I practically sound like I'm begging, but I can't take it back so I just roll with it.

He can see it in my eyes too, the avoidance, my attempt to get around talking about the emotional baggage I keep locked inside me. He starts to open his mouth to say who knows what, probably something that will make me feel more and cause me to panic even more, I'm guessing. But I silence him as I lean up and press my lips to his, so aggressively we knock teeth. It's anything but sexy and hot; however, I've never really given a shit about that stuff and there'd be no point in starting now.

Kissing him almost desperately and pulling at his hair, I lift my head up and swing my leg over his side, forcing him to lie flat on his back so I can straddle him. I keep our lips sealed as I run my fingers up and down his tattooed chest, continuing my exploration of his lean muscles until I reach the top of his boxers.

'Violet,' he says through groans as I slip my hand beneath his waistband. 'Maybe we . . . we shouldn't . . .' His head tips back and I put a sliver of space between our lips, watching him starting to lose control.

'You know, I'd be hurt by your protests, but,' I slip my hand further into his boxers and rub his hard on, 'it's pretty clear your words don't match what you really want.'

He grips my waist, as if securing me in place, either keeping me near, or allowing himself to have control enough over the situation that he can bail out whenever he wants. 'It's not that I don't want to . . . I just . . . don't think we should . . .' He searches my eyes for something and I'm guessing doesn't see it because in the end he seems disappointed. 'Not when you're upset.'

'I'm not upset.' I scowl at him. 'Why do you always think that whenever I want to have sex?'

He presses his lips together to restrain whatever's on his mind. I seize the opportunity to slant back, tug my dress off, and toss it aside so I'm only in my bra and panties.

'I promise this has nothing to do with anything else than me wanting to get laid.' Liar. Liar. Liar. And a bad one at that. I know it – he knows it. But he'll give in – he always does. And part of me might love him for it and part of me hates myself for doing it to him, using sex as a temporary replacement for my adrenaline addiction.

An exhale later, he's pulling me to him and as our lips reconnect with a blazing spark of heat, I feel a split second of inner peace, like maybe this is really what I want, that I'm not just trying to bury my feelings by having sweaty sex. The feeling dissipates, however, the moment I come to the conclusion that maybe it's more than just sex. Denial. I'm living – dying in it. But I fear the truth won't set me free – it'll kill me. So instead I focus on kissing Luke, basking in the sensation of his hands wandering all over every inch of my body, leaving hot trails of heat across my skin. The way he keeps moaning my name every time I touch his skin and bite his flesh drives my mind into a state of euphoria. We don't hurry, taking our time, but eventually it feels as though I'm going to combust with need and I end up peeling the rest of my clothes off. Luke follows my lead, taking his boxers off.

Suddenly, he pauses. 'Wait . . . do we need—'

I cut him off by covering his mouth with my hand. 'I've been on the pill for a few weeks now, so we're good.'

He sucks in a breath, then seconds later he's flipping me on my back and slipping deep inside me. He takes my leg and hitches it over his hip as he thrusts in and out of me. Over and over again until I let out a soft cry, my nails digging into his shoulder blades. For a moment I'm gone. For a moment, I feel like everything is going to be okay. For a moment, I'm dropped into a blissful illusion where I'm free from everything and Luke is right there with me. But almost as quickly as the relief came, I crash back to reality. Luke has stilled inside me, his face buried in my neck, his sweaty chest pressed against mine. I can feel every heartbeat, every breath he takes. I count each one, try to match my own breathing to his. Content. I feel content and I want to ask him to never move.

Just stay still. Forever. Please.

Yet if I did dare utter those irreversible words, that'd just be me trying to live in a fairytale and I've lived too much to believe in such things. So I keep silent and eventually Luke pulls out of me, giving me one last deep kiss before he rolls onto his back and stares up at the ceiling with his arm draped over his head. He doesn't say anything, lost in his thoughts, drowning in some sort of internal agony that makes me feel guilty since I probably put it there. I want to say something to him, to take that worried expression off his face, to tell him I'm sorry I'm so broken and that I'll try to fix myself. But I can't find the words, not knowing where they exist, so instead I take the coward's way out and utter, 'Goodnight.' Then I shut my eyes and let my nightmares slowly drown me.

Chapter 4

Violet

I'm standing in the middle of dried up trees and grass, wilting rose bushes, and rows and rows of cracked tombstones. The sky is so dark it's nearly black and ash falls from the sky like snow.

I know why I'm here, what I'm looking for, even though I don't want to find it. A certain tombstone belonging to someone I care about and fear losing. I wander aimlessly through the cemetery, trying to fight the need to go to a specific tombstone, the one tucked in the corner beneath the only tree flourishing. But finally I reach it and have to look down and read the words engraved on the ash-covered stone.

'Luke Price,' I read his name aloud as I fall to the ground, ash falling down on me. Tears slip from my eyes,

but they're black and stain my skin like ink, stain my dress. 'No . . . No . . . I can't lose him. Can't do this again. I can't lose someone again.' My head falls as I sob. 'Please don't let me be alone again.' But the hollow sound of the world around me is the only response I get.

I'm once again ripped out of a nightmare, gasping for air as I bolt upright in the bed. I nearly black out from the lack of oxygen, struggling to shove the nightmare out of my mind, but it consumes my thoughts.

It's the fear of being alone, of losing Luke, of someone else I care about leaving me. Just dreaming about it feels like it killed me, what would happen to me if he really did leave me? Or worse, something terrible happened to him?

I lie soundlessly in bed for a while, so I don't wake Luke. Usually I wake him up with my gasping ritual, but he must be super-tired this morning. I stare up at the ceiling, telling myself that it's just another damn dream and to get over it. That Luke's not buried under the ground in his final resting place. That he's right here beside me, breathing rather loudly, shirtless, his rock-solid chest inked like a canvas, and that I'm not going to lose him. But the problem is, my parents *are* buried under the ground, and it reminds me of how

I felt right after I lost them, back when I would allow myself to feel the sting their deaths left behind. How afraid I was that I'd end up alone in the world and how painful it was when I realized my worry was reality – that I was alone. I got used to it, though, adapted the best that I could. What would happen though if I lost Luke suddenly? Could I handle it again?

My fears keep me awake until the sun comes up and fills our room with bright sunlight. Luke starts to wake up, turning over and rubbing his eyes before he sits up. His jawline is scruffy, in need of a shave, and there are dark circles under his brown eyes. 'How you feeling this morning?' he asks me with a yawn. He must see something in my eyes he doesn't like because concern masks his expression. Damn eyes. They've been giving me away lately.

I look away to avoid eye contact with him. 'Good, other than the killer headache I have.' I know my hangover isn't what he was referring to, but I don't want to talk about anything else. About last night. About my nightmares. About me using sex as a distraction.

It takes him a beat or two to answer. 'You think you're up for class today?'

My mood plummets even more at the idea of stepping into the outside world, full of looks, stares, and questions – too much to even picture. I shake my head and roll to my side, facing the wall instead of him. 'Not today.'

'Are you sure?' His hand finds my back, his fingers stroking the space between my shoulder blades. 'I could make something for you to eat . . . maybe that would help.'

I shudder from his touch – always do – but refuse to move. 'Yeah, I'm sure . . . I just want to stay home and rest.'

'But . . . I don't like leaving you here alone.'

'Seth's here, so I'm not alone.'

'Yeah . . . but he might have class later today.'

I glance over my shoulder at him. 'I'm pretty sure he doesn't.'

'Still . . . I don't like you being here without someone watching you. And Seth . . . As much as I like him, he's not the most responsible person. I'd rather I just watch you. I'd do a better job.' He gets this funny look on his face as if he's realizing something that baffles him.

I turn and place my hand on his cheek. 'Luke, I'll be fine. I won't leave the house or anything without telling anyone.' I tuck my hands under my head and bite my lip until it bleeds because it takes the emotional

39

pain briefly away. 'You can't watch me forever and it's not your responsibility to do so.'

'Like hell I can't,' he mutters under his breath as I turn on my side. It grows silent between us. He wants to say more – I want to. Yet we both don't – can't.

Eventually, his lips brush the back of my neck, right over the two stars tattooed on my skin, each representing a person I've lost in my life – my mother and father. 'I'd feel so much better if I was here with you.'

'And I feel so much more guilty if you missed another class with me,' I reply, as he places a gentle kiss over each star.

He nuzzles his nose against my neck and sighs in a surrendering manner. 'Fine, but call me if you need anything. And keep the door locked,' he says. 'I'll tell Seth to keep an eye on you and promise me you'll check in with him.'

I open my mouth to protest. 'I'll just be in the house, like I said, I'm not—'

'I know you won't go anywhere,' he says, placing a hand over my lips. 'But please just promise me that you'll check in with him so that I can have peace of mind.'

The plea in his voice makes it hard not to agree so I nod, then he reluctantly climbs out from the bed, making the mattress lift with the lack of his weight and making the bed feel empty and cold. I hear his footsteps cross the narrow room and he stops in front of the dresser.

'There's something else I need to tell you,' he says as he rummages through the drawer for some clothes.

The edge in his voice makes me hesitant to answer. 'Okay . . .'

'It's about last night . . . After we got home.' He shuts the drawer then just stands there in the middle of the room. I can't fully see him other than out of the corner of my eye, but he's making me uneasy. Did I do something strange last night? Well, more strange than normal for me? Did I speak about the dream maybe, when I was half asleep or something? 'There was a box on the doorstep when we got home from the party.'

The hair on the back of my neck stands on end and goosebumps erupt across my arms. 'And who was the box from?' I ask, even though deep down I already know – from the monster haunting my dreams. I'm just hoping – wishing – that maybe Luke will prove me wrong.

He sits down on the edge of the bed, the mattress sinking below his weight and the emptiness I'd been feeling diminishes again. 'It didn't say exactly who sent it . . . but there was a photo of you inside . . .' He puts his hand on my back and I feel a tremble in his touch. 'Please just come to class with me.'

I turn all the way over and face him. The fear in his eyes tells me I should be afraid; that whatever was in the box I should be afraid of. But I won't let myself do that, feel the fear. 'What was in the box, Luke?'

He keeps his intense brown eyes on me. 'I already told you . . . a photo of you.'

I steadily maintain his gaze. 'And what was I doing in this photo?'

He searches my eyes for something and I wonder what he sees exactly. Someone lost and scared or the façade I'm trying to wear, the one I've been wearing since I was five. 'I just want to protect you.' His fingers spread across my cheek and warm my skin. 'From all the bad and ugly in the world.'

'I already know too much about the bad and the ugly to be protected. And it's better to know than to be in the dark,' I tell him, although I'm not sure I believe my own words. There are many times in my past where I've questioned whether it was better to stay in the dark, starting out with when I was five and in the basement where my parents were killed. If I had stayed there until someone came to the house, I'd never have seen my parents dead. The memory of the blood, and my father's final words, wouldn't be branded in my head, like a hot iron rod singeing flesh. And then maybe the foster families wouldn't have been so afraid of me. Then maybe I would have grown up with a family and I wouldn't be here in this moment. But see, that's the problem. Because deep down, my heart wants to be here with Luke, which means all of that had to happen. Destiny, right? Well, I've been conflicted over destiny a lot lately. Because it led me here to Luke, but it took so much for me to get here. To go back would mean to lose Luke, but to admit that I wouldn't want to go back would feel like a huge betrayal to my parents. And if I did finally accept just how much I care for Luke, I'd be accepting that something might happen – maybe destiny again – that would rip him from my life and I'd lose him perhaps forever. And I'm not sure if I could handle that – handle destiny again. All I really want is . . . well certainty I guess.

'You were in this room . . . in the photo.' Luke finally divulges and there's a tremble in his fingers. 'I think he took it from across the street.'

Fear blazes through me, but I extinguish it quickly.

Bury it, dammit! 'So you think it was Preston who left the box and took the picture,' I state emotionlessly, refusing to feel anything toward Preston, whether hatred or fear. *I will not let him get to me. Won't think of him.* But just trying not to think of him makes my blood boil. My fingers curl inward, my fingernails stabbing my palms, cutting flesh, slicing through the pain, distracting it into something else. 'That's new and bold of him. Beats sending texts I guess.'

'I'm not sure it was him, but . . .' He trails off, his expression sinking.

'But I only have one stalker,' I finish for him, my voice sounding empty. *Empty, just like me. I hate it, hate myself for everything I've done. Why can't I just let it go and change?*

Luke starts to say something, but I cut him off. 'You should go. You're going to be late for class.' I roll over to my side again and face the wall.

'Violet, I really don't think you should stay here,' he says, his fingers falling from my face.

'We already talked about this. I'm not going anywhere and Seth's here. I'll be fine.' There's a forced iciness to my tone so he will leave me alone. I hate that I have to do it, but if I don't I know eventually he'll convince himself that he has to stay here and look after me and that's not what I want for him.

He doesn't say much after that and I lay still, pretending I've dozed off again while he gets dressed. Before he walks out of the room, he gently kisses the back of my head. 'I'll be back as soon as classes are over.'

'Don't you have to work tonight?' I ask. A couple of weeks ago, Luke got a job at the diner with the help of Greyson, helping out in the bar. I was a little worried what this would do for his recovery, but he assures me he's fine for now, although he wants to get a new job as soon as he can.

'No, not until this weekend.' He grabs his diabetic kit and stuffs it into his backpack, along with his books.

'Okay, see you later then.'

He whispers something about being safe then briefly waits, as if either wanting me to say something or wanting to say more, an excruciating almost painful habit that's developed between us. And just like always, nothing ever gets said and he ends up leaving in silence.

I only move again when I hear the front door shut and then enough time's passed that I know he's not coming back. Hopefully, by the time he returns home later today I'll have gotten myself collected enough that I can pretend I'm okay with everything. Put on my smiles. Skip around, clean the house. Be drunkenly stupid, pretty much, because that's what it takes now.

After about an hour ticks by, I get out of bed and take a quick shower then pull on a pair of holey jeans and a faded *Silverstein* t-shirt. I put my hair up in a messy bun and then head back to the room, passing by Seth's bedroom door. It's cracked and I can see that he's sleeping in his bed. Greyson's gone, probably to work.

I wander back into my bedroom, lock the door behind me and turn on my playlist and 'People Live Here' by Rise Against clicks on. I go over to my bed, lie flat on the floor, and crawl halfway under it until I reach the box I'm looking for. Once my fingers brush the box, I slide out with it in my hands and get onto the bed.

Like every day since I got it, I stare at it for at least a half of an hour before I get the courage to open it up. Then it probably takes me another half of an hour to reach in and take out the contents: a small stack of photos, a silver bracelet and a spiral notebook with notes my mother scribbled down. These were the things that Detective Stephner could let me take that belonged to my parents. They'd played no part in the investigation, had been checked for blood and DNA but came up with nada, so he gave them to me a couple of weeks ago – right about when we got back from California – thinking I'd want them. I'm not sure if I do, since I spend way too much time simply holding them and staring at them – I haven't even made it past the first page in the notebook yet. No one knows I have the stuff either, except the detective.

I'm still not even sure what to do with it. When it comes to my parents, I usually avoid thinking about it, hence the adrenaline addiction I've developed. I try not to think about them, remember them; I've never even visited their graves. It just seems too hard, you know, to face head on what happened, what I lost, what will never be. Letting go, moving on, instead of drifting somewhere between the past and the future, like I have been for most of my life. Face the future. God, I can't even imagine what that would be like.

I turn the bracelet over in my hand and then with a deep breath put it on my wrist. It's nothing special, just a silver bracelet with a plate that reads *Sempre*, which after some messing around with online translators, I discovered meant *forever* in Italian. Not sure why it's in Italian, since I don't know enough about my parents to understand why they'd choose that language, which makes me depressed.

All of this stuff does.

But I won't ever acknowledge it.

Can't.

God, I wish I could just be free from my thoughts and the past. But it's never going to happen, not when the past has its chains wrapped around my wrists, weighing me down and constantly holding me back. I know I'll never be able to let go of the pain and darkness inside until there is justice for my parents.

I end up tossing everything back into the box like it's made of fire, and then I close it up and shove it back under the bed where it belongs. I should stop looking at it – it's becoming an obsession. But just being in the room makes me want to take out the stuff and obsess over things I can't change.

'I have to get out of this damn room,' I mutter to myself as I hurry over to my closet and get my leather jacket and boots. I put them on then head out, grabbing the keys and my wallet off the kitchen counter on my way. I momentarily hesitate before stepping outside, with the slightest pang of guilt for bailing without telling Seth where I'm going like I promised Luke I would. I don't want to explain to Seth, though, why I'm freaking out at the moment. So I hop over the threshold and close the door behind me, the guilt building inside my chest like bricks of steel. I know going out alone isn't necessarily the safest thing for me to do, and deep down I know Luke has every reason for me not to go out by myself. Detective Stephner would agree with him. Preston's obsession with me is beyond creepy . . . that room with all those photos of me, some from when I was young. It's disturbing and anyone would worry, except me. Plus he continues to text me from random numbers and then of course there's the box from last night. I also wonder if there might be more to it that I'm not even getting told. The fact that the police send a cop car over here every night has to make me wonder, but what Detective Stephner would keep from me, I have no idea.

'I should just walk back into the house and lock the door,' I say, trying to convince myself, but it doesn't work and I end up trotting down the stairway. *Because I'm twisted, broken, messed up. A million different things.* The voice inside my head is not my own, but a choir made up of my foster parents over the years. *This is what I do. I mess up. I do everything wrong. I shut down because it's easy and I'm the kind of person that takes the easy way out.*

Needing a distraction from the voices, I retrieve my

phone out of my pocket and text Greyson, figuring I can tolerate hanging out with him right now. Plus, he can also tell Seth that I'm with him, that way I'm keeping my promise to Luke without having to go explain to Seth that I'm freaking out and need to get the fuck out of the apartment.

Me: Where r u at?

I head down the stairs, waiting for his response. It's chilly, autumn rolling in and crisping the leaves and grass. I can feel the Wyoming breeze stinging my cheeks and can hear wind chimes singing from somewhere nearby. It seems peaceful. I wish I could freeze. Never take a step forward, never take a step back. Just hold onto this moment, stop moving, stop breathing. Forever. But the phone buzzes from inside my pocket and I have to move again. Sucking in a breath of air, I swipe my finger across the screen, noticing that along with the text message, I have a voicemail. I have no idea when I missed the call but decide to open the text first, since it's from Greyson.

Greyson: At work. What's up? U ok?

Me: Yeah, just bored. Took a break from class today. Mind if I come chill at the bar?

Greyson: U know Benny will probably get u to work if u show up here. We're understaffed.

Me: Better than sitting in the house.

Greyson: Alright, come down then. I'm bored anyway. Bars always slow in the afternoon. Not even sure why Benny insists on keeping it open. The dining side is mad crowded though.

He keeps it open for people like me who want to start drinking early because that's what I'm going to do if I go there.

My hand trembles at the revelation. *Is that where I've gotten? Am I that bad? Do I care? About anything?* I'm not sure – I'm not sure about anything anymore. I used to be so anti-drinking. And I dealt drugs but rarely dabbled in substances, mainly because it fucked with my head and my head's already too fucked up to begin with. But ever since the thing with Preston I've been living in a cloud I chose to create, because it helps me forget all the dirty things I did with him . . .

'Wow, I'm a real freaking mess.' Reality slaps me across the face, cold and hard. I stand there on the steps for a while, motionless.

Always motionless.

Never moving.

It's not anything new, but it still gets to me every time I think about it – what I've become – and my fingers are a little unsteady as I type a response.

Me: C ya in about 15 min.

I listen to the voicemail as I trudge the rest of the way down the stairs, the weight of my life crushing down on me. Things only get worse when I listen to Detective Stephner's voicemail. At first I think it's just him giving me an update, even though I'm usually the one that calls him. But when I realize what he's saying . . . no, I had to have heard him wrong. I have to replay the message. I replay it again and again.

'No . . . It can't be . . .' His words slam against my chest, crash over me like a fierce ocean wave that makes me feel like I'm drowning. And instead of fighting it, I just stand there letting the water take me away.

Mira Price has been arrested.

Mira Price has been arrested?

I'm startled, shocked, taken completely off guard. I didn't anticipate this ever happening, at least I'm realizing this as of this moment. And I definitely didn't anticipate this kind of reaction from myself. Or maybe I was just in denial. Maybe deep down I knew all of this was lying under the surface, and that when it happened I was going to have to admit many things to myself.

That Mira Price has been arrested for the murder of my parents, and that regardless of this my parents are never coming back.

Nothing will ever bring them back.

By the time I arrive at the bottom of the stairway, I feel like I'm sinking into the ground. It takes all my energy to keep my knees from buckling, but in the end I drop, right on the sidewalk. I can feel the rough surface of the concrete rubbing away layers of my skin from beneath my jeans, but the physical pain is nothing.

Nothing.

The physical pain is my sanctuary.

It's the emotional pain that's going to kill me.

Breathe in. Breathe out. I'm stronger than this . . . or am I? No, I need something to kill the emotions stirring in me . . . the confusion . . . the helplessness of the unknown . . . Where do I go from here? What I need is a window, up high. Something dangerous. Something. Something. Something. To turn off the emotions prickling up in me, sharp as needles, potent as knives, tearing me apart. It hurts. Aches. Is killing me. I swear I'm bleeding from the inside . . . too much pain. The pain grows more powerful as I think of what lies before me, the future I have to face.

Finally, I manage to suck it up and bury the pain just enough that I'm able to stand up. Then I walk aimlessly down the sidewalk with an idea rising in my head, one that might help me get through the day.

Although I might not walk out of it alive. I want to find the tallest building, to step onto the edge with my hands spanned out to my side and to lean forward until all emotion inside me is replaced by fear. The idea is terrifying and makes it that much more appealing.

Makes it what I need.

Crave.

Feed my addiction.

I just wonder how long I'm going to be able to keep going like this until I push it too far.

Chapter 5

Luke

I feel like shit today. Not only is the stress of the box and the photo getting to me, but I'm worried about Violet, more than I already was. She's getting more distant and last night when we had sex it felt like she was somewhere else, drifting farther away from me and one day I'm afraid I won't be able to reach her.

It stung like a motherfucker and reminded me of myself from not too long ago, when I was having sex to feel like I had control over things. I hate that that's where we've gotten, but I don't know what to do about it. Ask her to get help? Maybe. But I feel like I'd be a hypocrite, like I don't have the right to say anything about it.

Classes drag on and on as I overanalyze everything.

I keep checking the time every fucking minute, which makes it feel like it's moving even slower. I text Violet to check on her and when she doesn't respond I call her. It goes straight to her voicemail, which is alarming enough in itself, but add an hour of not being able to get a hold of her and I'm fucking freaking out. And I can't get a hold of Seth. I don't like the feeling, but I can't seem to control it, and finally after looking at the clock for about the fiftieth time, I leave class right in the middle of Professor Haperson's lecture. It's completely unlike me, Mr Structure, and I get a lot of weird looks in response, especially from Kayden Owens, my best friend since I was a kid. He's probably thinking about the last time I disappeared, just blew off class and football practice for a couple of weeks without so much as an explanation, which was also completely out of character for me, Mr Structure. I still haven't given him an explanation yet, but that's mainly because half that explanation belongs to Violet and I'm not going to tell her story without her permission.

Sure enough, I'm halfway across the campus yard when I get a text from Kayden.

Kayden: What's up? Why r u bailing?

Me: I have to check up on something.

Kayden: Something or someone? Because it seems

like you've been having to ditch class to check up on that someone a lot lately.

I pause. I'm not sure if he means it rudely or not, but I'm kind of getting the feeling that he may think that a lot of my fuckups are connected to Violet, which makes me a little defensive. Whether they are or not, it doesn't matter. Violet's parents are dead because of my mom. Whether she did kill them or not, she was there that night and played some kind of part in the reason Violet grew up with foster families. But Kayden doesn't know that, so I guess his accusations toward Violet are understandable.

Me: Look, there's a lot of stuff u don't know about Violet and I.

Kayden: I figured, but I still worry man . . . u seem a little off course lately, which is really fucking unlike u.

Me: I know, but I wouldn't be if it wasn't important.

It takes him a moment to respond and by the time I get his reply, I've made it to my truck and gotten the engine started.

Kayden: Well, if u need help with anything, let me know.

If only he could help. Perhaps I wouldn't feel like I

was continuously falling off a cliff, unsure when I'll ever land or where I'll land.

Me: Thanks man, but I can handle it for now.

Biggest lie I've ever told. I'm not handling it at all. Not even a little bit. In fact, Violet seems to be getting worse and worse, and it feels like I'm just standing there watching her destroy her life . . . I feel so damn helpless.

'Fuck.' I curse aloud as I drive down the road, frustrated and pissed off at myself for not doing a better job of keeping an eye on her. There are so many bad things that could happen at the moment, anywhere from her harming herself to Preston getting a hold of her. It sends a chill down my spine and slams me in the stomach hard. I can't lose her – can't lose the only person I've ever cared about. It's terrifying to think about and I find myself wishing – hoping – that one day, somehow, things won't be like this. That they'll be better. Normal.

Please just let things get better.

Chapter 6

Violet

This is my last attempt to try and make the pain go away; the last attempt to fill the void in my heart. I just hope it works, because nothing else seems to.

I'm standing on the edge of the raging river, watching it flow powerfully over the rocks, curving around the bends, dipping beneath the bridge, beauty at its finest. I wish I was a painter so I could capture the beautifulness. Or a photographer. I wish I were a lot of things; or at least knew what I wanted to be, then maybe this would be easier – life could be easier. If I had direction, a purpose, other than always drifting like the leaves in the water.

I blink the long sequences of thoughts from my mind, ones created from the adrenaline coursing through me, along with an abundance of alcohol. Then I force myself to step up to the edge, where the rushing water meets the sandy shore. I'm only procrastinating, distracting myself from what I came here to do, another attempt after several failed ones. I'm not sure, but today it's been hard to calm myself down. I'm not sure why. Am I more scared than usual? No. Have I changed my mind? Definitely not. Once I decide I need to do this I'm beyond going back. I've reached the emotional point I can't deal with – don't know how to deal with – and this is the only way I know how. It's what I've been doing for years and it's no longer a habit, an escape, but a part of me, engrained into my skin like my tattoos.

'I need this,' I whisper and then with a deep breath I wade into the violent water. It soaks through my clothes and hits my skin instantly, a thousand tiny needles, warning me to go back. But I keep going forward, until I'm submerged to the waist . . . the chest . . . the neck . . . I can barely keep my legs under me now, the power of the water fighting to tug me under, suck me up, take me away. Part of me wants to let it, wants to lift my feet up and get carried away into the unknown. I have no idea if I'll survive and that's kind of the point. The terrifying, intoxicating point. But the little will left inside me, the one that whispers that it's not just me anymore, begs me to put up a fight.

'I don't know if I want to anymore.' I call over the water. 'I'm so tired of fighting just so I can tread with my head above the water.' The sound of my voice gets lost in the roar of the water as I stand there waiting for . . . well, I'm not sure. An answer to what I should do? Where do I go from here?

There's no answer though, and the only choice I have is to wade back to shore. Maybe it's not the only choice though. After all, I could just give up right now, but I'm not. I'm choosing to go back to my life, to my home, to the people in it. What does that mean?

Unsure, I start to turn around toward the shore again, but mid-turn, my feet get ripped out from under me. A breath later, as my head slams against a rock, I'm engulfed in water. I try to grab onto something, desperately seek to get my footing, but I don't stand a chance. The water's too strong and my head is fuzzy from the bump. I can barely see anything . . . water . . . rocks . . . water . . . myself swirling in the center of it.

Oh my God, I'm going to die.

I've never had that thought before. Never truly

thought I was going to die through all the things I've done. I've pushed myself to the edge, but I always knew the point where I'd cross the No Going Back Line and never crossed it.

But now I've crossed it.

And I'm going to fucking die right now.

I want to cry because I'm not ready for this, not ready to go. I try to open my mouth to yell for help, remembering that there were people just up the shore, but every time I open my mouth, I swallow huge gulps of water that I choke on. So instead I fight for my life. I fight like a Goddamn person who wants to live more than anything else in the world. I'm surprised how much I fight. How much I want to make it back to the shore. How much I want my life. How much I see the things I want . . . see the people I want. I swear in the midst of it I hear my father's voice, telling me to be strong. I swear I see him too, swimming toward me, to help me get back to the shore. It's just an illusion, though, the person's face shifting into someone else as they get closer.

But it's someone.

Someone who maybe can save me. Because God, I want to be saved.

There are people yelling in the distance and I can

see the person getting closer. I reach for them and they reach for me, our fingers so close as water swishes over my head and rocks slam at my body. But suddenly a wave rips over me and just like that, they get ripped away, like the water rips me away.

Chapter 7

Luke

I manage to keep myself together as I drive toward the apartment, hoping she'll be there, crossing my fingers that out of all the bad things that could be going on, it's actually something that's okay.

Please, just let her be okay.

I'm halfway there when I get a text. Taking my phone out of my pocket, I see it's from Greyson.

Greyson: Hey, I have something of yours.

Me: Huh???

Greyson: A girl with black and red hair, a pierced nose, tattoos, a smartass personality. Goes by the name of Violet.

Relief washes over me. She's with Greyson. Thank God.

Me: Glad she's with you. I've been trying to get a hold of her.

Greyson: Yeah, she's been busy. With what I have no clue, but she showed up here in wet clothes, with a swollen eye, a cut on her wrist, and drunk beyond comprehension . . . It's really bad, Luke. I'm not going to lie. Something must have set her off today. Not sure what though since I can't get her to talk about it.

A ripple of guilt sweeps through my body, so powerful I have to pull over the truck and collect myself before driving down the road to avoid getting into an accident.

Me: Where are u guys exactly?

Greyson: At the diner. Thankfully the bars pretty empty so I can keep an eye on her, but it's going to pick up around three or so. Can u pick her up? I'd take her home myself but we're understaffed as it is.

Me: On my way now.

I drive like a bat out of hell down the streets of Laramie, breaking too many traffic laws to count. But I'm flipping worried, not just about Violet being drunk, but because she showed up at the diner with wet clothes and bruises. I know enough about Violet to understand that she could have done this to herself. I thought she'd been taking it easy on the adrenaline seeking, but now I'm not so sure.

It takes me half the usual time to get to the diner and by the time I get there, I'm all jacked up on my own adrenaline, my mind racing with a ton of ideas of what Violet was doing while I was at class. I never should have left her home alone. I should have stayed with her.

I hop out of the truck and hurry to the back door of the diner. It's cloudy, the sky grey, the wind chilly, and I swear to God I can hear thunder rumbling in the distance like a goddamn omen. When I open the door and walk inside the diner, the first thing I notice is how quiet it is. It's unsettling and the feeling only amplifies when the first noise I hear is the muffled sound of cries. I turn the corner and step out into the shelf area that's tucked between the kitchen and the bar and find Violet huddled in the corner with legs pulled to her chest. Her hair is a tangled mess and there's dirt on her clothes. Her bloodshot eyes are focused on empty space and tears are streaming down her cheeks. So much sadness pouring out of her yet she looks so empty inside.

'Jesus Christ.' I don't even mean to say it aloud. It sort of slips out, but it's a little bit of a shock to see her like this. I've only seen her cry a couple of times and she hated that even I saw it. Out here in the open where anyone can see her . . . whatever happened must have been bad.

I approach her like she's a skittish cat but she doesn't even notice me until I'm pretty much standing in front of her. Then she tips her chin back and looks up at me, eyes big and watery, so lost, swarming with confusion.

I have to work to keep myself composed. 'What's wrong?' I ask, crouching down in front of her. When she doesn't respond right away, I reach for her, but she shakes her head and hovers back, turning her face to the side. I see the swollen area Greyson was talking about. Already deepening to a bluish purple, which means whatever happened, she was probably hit hard.

'Please don't touch me,' she whispers. 'Not right now.'

I'm feeling about as lost as she looks when I spot the scratch on her wrist Greyson told me about, only it's not a scratch but a wound, jagged and open across her flesh and still bleeding a little. A switch flips inside me and I nearly lose control over myself as I grab her arm.

'What the fuck happened right here?' I demand, not

meaning to sound so angry, but I can't help it. I hate that she does this to herself, hurts herself. She deserves so much better than that, yet she can't see it.

She winces from my grip and I realize how roughly I'm grasping onto her, so I loosen my fingers a little. 'Sorry, but . . .' I swallow hard and shake my head. 'It looks like you did this to yourself . . . like you cut yourself.'

'I did,' she responds hollowly. 'I'm sorry . . . but I tried to turn it off another way, but this time . . . this time it was too much and I couldn't deal with it . . . couldn't make the pain stop no matter how hard I tried, so I went further . . . did things I never thought I'd do.'

I grind my teeth as I attempt to keep myself composed, but the idea of hurting herself makes me sick and angry. Not angry at her but at everyone else that helped destroy Violet over the years. All her foster parents that abandoned her. Preston. My mother.

'What happened?' I sit down on the floor in front of her, still holding her arm. I can hear someone in the kitchen, banging pots and pans around, but Violet seems to not notice. 'And where's Greyson?'

'He's working in the bar,' she tells me, staring at the space of floor in front of her feet. 'He doesn't know I fell apart like this . . . I waited until he got too busy to check on me.' She sucks in a breath, attempting to stop the tears, but they keep pouring out.

'How did you . . .' I gently brush my finger across her wrist where remnants of the wound are. 'How did this happen exactly?'

She inhales then exhales before finally her gaze resides on me. Her expression is empty – so detached it's chilling. 'I cut myself.' She slides her arm out of my hold, tugs the sleeve of her jacket over it, then hugs her wrist against her chest. 'I tried everything . . . standing on the top of a building, leaning over the edge, dangling my feet over it. When that didn't work, I tried to cut myself.' She shrugs indifferently. 'But it didn't help.'

I'm trying to ignore the fact that she's acting way too nonchalant over the fact that she hurt herself, but it's really fucking difficult. I just want to yell at her, tell her to stop, tell her she's too important and too good to be doing that shit to herself. 'How did you get the bruise on your face?' I gently brush the spot with my fingers.

Her face twists with perplexity as she reaches for her cheek, almost as if she's forgotten it was there. 'Oh that . . . I bumped it on a rock when I dove into the river.' I notice she has a hospital band on her wrist. 'It kind of hurt.'

I slip my fingers through the hospital band, my eyes widening. 'What the hell is this?' I ask, but she just shakes her head, refusing to tell me. Shaking my own head, I move my hand to her face and cup her cheek, trying not to be so angry, but I can't help it, not when she doesn't seem to care about herself. Doesn't she know how important she is . . . to me? How could she, though, when I've never actually told her . . . told her . . . that I . . .

That I love her.

'Your skin is freezing . . .' My hands travel down her body, to her neck, arms, her fingers, which are equally as chilled. 'You're freezing, baby . . . What happened to you?'

'It's cold outside and I walked here in damp clothes from the hospital.' She contemplates something. 'But I think the alcohol numbed me for the most part because I can't even feel it.' She pauses, head angling to the side as her brows furrow. 'It's weird, but I don't even remember walking here very well.'

I hate that she's clearly blacked out, either from the adrenaline overload or the alcohol and that in the middle of it she somehow ended up at the hospital. God, so many thoughts race through my mind about what the hell happened while I was at school. But what drives me even crazier is that she was wandering around alone when she's got a stalker after her. And while she's drunk. Not only is it dangerous but all the drinking she's been doing is bad for her health. Something I discovered firsthand almost a month ago after I'd made the decision to quit drinking. I'd gone to the doctor to get put on a pill that would help me go through detox. He did a check up and said that with my diabetes, I was pretty much lucky as fuck to still be walking around with all the binge drinking I've been doing. I think a year ago, I wouldn't have gave a shit, but now, with Violet around, with someone that I care for needing me, it makes me want to get better.

I just wish I could get her better too.

'Let's get you home.' I wind my arms around her to pick her up. She doesn't put up a fight and pretty much sinks into my arms with a heavy sigh, as if she's been waiting for me to do exactly this.

'This feels nice,' she murmurs as I carry her toward the door, her eyelids fluttering as she fights to keep them open. 'Luke . . . please don't ever leave me.' Her voice cracks in a way that rips my heart open. 'I don't have anyone anymore.'

'Yes, you do. You have me and I promise I'm not going anywhere. Ever,' I say without as much as an afterthought. I kick the door shut then start across the parking lot toward my beat up truck parked out back.

'You say that now . . . but you might change your mind after . . .' She yawns and buries her head into my chest.

'After?' I ask as I try to get the passenger door open without putting her down.

'After what's about to happen . . . so much stuff . . . ahead . . . for us . . .'

I pause, tension filling my body. *What the hell happened today?* 'What's about to happen?'

She doesn't answer, passing out in my arms, leaving me clueless as hell. Why would she think I'd leave her? And what could have possibly set her off this bad today? Could the two possibly go together?

God, what if I'm the reason she's breaking apart?

Chapter 8

Violet

When I open my eyes again I'm tucked in my bed, the sunlight sparkling through the window, which means that I must have slept through at least a day. I'm wearing one of Luke's t-shirts, the scent of him overwhelming my nostrils in the best way possible and for a moment, everything is okay. But then I take in the rest of myself; tangled hair that smells like dirty water and my entire body that feels like I've gone through the wringer with a champion boxer. At first I can't remember how I got here, but then slowly, bits and pieces come rushing back to me. The call from Detective Stephner . . . what happened . . . what he needs me to do . . . how I reacted to it all . . .

I lift my wrist up and examine the spot where I

started to cut my wrist with a shitty pocketknife I've had for a while, but I ended up backing out. Then I touch the side of my head where I hit the rock in the river. I can't even remember how I got out of the rapids. I think the person swimming toward me pulled me out . . . Then a bunch of people showed up and there were sirens there to take me to hospital. I lied through my teeth to the nurse about what happened; that I was standing on the edge trying to take a picture of a nearby bridge when I fell in. I think because I don't have insurance or anything it was easier for them to let me leave without questioning too much what happened. Plus, I can be a damn good liar when I need to.

After the hospital, I walked. And walked. And walked. So confused about life and what I wanted from it, because clearly I wanted something, otherwise I'd have let myself drown and join my parents in the ground. But I couldn't figure it out, just kept thinking of Luke. Then I found the diner. And Greyson . . . And then Luke was there in person, seeing me like that . . .

'Shit. Luke.' I blow out an exhausted breath as my emotions, the ones I was trying to get rid of, come rushing back to me, along with everything else. I pick up my phone from the nightstand and check the date

– yep, I've been out for a day. 'Fuck.' I rub my hand across my face, wincing from the pain, but then freeze when I notice the silver bracelet with the word *Sempre* engraved on it. 'I swear I took this off,' I mutter. 'What the hell?' I force myself to sit up, but it's like I've stepped onto a merry-go-round on crack. The room spins round and round and I nearly pass out and topple onto the floor. I grab the edge of the nightstand to brace myself and in the process, bump the lamp. It falls to the ground, not breaking but making a loud noise.

As I'm trying to get myself back up to sitting position, the door swings open and in walks Luke. 'What are you doing?' he asks, taking in the lamp on the floor and then me hunched over, attempting to get to my feet.

I wince as I collapse back down on the bed. 'Trying to stand up.' I fake a light tone. 'But it seems as though my legs have forgotten their purpose in life.'

He scowls at me. 'This isn't funny, Violet.'

'What? Me not being able to walk?' I'm uncertain how to react to his anger because it's not typical of him. 'It is kinda, sorta funny, don't you think?' I hold up my finger and thumb about an inch apart. 'Just a little bit.'

He shakes his head, clearly still irritated with me. 'Stop making jokes.' He sinks down on the bed, causing the mattress to concave and me to slide toward him. 'I don't even . . . I can't even . . .' When his gaze welds with mine, I want to shrink back and hide under the blankets. I've been scolded many, many times by people throughout my life, but never like this, never with so much passion, disappointment, terror and worry in their eyes. 'What the hell were you thinking? Leaving the house . . . going into the water . . . God dammit!' His hands ball into fists and he looks like he wants to break something.

I flinch from the harsh tone of his voice, but still sit up straight even though my back hurts. 'I was thinking how much I didn't want to think anymore. How much it hurts to think. How hard it is.'

'You promised me you wouldn't leave the apartment and you'd check in with Seth, none of which you did.'

'I don't need a babysitter, Luke. I've told you this time and time again.'

With a hard expression, he raises my arm and flicks the hospital band. 'Clearly you do . . . do you know how fucking worried I was when I couldn't get a hold of you?' He shakes his head, his jaw set tight, and his balled up fists are trembling. 'And then I find you drunk, soaking wet, with a hospital band on your wrist, and that makes it that much worse.'

I slip my hand from his hold, feeling ashamed of what I did. Luke knows, like knows, *knows* my dirty little secret. Unlike the nurse at the hospital, I can't just lie to him and tell him everything was an accident. And honestly I don't want to. 'I fucked up. It's what I do, Luke. I'm sorry, but there's not much else I can say.'

His gaze bores into me as he scoots closer on the bed until our knees touch. Then he rests his forehead against mine, like he needs to touch me. 'Why did you fuck up?' he says, his voice much more gentle.

One simple question. But it's packed with so much emotion and I feel like I'm drowning again. I open my mouth to tell him I don't want to talk about it, but then I realize that whether I want to or not, I need to. I made my choice when I decided to fight instead of drown that I was going to deal with this.

'Detective Stephner called today,' I say quietly. 'Something's happened with the case.'

He's struggling to keep a neutral expression as I lean back from him. 'Okay . . . What is it?' he asks.

Everything I felt when I heard the voicemail rushes

through me. The fear. The relief. The worry. The excitement. The disappointment of realizing that even if they do solve my parents' case, my parents will still be gone – nothing will change that. I still have no one. No mother. Father. No relatives. Nothing. And that the past still exists, that this didn't free me, that I might never be free. And then the revelation and the fear that I could lose him also set me off, was what nearly killed me.

But I chose to live. Chose not to drown. That has to mean something, right? That I don't want to die.

'They arrested your mother two days ago and transferred her here.' My voice unsteady as I feel my life shifting and altering, to something that's unfamiliar and terrifying. 'They want me to come down and do a lineup, see if I recognize her . . . I don't think I will be able to but it's something I have to do.' I shrug like I'm talking about something as casual as the weather. 'If all goes well, there'll be a trial. She'll be in prison . . . if all goes well, they'll figure out who killed my parents.' I swallow hard. 'Nothing's ever going to be the same again . . . I know it isn't . . . it's going to change everything . . . and I know . . . I know I'm going to end up alone.' I feel so vulnerable admitting the truth, ashamed, weak, so many things. 'I just want to be stronger,' I admit. 'Why can't I be stronger, like I used to?' *Because I didn't have anything to lose to begin with.*

His eyes skim every inch of me, making me tingle all over and he's not even touching me and it seems like he wants to say something, but can't figure out what it is. The silence stretches between us. It seems like the longest silence ever, the kind that seems like it's never going to end and I know that the longer it goes on, the worse the words that follow it will be.

Finally his lips part and words spill out. 'I love you.'

At first I think I've heard him wrong, but his eyes widen as I process what the fuck he just said.

'Huh?' I blink, stunned as shit. 'W-what did you just say?'

More silence stretches between us, only this time it's filled with our erratic breathing. It makes me want to retract my initial statement. This is the longest silence that's ever existed. And it's awkward as hell. Luke looks utterly perplexed, his brows dipped in, his thinking face on as if he's replaying what he just said over in his head while thoughts race through my flabbergasted mind. *Did he just say he loves me? Loves me? No one's ever said that to me since I was five, since my parents were still alive.*

'Oh my God.' They're the first words that leave my mouth. I don't know where they came from or what I mean by them. All I know is that it feels like the wind's been knocked out of me and I feel like I'm being strangled.

'I didn't mean to say that,' he finally says, but it doesn't seem like he regrets saying them either. He's way too calm. Way, way too calm while I'm freaking out. 'I mean, I did mean to say it, just not right now.' He forces a half smile as he tucks a strand of my hair behind my ear. 'Way bad timing, right?'

I gape at him, my mouth hanging to my knees, at a loss for words. He's acting like this isn't a big deal, but it is. A huge, fucked up, confusing deal that I don't know how to comprehend or handle.

I remain quiet to the point that it feels like I want to bang my head on the wall just to make some noise. I keep staring at Luke, unable to take my eyes off him. Part of me, the one connected to the side of my mind that still wants to believe in fairytales, unicorns, and all that imaginary shit, tells myself that the only reason I'm sitting here with him still is because my legs hurt too much to get up and walk away. But the other part of me, the one connected to the part of my mind that laughs at me when I'm trying to lie to myself, tells me that I'm still sitting here because I want to be here. And that in itself is horrifying.

'Violet, please say something.' There's a plea in Luke's voice, begging me to . . . break the awkwardness? To maybe say it back? I don't know if that's it, but what I do know is that I can't. I don't even know what love is.

'I need to get down to the police station.' I stare at him a second or two longer before tearing my gaze off him. 'Detective Stephner is probably wondering where the hell I am by now.' I don't know how, but I manage to get my legs under me and stand up without falling back down. Then I slowly step toward the dresser to get some clean clothes.

'Are you sure you don't want to wait until the tomorrow?' he asks. 'Get some rest before you go?'

'I just want to get this over with.' I select a red shirt, a pair of jeans, and a matching bra and panties. I think about asking him to step out so I can change, but worry that'll just make this situation even more awkward. It's not like I normally ask him to step out. In fact, I sometimes strip in front of him to tease him. So I remove my shirt and toss it on the floor, the bracelet getting caught in the fabric in the process. 'Hey, you didn't by chance find a silver bracelet, did you? And put it on me?' I ask as casually as I can as I work to untangle the bracelet from my dress.

'No . . . Why . . . And what bracelet?'

'Just a bracelet . . .' I clear my throat, knowing he's going to be upset that I didn't tell him about the box a while ago, but figuring I'm going to have to if I want to get to the bottom of why the bracelet was on my arm. So I tell him, not just about the box but how I swear it wasn't on my wrist when I left the house yesterday evening.

He scratches his head as I finally take off the bracelet and tug it from the dress, ripping the fabric a little. 'Are you sure you didn't have it on and maybe just thought you took it off?'

Once I get the bracelet out of the fabric, I set it on the dresser. 'Maybe . . . but I don't even like it on me at all so it'd be weird if I did leave it there.'

His frown deepens while studying me as I struggle to get my bra on through the pain radiating through my back. 'Well, it could just be that you accidentally forgot to take it off, but I still think you should say something to the detective, considering the box that showed up the other night . . . Preston's getting more.' He grinds his teeth. 'More daring.'

'God, what if he was in the house . . . but how could he even get it on me without me knowing . . .'

I trail off as images of me in the river and a figure in the distance appear in my head. The crowd standing around me as I lay on the ground, choking up water. Was he there? In the middle of them? No, there's no way Preston could have been there, yet I swear I see his haunting face in the memory. I think about telling Luke my conclusion, but I've already stressed him out enough for the day, so I decide to just tell the detective. 'Okay, I'll bring it up.'

Luke relaxes then stands up from the bed. 'Here, let me help you get that on.'

I tense as he crosses the room, stopping so close, and heat pours over my skin like warm honey. Within seconds he has the bra done up, then without saying anything, he takes the clean shirt from my hand and helps me pull it over my head. He lets me use his shoulder to support my weight while I put my panties and jeans on.

'You want me to go with you?' he asks as I fasten the button on my jeans.

'To the police station?' I flip my hair out of the collar of my shirt, getting a whiff of the damp stench flowing off the locks. *Jesus, I need a shower.*

Luke nods with uneasiness. 'Yeah, I can give you a ride and then wait for you in the parking lot.'

'What if it takes a while?' I slip my foot into one of my boots, then lean over to tie it, moving slowly because of the pain.

After watching me struggle for a few seconds, he crouches down and ties my boot for me. 'I'm sure it will, but I don't want you going there alone, especially after everything that's been going on.'

'I could ask Greyson to come with me maybe.' I'm trying to give him an out because there's no way he could want to go with me, not with what I'm about to do. 'That might be easier.'

Looking up from me, he arches a brow with accusation. 'For who exactly? You? Or me?'

'You . . . I mean, it's your mom . . . in jail . . . and I'm going there to try and help keep her there . . . won't it be weird?'

Shaking his head and not saying anything, he helps me put my other boot on. Then he stands back up and looks me directly in the eye with passion pouring off him as he places his hands on my shoulders. 'Violet, let me get something straight. Right here. Right now. My mother physically, mentally, and emotionally beat me and tormented me.' His voice cracks, but he quickly clears it and keeps going. 'She broke my sister Amy, let someone rape her . . . is part of the reason why

Amy decided to take her own life. Every single day living with her was like spending a year in hell. I fucking hate her, wish I was the one putting her in jail, so believe me when I tell you that I want this to happen too – I want her to be locked up forever.'

I know a lot about Luke through tidbits of stories we've shared with each other whenever we're in our room in the dark, but never so bluntly, so openly like this. I have to catch my breath before I speak. What I really want to do is kiss him, but I'm too afraid after what he just said . . . with the whole I love you thing. Afraid of what it'll mean . . . to him . . . to me. 'Alright, come with me.' Then I take his hand and we walk side by side and, for the briefest second, I feel like I'm stepping into the future for once instead of drowning in the past. Maybe this is why I chose not to drown. But then I remember where I'm going and the past catches up with me again.

Chapter 9

Luke

I can tell she doesn't want me to go inside the station with her but it worries me, her going in to face the woman who was part of one of the worst days of her life. To see her again . . . I can't even imagine how that's going to make her feel. Violet's pretending like it's not a big deal but I know it is. No wonder she had a break-down yesterday.

I don't think that Detective Stephner would appreciate me being in there, though, so I make it easy for Violet and tell her I'll wait for her in the truck. Instantly my mind starts to race with thoughts of what's going on inside, what I said to Violet today, with what's going to happen with us. Not just with my mother being caught finally, but after what I said to her. I love her. I've known that for weeks now, but I've been waiting until we were both ready before I said it aloud, wanted to be on better terms in both our lives and our relationship. But it sort of slipped out. I'm not even sure how, other than I was thinking about my shitty life with my mother and how glad I was that she was finally going to be behind bars. I started thinking of my life now and how much better it is, how much happier I am, even with all the complications. And how glad I am that I have Violet. Then Violet said something about how she was worried she'd be alone and suddenly, the words sort of slipped out because I wanted her to understand that I would never leave her. That she means way too much for that to ever happen, but instead of bringing her comfort it frightened her and, honestly, it kind of stung.

'Dammit. Did I fuck this up?' I grip onto the steering wheel, trying to calm down and think of something else, but it's all I can think of. When my head feels like it's on the verge of exploding, I decide to call my father to let him know what's happening, figuring it'll be a distraction from my obsessive need to analyze Violet's and my relationship.

'Hey, Luke,' he answers after three rings.

'Mom's in jail,' I tell him. 'They arrested her for

. . . for her involvement in Violet's parents' murders.'

'Luke, I'm so sorry,' he says sympathetically.

I lean back in the seat of the truck and stare out the window at the stars. I remember when I first got my license and this truck, how I used to sleep in it just to avoid going home. I'd just park somewhere out in the mountains and turn on some music and stare up at the night sky, basking in the peace of not having to be anywhere near my mother. 'You don't need to be sorry. I'm glad she's locked up.'

'That's not what I'm sorry for,' he tells me with a heavy-hearted sigh. 'I'm sorry you have to go through this . . . that you and Violet have to go through this. It has to be tough . . . your mother . . . her parents . . . God, I can't even imagine how Violet feels right now.'

'I can't either, since she won't talk to me about it.' I've never been one for talking about personal stuff going on in my life so I surprise us both when I say this. I didn't even mean to say it aloud, but between the stress and lack of sleep, my brain's been working a little slow the last couple of weeks.

'That's pretty understandable, considering the circumstances.' He pauses. 'How are you handling it?'

'I already told you I'm glad that she's in jail.'

'Not with that. I mean, handling Violet being distant.'

I shrug even though he can't see me. 'Fine, I guess.'

'Luke . . . you don't sound fine.' There's hesitancy in his voice, something that exists because our relationship is still rocky. I feel like I'm just getting to know my dad after years of him being pretty much nonexistent in my life and I think he feels guilty for being nonexistent, especially after finding out some of the stuff that went on with my mother while Amy and I were growing up. 'You know I'm here if you need to talk.'

I plan on telling him that I'm fine again. That I called him just to give him a heads up on what's going on with my mother, but suddenly words are leaving my lips that I don't mean to say. 'I told Violet I love her.' *Fuck.*

'Oh.' He's silent, thinking about who the fuck knows. Probably that his son is still screwing up, something I've proved to him quite a few times with my drinking and gambling habit.

'I told her right after she told me about Mom,' I say then add with a sarcastic laugh, 'Perfect fucking time, right?'

He chuckles on the other end of the line 'I told

Trevor I loved him during his grandmother's funeral.'

'Well he married you so it must have worked.' I aim for a light tone but suck at it big time.

He chuckles again. 'I was just telling you so you'd know that when it happens it happens and sometimes we can't help it when we fall in love. It just sort of blindsides us, you know.'

He's completely right. When I first realized I was in love with Violet, it came out of nowhere. It was like one minute I liked her and wanted to help her and the next minute I loved her and would do anything for her. 'I've known for a while.' I free a trapped breath, deciding if I want to go down this road with him, where we talk about our feelings and personal shit. What the hell am I doing? This doesn't sound like me at all. But am I really me anymore? My eyes wander to the rearview mirror, the person staring back at me isn't me either. They look healthier. More stable. My eyes less glossy, skin less pale.

'That you loved her?' He carries on with caution.

I squirm at the sound of the love. Unlike Violet, I did hear it a lot from my mother while growing up, but it always felt wrong when she said it . . . and the way she showed it. 'Yeah . . . I've known for like a month and have been waiting for the perfect time to say it to her. But like I said, I fucked up on that one big time.'

A gap of silence passes.

'What did Violet say after you told her?' he asks.

'Not much.' It's painful just remembering it, the endless silence that followed. 'There was a fuck-load of awkward silence and then she said she needed to go down to the police station to see if she could identify Mom as the person in the house that night.'

'So where are *you* now?'

I pick at the crack in the steering wheel as I look over at the police station, noticing a guy standing beside a tree near the entryway, smoking a cigarette. I wouldn't even have noticed him probably, but he's staring directly at my truck. 'Outside the station waiting for her.' I lean forward trying to get a better look at the guy, but it's too dark to see his face. For all I know, it could be Preston. But would he dare come to a police station?

My father grows quiet as I continue to stare the guy down and he looks as if he's doing the same thing back. I think about getting out, start reaching for the handle, when he takes a drag of his cigarette, then flicks it on the ground and walks off toward the parking lot. I open the door to get out, but by the time I get my boots planted on the ground, he's walked up to a Ford Taurus where a pregnant woman is waiting for him. He kisses her then opens the passenger door for her and the light from the lamppost in the parking lot hit his face. It's not Preston, but it's a realization of how worried and paranoid I am and how much I never relax.

I just want to be able to relax again. Not worry.

'So Trevor and I were thinking about taking a trip out there soon.' My father interrupts my thoughts and I look away from the guy and fix my attention on the night sky again. 'Maybe we could fly out in a couple of weeks . . . help out with anything you guys need help with.'

'I have football games on the weekends,' I tell him, which is true, but I'm also not sure I want him to come out yet, not sure if I'm ready for that.

'That could be fun,' he says with a hint of excitement. 'I've never seen you play before.'

I want to say *that's because you abandoned me*, but I've been trying to work on that shit ever since I had to borrow money from him to bail me out of a gambling debt, which he won't let me repay. And I don't want to be the kind of son that uses his father for money.

'I have to work on Sundays too,' I say. 'But if you're okay with that then sure. Come out.'

'Are you still working at that bar?' he wonders with concern. I don't blame him for worrying. Recovering drinker working at the bar. It's not the ideal situation but I'm looking for something else that will work with my school schedule, games and practice. But still, the fact that he's bringing it up is kind of annoying me.

'I applied at a few other places,' I explain, shaking off my annoyance the best that I can. 'But haven't heard anything yet.'

'You're not thinking about . . . about gambling again, right?'

Honestly, I haven't thought about it a whole lot, but that might be because I've been so focused on Violet. 'I'm good. I promise.'

'Okay . . . I just wanted to check up on you . . . I worry, you know, about you,' he says and I can detect the smallest bit of relief in his voice as if he'd been worried I'd been going back to my old habits. 'I'll get some tickets booked so we can fly out in a few weeks and let you know what time our flight lands.'

'Sounds good.' It's strange. My dad is coming to Laramie, to see me. Not long ago I would have fought it, but now I just have to accept what is otherwise I'll go back to the Luke that hangs onto everything and drowns his pain away with booze.

'And Luke?'

'Yeah?'

'If you need anything call me.'

Just a few words, but they mean a lot. Getting way too fucking emotional, I reply with an 'okay', then hang up, telling myself to stop acting like a pussy and suck it up. To distract myself, I crank up some music and start searching through job ads online on my phone, but I start to grow restless as more time ticks by. Thirty minutes. One hour. Two. God, I wish I knew what was going on in there. Wish I knew that Violet was okay and that seeing my mother wasn't breaking her.

Chapter 10

Violet

I've never been a fan of police stations. The noises: phones ringing, loud voices, commotions. It smells like takeout and I'm starving. It's driving me crazy and is bringing back the few times I had to visit some while I was growing up, both for myself the few times I got into trouble and for my parents' case. It's unsettling and making me fidgety. And it's not helping that it's taking forever. I've been sitting outside Detective Stephner's office for a couple of hours, waiting for him to show up and tell me it's time to go back – time to get this over with. I feel bad for Luke sitting out there in his truck, probably wondering where I am and I can't even call him since I left my phone at the apartment.

I think about going outside to tell him that maybe he should just wait for me at the apartment, when Detective Stephner comes strolling up to me from one of the cubicles. He has a folder tucked in his hand and a cup of coffee in his hand and is wearing a suit, the jacket open, revealing his tie with Christmas trees on it.

'You know it's not Christmas, right?' I elevate my eyebrows at him, sarcasm dripping from my voice as he tosses the coffee into the trash bin beside me.

His forehead creases as he sifts through some papers in his hand. 'Huh?'

I point at his tie. 'It's October, shouldn't those be like pumpkins or something?'

He distractedly glances away from the papers and down at the tie. 'Oh that.' He laughs, scratching his head. 'Yeah, my wife must have laid out the wrong one for me this morning.'

'Your wife lays your clothes out for you? How very nineteen fifties of you, and kind of sexist.'

He sighs, because I always do this to him – press his buttons. I'm not even sure why. He's not as bad as the detectives I've had to deal with in the past, but being here in the police station brings back too much painful memories for me and this bitterness sort of spills out.

'She likes doing it,' he replies with a hint of aggravation. 'I don't ask her to do it.'

I gesture at his tie. 'It looks really clear that she enjoys it, which is why she dressed you in Christmas stuff in October.'

'Why do you do this every time you come in?'

'What? Yank your balls?'

He gives me a blank stare. 'You know, one of these days that mouth of yours is going to get you in trouble.'

I stare back at him, my expression matching his. 'That's for the words of wisdom.'

He sighs again, giving up. 'Okay, are you ready for this?'

I shake my head. 'Nope.'

He sighs again. 'Violet, we talked—'

I cut him off. 'I'll never be ready for it, but I'll do it. I was just stating a simple fact.' I stand up from the chair, my knees wobbling and my stomach bouncing with my nerves, a bundle of butterflies that must have awoken specifically for this moment.

'Alright, follow me,' he says, heading across the busy room full of cubicles and desks and toward a hallway with florescent lighting. There are still a lot of people at the station and I catch a few of them glancing up at me as I pass. I wonder if they know who I am, if they know my sad, depressing story. I wonder if it makes them afraid of me. 'Oh and I wanted to let you know that I got the package with the photo and am looking into it.'

'Okay . . .' I'm barely aware of what he's saying as the reality of what's about to happen bears down on me. With each step, it feels like the walls are closing in, crushing, suffocating. I can barely breathe. Think. Function. This is it. I'm really going to go see the woman whose song has haunted my nightmare for years? How is it going to make me feel? Can I handle it?

Whoosh.

It's like all the air has been ripped out of my lungs. I suck in a deep breath, my vision spotting, and my knees start to buckle. I brace my hand on the cold brick wall to keep from collapsing onto the floor.

'Shit,' I say between gasps. *This can't be happening right now.* 'Shit. Shit. Shit.'

'What's wrong?' Detective Stephner asks, leaning over with concern in his eyes as he studies my face. 'Violet, just breathe. It'll all be over soon.'

I shake my head and back away down the hall. I didn't prepare myself for this . . . this massive wave of emotional turmoil. I want to be stronger, want to have inner strength like the old Violet, but she was only a façade, a costume I'd wear to make it easier to pretend everything was okay when it wasn't. But that costume was torn to pieces and my true self left standing vulnerable and naked. I want to run away and fix the problem the only way I know how, but after today, realizing that I don't want to die, I'm not sure it would calm me down even if I tried. 'I can't do this . . . not when I feel like this . . .'

'Do you want me to call someone to be here with you?' he asks, following me down the hallway, but he knows I don't have anyone, hence a hint of uneasiness on his part.

I work to catch my breath. 'I need . . .' What do I need? 'Luke.'

He appears extremely reluctant about the idea while I arrive at a strange state of calm from the statement. 'Violet, that's not a good idea . . . he's the son of the potential suspect . . . and . . .' He shifts his weight. 'Having him in here could be harmful to the case.'

'Can't he just come sit in a chair in the waiting room?' The air is returning to my lungs at the realization that this is what I need. Yes, it's what I need – Luke. He always makes me feel better, at least better than what I'm feeling. I need him.

God, do I need him.

Wow, that was hard to admit. I just hope he meant what he said – that he wants this as much as me; with Mira, with us. 'I mean, he's out in the parking lot right now, so it wouldn't be that much different if he just stepped inside.'

Detective Stephner scratches his head as he glances around at the busy cubicles around us. 'Maybe . . . out in the waiting room, but I'd have to ask my partner to sit with him . . . to keep an eye on him.'

I nod with eagerness. 'Okay, I'll go get him.'

'I'll escort you there,' he says, trailing me as I hurriedly make my way through the cubicle area.

'I'll be fine,' I tell him as I veer left and head past the sitting area and toward the entrance doors.

'It's not for you,' he tells me, moving forward to open one of the doors for me.

'Afraid I'll run?' I ask, wrapping my arms around myself as I step outside into the chilly night breeze.

He shrugs, staring out at the parking lot where Luke's rustic truck is parked. 'Wouldn't be the first time.' The door slams shut. 'I'll wait for you right here.'

I trot down the stairs, my heart hammering inside my chest. I remember the many things I had to do by myself when I was younger. At doctor's appointments, one of my foster parents would wait for me in the waiting room. My visits with the police in the beginning, I was chaperoned by my foster mother at the time, which meant she'd sit on a chair nearby and file her nails. I remember sitting in the chair and just wanting to hold someone's hand. I tried to hold her hand once, from which she casually slipped hers out. All I wanted was someone to comfort me.

What I wanted was my mom and dad. But that wasn't possible since the reason I was there alone was because they were dead.

As I approach Luke's truck, I can hear music playing and see smoke lacing out the cracked window. When I open the driver's door, he's messing around with his stereo and I end up scaring the crap out of him. He jumps, looking as though he's about ready to hit me.

'Jesus, you scared the shit out of me.' He puts his cigarette out on the ground, caution in his eyes as his gaze elevates to me. 'Are you ready to go?'

Shaking my head, I point over my shoulder at the police station. 'I need you to come in there.'

He instantly frowns. 'Is something wrong?'

'Not really, I just . . .' I chew on my bottom lip. God, asking for help can be so difficult. *Just do it* for

God sakes! 'I just don't want to be alone when I do this.'

As hard as it is to ask for help, his expression makes me feel the slightest bit better. 'Okay.' He grabs his keys, gets out of the truck, and shuts the door.

'You have to wait in the waiting room, though . . . because . . . well, you know.' There's a bit of awkwardness, at least with me, having to remind him that it's his mother in there.

But Luke tangles his fingers with mine like it's the simplest thing in the world. If only everything was that simple, but even walking on my own anymore is getting complicated. Still it helps that Luke is there, helps that he tries to make it as easy as possible when the detective makes him sit out in the waiting area as if he's the criminal, helps that when I get back to the room with the two-way mirror, I know that he's right out there in the same building, within running distance.

It makes it easier to breathe.

The room I'm standing in is small and dark, except for the light coming from the other side where they're going to bring Mira Price in. The air smells like cigarettes and coffee and there are a few metal chairs behind me that I could probably sit down in, but I'm afraid if I move, I'll run, so I stay planted in front of the window.

I swear to God I'm standing there for hours, when really it's probably only a few minutes, maybe even seconds before the detective joins me.

'You ready for this?' he asks, glancing down at the papers he's been carrying around.

No. 'Yes.' I fidget with the leather band on my wrist, the one I put on to cover up what I did earlier. 'What exactly am I supposed to do, though? Just tell you yes or no if I can remember her?'

He nods, distracted by the papers. 'If she was the one there that night and you can identify her, then you'll tell me. But it's very important that you're sure, okay?'

I nod. Like I would ever say anything else. Falsely identify Luke's mom, that's something I'd never want to do.

'And we can get her to speak, too . . . I know you said you heard her speak, right?' he asks as a door on the other side opens up.

I swallow the lump in my throat as I step up to the glass window. 'Sing . . . I heard her sing . . .' I trail off as a woman enters the room.

This is it.

This is it.

Holy shit, this is it.

She walks awkwardly as if her feet are too heavy for her legs, her shoes dragging across the floor. Her head is tipped down, her brown hair a veil around her face. She's wringing her hands in front of her, nervous and scared. The first thing I think is that this can't be the woman there that night. But I quickly learn that my initial observation of Mira Price is wrong because when she reaches the center of the room and turns to face the window, her expression is calm, her shoulders are squared. And those eyes . . . Those goddamn eyes that are as hollow as my heart used to be. They're the color of Luke's too, but still look so different – so lacking life and emotion. No, they're not the same at all.

Mira's eyes look hauntingly dead, pale, expression-less, and when she smiles it's as if she's pleased to be on the other side of the glass. But I'm just not sure it was her singing in the dark that night, and a sadness weeps inside me as I realize this and what it means – that I can't identify her.

A tear or two falls from my eyes but I can't seem to take my focus off of her. Her eyes are locked right in my direction too, even though she can't see me. But it feels like she can, feels like I'm five years old again, hiding in the dark and she's looking right at me, but never says a word.

Then her eyes grow more intense, her posture more confident. There's a shift in the air, an omen perhaps, one that I should run away from, but I don't budge. Her lips start to move, twist and conform as if she's sickly pleased with what she's about to do. When her voice leaves her mouth, it's as if I've been jerked back to my childhood home and I'm all alone. A few simple sentences, that's all it takes, for my world to forever change.

'Lean into me. Lean into me,' she sings slowly, looking right in my direction as if she can see me through the window. 'Take. Help me. I need to understand. Help me. I can't do this without you.'

Someone starts to scream. Shout. Bang on the glass. It's hurting my ears . . . my hands . . . feels like I'm bleeding out, gushing wounds . . .

'Violet! Violet! Calm down!' Arms wind around my waist, the touch bringing me back to reality. I realize that the screaming and banging is coming from me. That I've lost it. Smashed my hand against the glass so hard that it feels like it's broken. Detective Stephner has got a hold of me and is trying to get me to calm down. He yells something to someone, but I can't focus on his words. I can only concentrate on the excruciating pain, the blinding rage, the scorching hatred for the woman singing on the other side, tormenting me with her lyrics, her voice, her eyes. My veins burn with the overpowering need to break through the window and hurt her, make her pay for what she did. I've never felt so much in my entire life and if the detective let me go, I don't know what I'd do. Break through the glass maybe, just to get to her.

But Detective Stephner manages to get me out of the room before that happens, and I no longer have to see the fucking devil standing ten feet away, where the only thing separating us is a thin piece of glass. Yet the rage within me blazes and scalds me from the inside and I keep fighting to get away from him.

'Let me go!' I kick my legs, trying to break free, and end up knocking over a chair as we step out into the cubicle area. I'm causing a commotion, but I don't give a shit. Let them all stare – I'm used to it. 'She killed them! That stupid fucking song!'

'Calm down . . . It's going to be okay.' He tries to console me as he maneuvers me around the desks and heads toward the front area of the building.

'Where are we going?' I gasp for air. 'Are you kicking me out?' Right as we say it, we round the corner and enter the waiting room where Luke is sitting. He's staring at the ground, his head hung low, but his focus snaps up when we enter because I'm being extremely loud.

'What happened?' he asks as he rushes over toward me, scanning me from head to toe.

There's an awkward transfer as Detective Stephner hands me over to Luke and I think in his own way Detective Stephner is helping me, as if he knows Luke is the one thing I need right now. 'I need you to come with us to my office.'

Luke's arms wrap around my waist and it takes some of the pain away, but not all of it. 'Why?' Luke asks Detective Stephner.

The detective looks at Luke. 'Because I need to talk to Violet some more, but you're the only one who she seems to listen to. So calm her down and bring her back please so we can have a rational conversation.'

'Asshole,' I say, even though I'm not really angry at him. Just angry.

The detective shoots me a warning look then walks off.

After he vanishes around the corner again, Luke pulls me closer to him, my back pressed against his chest. 'What'd she do?'

'She sang that stupid fucked up song . . . no one even asked her to . . . it's like she wanted to get caught or something.' My breathing is ravenous, my heart tremulous. *Everything* about me is unsteady at the moment and the only thing holding me up is him.

'No, she wanted to fuck with your head,' he says through gritted teeth. 'That's what she does.'

It's strange to think how much he knows her, the monster standing on the other side of the glass. He's firsthand felt her pain, felt the damage she can inflict, and as strange as it is, it makes me feel connected to him, calms me down the slightest bit.

He exhales. 'The scream . . .'

'That was me,' I admit, struggling to breathe normally again. 'I lost it . . . I didn't even know what was happening to me . . . I just sort of snapped.'

'Baby . . . I . . .'

'I'm fine.'

He places a kiss on the back of my head. 'No you're not. What can I do to help?'

'You're here . . . that's enough for now.' And I mean it. Luke is having this strange calming effect over me, like he's holding me above the water when I feel like I'm about to drown again. 'We should probably go back though before Detective Stephner thinks I've bailed.'

He nods then reluctantly releases me. I want to grab his arms and wrap them back around me, but he steps up to the side of me and slips his arm around the back of me. I look into his eyes, similar to the ones that belonged to the monster on the other side of the glass, at least in the shape and color. But that's it and everything else about them – everything else about him – is different. He makes me feel comforted instead of utterly terrified. He makes me feel safe when no one else can.

See, this is what I'm afraid of. Losing this. What would I become if it was gone?

The answer is terrifying to think about.

Chapter 11

Luke

I heard the scream. God, I heard the scream. It sounded like Violet's and I wanted to run to her but the receptionist wouldn't let me back. I could only breathe freely again when I saw Violet again. Then Violet told me what my mother did and I expected her to leave me, walk out on me right there. But she seems to be having the opposite reaction, wanting to be closer to me instead of further away.

She lets me lead her back to Detective Stephner's office, my arm around her back and her head resting against my shoulder. She's practically glued to my side, which I one hundred percent don't mind. I just wish it was under different circumstances. Wish it wasn't for this.

The rundown from the detective is quick. Even though he doesn't full-out say it, he basically tells us that right now there's probably enough evidence to build a case against Mira and that things will start to move. They are going to be questioning her, to try and find out who the other person was at Violet's house that night.

After the detective is finished, he dismisses us, but stops me before I walk out. He kind of guides me back into the room as Violet wanders out into the cubicle area, unaware that the detective has pulled me back. 'Just so you know, when this gets going, you might be contacted to be a witness . . . from both parties. I thought I'd let you know, considering,' he nods his head in Violet's direction.

I know what he's saying. That not only could I help put my mom behind bars, but I could also help free her. Like I would ever do that. But the idea of going up in front of her to help put her away has me feeling like the scared little boy inside me, the one that grew up with that horrendous woman. Could I do it? Get up on a stand and talk about my mother with her sitting there watching me?

'Thanks for the warning,' I tell the detective then walk out of his office, my head swimming with thoughts, a lot that make me hate myself for being so fucking weak, so afraid of the woman who raised me – or the woman who I lived with when I was younger. Raised doesn't seem like the right word at all.

'What was that about?' Violet asks as I walk past the cubicles and up to her.

I circle my arms around her waist. 'Nothing. He just wanted me to keep an extra eye on you.'

'You already do enough for me.' She rests her head against my chest. 'What more could you do?'

'A lot, lot more,' I assure her as we start for the door. 'Come on, let's get you home.'

'Home sounds good.' She sounds as exhausted as I feel.

A few minutes later, we're in my truck, getting ready to drive down the road toward home. I'm about to pull out onto the street, when I notice Violet is cradling her arm against her chest.

I tap on the brake and stop in the exit area. 'Wait. What happened to your arm?'

Violet blinks her attention away from the window, looks down at her arm, then back at me. 'Oh . . . I hit it against the window when Mira sang . . . I can't even really remember doing it . . . I just sort of lost it.' Her eyes flash with an unnerving frustration that sends a chill down my spine. 'See, this is why I have to do the things I do, Luke.' She raises her arm and winces. 'Otherwise I end up snapping and lose my shit.'

I want to be comforting, but I can't when she's talking about hurting herself. 'There are other ways. Trust me, I know . . . remember how much I used to get into fights and I haven't in a while. It's because I found something else.'

'Like what?'

'Working out. School. Taking care of myself.' I pause. '*You*.'

She frowns at the last thing I say. 'I don't want to be a chore for you.'

'A *chore*? That's what you think you are?' I shake my head when she doesn't answer then shove the truck into park and scoot across the seat toward her. I'm not even sure what I'm going to say, what I want to say, but stuff just starts pouring out. 'First off, you're anything but a chore. I lov— like being there for you.' I hold her arm in my hand and she winces from my touch but her muscles unstiffen. 'I just don't want you hurting yourself anymore.' I shut my mouth and concentrate on examining her arm. I plan on keeping my lips sealed, but there's something in me, a pressure building and I need to let it out somehow. Maybe it's because I told her I loved her today, that it's had some sort of snowball effect, but whatever the hell it is my mind goes fucking crazy and my mouth continues to say things it shouldn't. 'We could be good . . . me and you . . . good together. And my mom's going to jail now . . . we'll make sure she's behind bars forever . . .' Another loud breath. 'And I know there's so much more shit ahead for us, so many more things to deal with, but I just need you to take care of yourself better. We can work on it, you and I, together. Getting better, I mean.' I stop talking, shocked as fuck that all that shit came barreling out of my mouth. Apparently tonight is confessional night with all the shit I'm putting out there.

It's quiet for a while and it takes me some time to let my gaze lift, after pouring out my heart and soul like that. Her eyes are unreadable, her expression neutral, her body still. I have no idea what she's thinking, but fuck, I wish I could just once know what she's really thinking.

'I'll try,' she finally utters, her voice barely audible. She's not looking at me, but out the window at the streetlights and closed buildings.

'Promise me you will,' I say, sketching my finger

along her wrist. She may look completely calm, but her pulse is hammering underneath my touch – she's terrified on the inside.

She swallows hard but still doesn't look at me. 'Yeah, okay. I promise.'

I'm not sure if I believe her – hate that it's like that. But all I can do is hope that she's telling the truth and be there for her if she's not.

Chapter 12

Luke

The next few days go by fast, probably because I have a lot on my mind. Violet, school, my mother, Violet, the case, Violet, the game, Violet.

Violet.

Violet.

Violet.

She consumes me more than anything else. I worry about her, want her near me at all times, but that's kind of been a problem since she seems to be putting some space between us ever since the night at the police station. I'm not sure if it has to do with my mom or that my mouth didn't want to shut up; that all that emotional shit I put on her was too much.

Still, if I had my way, I'd take her everywhere with

me. Besides, it'd be good for her. She's been spending too much time cooped up in our room, especially since the news of my mother being arrested hit the news. Somehow a reporter or two found out that Mira was my mother and that Violet and I were dating and things went batshit crazy. Phone calls, knocks on the door, all wanting to ask their questions. I've wanted to punch one or two in the face, but have resisted the urge, even though it's hard as hell, the need to protect Violet always burning in me.

'Dude, your mind is fucking gone, isn't it,' Seth says. We're out on the balcony smoking and he's sipping on a beer while I'm drinking a soda.

I rub my hand over my hair, scattering ashes all over myself. 'Yeah, I know.' I brush the ashes off the sleeve of my grey shirt. 'I've just been thinking a lot about stuff.'

He rests his arms on the railing, the cigarette smoke lacing the air. 'Violet stuff?' he questions and when I nod, he adds, 'What is it with you two? You both refuse to tell anyone what's going on with the police and stuff, but Greyson and I can tell there's some huge shit going on. And Violet comes home with a cast on the other day, but won't tell either of us how she broke her hand.'

She ended up breaking it when she was pounding against the glass at the police station, after my mother taunted her so badly she snapped. The next day after we'd left the police station, I'd taken her to the hospital despite her protests because she was in so much pain she could barely move the damn thing.

'That's not my stuff to tell.' I take the last drag of the cigarette, then drop it on the ground and put it out with the tip of my boot. 'Look, I'd love to share, but I'd feel wrong doing so.'

He rolls his eyes. 'Bullshit. You've never been one to share.'

'True.' I turn around and face the sliding door, putting my arms on the railing. 'But this time, I have a good reason not to.'

He doesn't say anything, finishing off the rest of his cigarette while I head inside. 'So Greyson and I will be at the game this week,' he says as I step into the living room.

'Figured as much, since Callie's going to be there,' I reply. Callie is Kayden's girlfriend and one of Seth's best friends. It's not too uncommon for them to come and cheer Kayden on.

'Well, we're going to cheer you on, too.' He shuts the door and takes off his jacket.

I feel a little uneasy as I make my way to the fridge, thinking about getting a beer, just to take the edge off from the conversation. For years I never had anyone come to games, to graduation, to any event. I got used to it and now suddenly I have Seth and Greyson, not to mention my father and his husband coming to a game in a couple of weeks. It makes me feel restless inside and like I'm losing control over my life and it makes me wonder if this is what Violet feels when she does the dangerous things she does. Maybe my drinking is the same as her adrenaline addiction.

I grab another soda from the fridge and pop the top, my thoughts on Violet who's been in the shower, way too long come to think of it. 'Well, I'm glad you're coming I guess.'

Seth gives me a sarcastic look as he plops down on the sofa. 'Oh really? Then why do you sound so depressed?'

'Not depressed.' I take a swig of the soda as I back toward the bathroom. 'Just a little surprised. That's all.' With that, I walk out of the room and into the hallway.

When I get to the bathroom, I open the door, glad Violet didn't lock it. The shower's still on, the curtain closed, the air foggy.

'Violet,' I say as I shut the door behind me. I'm worried with how quiet it is. She's been pretty mellow since Mira was arrested, but that healing cut on her wrist and cast on her arm is a reminder of how unstable she is. And even though she promised me she'd try to stop, I understand addiction way too well. Stopping is difficult, maybe one of the hardest things I've ever done. I think drinking, gambling, fighting might always live in my veins, but it doesn't mean I have to continue to feed them.

'Yeah, in here,' she replies over the sound of the flowing water.

'Okay.' I relax back against the door and fold my arms. 'I was just getting worried . . . You've been in here for a while.'

'I'm fine . . . you need to stop worrying about me so much.'

Yeah, that's never going to happen. I don't say it aloud though, figuring I've overloaded enough lovey-dovey shit on her since dropping the L word. We haven't mentioned it, but we're both hyperaware that it did occur – I can see it her eyes when she looks at me and feel it in the acceleration of my heart every time I look at her.

She draws the curtain back and sticks her head out.

Her hair is wet and has suds in it and beads of water cascade down her face and neck. 'I can't figure out how to wash my hair and get all the soap out without using my casted arm.' She sticks her arm out that's wrapped in a cast, the cast wrapped in plastic. 'This thing is a pain in the ass and not going to hold all the water out if I submerse it completely.' She muses over something with a thoughtful look. 'Although, it did come in handy the other day, when I pretended to bump my arm into this bitch, Daisy Miller, when I was on my way to the main office. I'm not sure what that chick's problem is but she bumped into me and then tried to act like it was my fault, so I replied with a nice knock in her side with this thing. She really wants to get her ass kicked, I'm telling you.'

I can't help but chuckle. I went to high school with Daisy Miller and she was a bitch like Violet said, but everyone let her walk all over them, except for me, but I never took shit from anyone. And neither does Violet, so I'm not surprised she reacted by 'accidentally' hitting her with her casted arm.

'Yeah, Daisy's a bitch,' I say. When she gives me a funny look, like how the hell do you know her, I add, 'Kayden used to date her when we were in high school.'

'Really?' She makes a *ewe* face. 'That's disgusting.'

I shrug. 'He was going through some shit or something . . . I think that's why he did it.'

'Aren't we all,' she mutters, then sighs. 'So any ideas on how to make washing my hair easier?'

'I could get in there and help you.' I'm partly joking but then she nods and the joke sort of evaporates and settles over me. Showering seems so intimate, so very couple-like, and it's fucking terrifying how much I want to do it with her.

'Hurry please, though.' She steps back into the shower and lets the curtain go. 'I have shampoo in my hair right now that I can't get out.'

It grows silent as she waits for me to get in. I strip my clothes, wondering if a) she's as nervous as I am and b) how the hell I turned into the kind of guy that gets nervous about showering with a girl. Yeah, I've never done it before, but still, it's just a lot of nakedness and water. Not a big enough deal to get all worked up.

Still, I feel out of my element as I draw back the curtain and step inside. My eyes are fixed on Violet as I seal the curtain shut. She's standing in front of the downpour, her cast arm in front of her, water rivering down her neck, her breasts, her stomach, her entire body wet and sexy as hell. Little beads of water dot the tattoo she has going down her side, of intricate flowers that wind and create viney patterns and I have the strongest hunger to lick them off. I catch her eyeing me too, her gaze lingering on my chest before colliding with my gaze.

'How do you want to do this?' Her chest heaves as she takes a deep breath.

It takes me a second or two to process exactly what she means, my mind immediately filling with a hundred different dirty ideas, every one of them including our naked bodies pressed together. But she's talking about her hair.

I step toward her, the warmth of the shower hitting my legs as the water splashes on me. 'Here, tip your head back,' I tell her. She obeys, angling her neck and dipping her hair into the water. She starts to lose her balance and she sticks her good hand out to stop herself from falling. I hurry and wind my arm around her back, support her weight. 'You can let go . . . I've got you.'

She swallows hard then lets go of the wall. Her eyes are fastened on mine as I run my fingers through her hair, washing the soap out. Her gaze fills with confusion, like she's looking for something in my face or eyes but can't figure out if it exists. I'm about to ask her if she's okay, when she mutters, 'You're always keeping me from falling.' Her eyes snap wide as soon as she says it, clearly the words an accidental falter of the lips. But it's already too late. They've already struck my heart, pierced my soul and I lean down and press my lips to the base of her throat. I slide my lips up her neck, licking and nibbling at her flesh, moving slowly, relishing the taste of her. She lets out this uncontrollable whimper that I've only heard once from her, but that drives my body into a mad frenzy. I kiss her lips fiercely and she kisses me back with equal intensity. Our wet bodies are pressed together, the air damp, heavy, filled with heat. She's still tipped back as I hold her up, tasting her, but I want more.

Slanting back, I guide her with me until we're both standing up straight. She looks like she's going to protest, but I back her up against the wall and lower my lips, licking up the water on her tattoo, just like I wanted to. She moans, relaxing under the touch of my tongue as it travels up her body, taste her flesh until I reach her mouth and crash my lips to hers. Her good hand grips at the back of my neck, pulling me close as my tongue searches every part of her mouth.

'Luke,' she groans, her leg lifting up and hitching around my waist. Something snaps inside me and every part of my body wants to be connected to her.

We haven't had sex since the thing at the police station happened. I'm not sure why, other than it seems like we've both been tangled in this emotional web of confusion and trying to figure out stuff.

'Tell me it's okay,' I whisper against her lips.

She doesn't respond with words, instead rocking her hips against mine and moaning. 'It's more than okay.'

My fingers slide up her leg, grip her thigh, grasping her tightly as I hitch her other leg around my waist. Her legs open up to me and her arms loop securely around the back of my neck. My lips collide with hers, pulling her nearer, our bodies aligned, but it feels like I need her closer.

She continues to kiss me, biting my bottom lip as I brace one of my hands against the wall and slide deep into her, our wet bodies colliding, our hips meeting rhythmically. Steam surrounds us, consumes us, makes it difficult to breathe. The feel of her lips . . . her warmth . . . the inside of her . . . watching her head fall back and her eyes gloss over as she comes undone in my arms temporarily takes all the bad away and pushes me toward the edge. Moments later, I join her, struggling to hold us upright. We're breathless, our chests crashing together with each breath we take.

'That was . . .' She trails off, breathing profusely.

'Perfect,' I finish for her.

'Such a softy,' she whispers. Usually she jokes when she says this, but now she just looks tired and kind of content.

I want to call her a softy, take the upper hand, because that's what we do, but I keep the remark to myself, figuring I don't want to do anything to ruin this good moment.

A really, really rare, but good fucking moment. If only I could find a way to make more of them.

Chapter 13

Violet

Things haven't been that bad for the last couple of weeks and that's saying something. I haven't heard or gotten any surprise packages from Preston either and the texts have stopped. Mira Price is behind bars for now, something that I've wanted to happen since I was five. I'm still dealing with my visit to her on an emotional level, the cast on my arm constantly reminding me of what happened. But it's strange. I'd been so angry and unstable at the police station, to the point that I'd broken my arm, but as the days go by, it almost feels like some of my internal scars are healing, right along with my broken wrist. I feel like a part of me was sort of set free in my outburst. Seeing Mira in that room, knowing she was there – knowing she's still there – is a small bit of justice for my parents, if only they could just catch the other person. I know that it won't bring them back and that's still another thing I'm dealing with, but after the drowning incident I'm trying to avoid testing my life at the moment, choosing to live life I guess.

The detective called me into the station for a little chat the other day to give me an update, which was basically so he could inform me that Mira was being an uncooperative pain in the ass. He's kept looking down at my casted arm and then suggested that maybe I should go see a therapist to help me go through this. I'd told him I was fine, since the idea of going and spilling my thoughts to someone is something I never wanted to go through. I remember the looks people used to give me when they found out I'd spent twenty-four hours in the house with my parents' bodies.

Pity.

Horror.

Fear.

But it turns out I might not have a choice. The publicity of the entire thing has got the university involved and it was 'recommended' by my school advisor that I talk to their counselor. Already being on thin ice, I agreed and I have my first appointment today.

The woman sitting behind the desk when I walk into the office is a bit different than what I expected. She's got fiery red hair, the kind you have to dye to make it look like that. And I can see a tattoo peeking out from the collar of her shirt. She's dressed in a pant suit though and her hair is pulled up into a bun, like she's half-business woman, half rebel, which kind of matches the dark but beautiful artwork she's got hanging up on the walls.

'Oh hey,' she greets me when I walk in as if I'm a friend not a client. 'Violet Hayes, right?'

I nod. 'Yeah, that'd be me.'

She smiles then leans over her cluttered desk to shake my hand. 'I'm Lana. Glad you could make it. Have a seat.'

I plop down in the chair and drop my bag to the floor, a bundle of nerves as I pick at my fingernail polish then start biting at my nails. I'm telling myself to put my walls up, be tough Violet, because this isn't a safety zone – this isn't like the time I spend with Luke.

'So what brought you in here today, Violet Hayes?' Lana asks as she sorts through a file on her desk.

'You don't know that already?' I put my hands on my lap. 'Because I'm guessing you do. Everyone knows me. Violet Hayes, creepy girl who lived while her parents were murdered. Stayed in the house for twenty-four hours.'

She smiles up at me, surprisingly not annoyed by my bitchy attitude. 'Sounds like you're a tough chick.'

'No, just blunt.' This is going to be harder than I thought.

'Hmmm . . . maybe . . . But maybe not.' She looks down at the folder again, reading a paper that's inside it. After looking it over briefly, she shuts it and slides it aside before overlapping her hands and putting them on the desk. 'So other than what the news says about you, what do I need to know about you?'

I give a relaxed shrug. 'Doesn't the news tell you enough . . . tell you what's wrong with me?'

She gives me a soft smile. 'I'd like to hear what you think about you, not anyone else.'

I honestly don't know how to answer her, not used to this kind of situation. 'There's not much to know.'

'Do you have a job?'

'Yes.'

'And you go to school. You've been really good with attendance up until a couple of months ago. Do you want to tell me why?'

I shake my head. 'Nope.'

'Okay then.' She lets it go easily and I'm relieved

that she does – I've already heard enough about that from other people. Maybe this won't be so bad after all. 'And what about boyfriends? Do you have one of those?'

I shrug, the walls I've put up starting to chip away. 'Maybe.'

She appears lost. 'Maybe?'

'It's complicated.'

She nods like she understands, but how could she when I haven't told her anything? 'What about friends?'

I fold my arms across my chest. 'I might have a few of those.' *Maybe.*

She mulls over my answer then picks up a pen and grabs a notebook from her drawer. 'And what about family?' She starts to write something down.

'Dead.' The walls crash down. 'I'm a foster kid.'

I catch her hesitating, but she quickly recovers. 'Are you close with any of them?'

I almost laugh. *Not by choice,* I want to say. *Because one won't leave me alone.* 'Again, no. Adults really aren't a fan of this.'

She glances up at me. 'Of what?'

I point at myself. 'Of a girl that scares the shit out of them.'

She writes one more thing down, then sets the pen

and paper aside and focuses on me again. 'Why do you think everyone's afraid of you?'

'Because that's what they say.' I'm uncomfortable, my inner demons and addiction clawing to come out and regain control over the situation the only way I know how. 'I don't blame them either. It's creepy what I did.'

She considers what I said for the longest time. 'You know, regardless of what you think, your reaction wasn't odd.'

I snort a disdainful laugh. 'I just sat there in the house with their bodies for almost a day. Even I think I'm creepy.'

'Maybe that's the problem then,' she says, reaching for a tin of mints on her desk.

I feel oddly on display for her, like I'm sitting in a glass case and she can see every part of me, inside and out and there's nowhere to hide. It's not the most settling feeling and I can't figure out a way around it. 'What is? Me being creepy?'

'No, how you think that about yourself.' She pops a mint into her mouth and closes the tin. 'Sometimes we hear people say stuff about us so frequently that we start to believe it ourselves, even if it's not true.'

'No, it's true.' My voice is tight, unable to accept what she's saying.

She sets the tin aside. 'We'll see,' she says, then picks up her pen and jots something else down. 'I'd like to see you next week, if that's okay. Same time and day?'

I want to tell her no, be a bitch so I don't have to come back and let her analyze my mind, but I find myself muttering okay, then I take the card she offers me before bolting the hell out of that office before she can say anything else.

The more I walk, the more I replay what she said about the problem. That I believe everything everyone's told me. The more I think about it, the more it pisses me off, like I'm that weak-minded that I just believe what everyone told me. And that's the thing. There's only so many times you can get told how unwanted you are, before you start believing it's true.

I hurry across the busy campus, yellow and brown leaves crunching under my boots as I stomp across the lawn, telling myself I'm not going back even though I agreed. I have a feeling that the next visit is going to go much deeper than our short preliminary appointment and Lana makes me too uneasy, probably because she cuts straight through the bullshit. I can tell I'm not going to be able to be the hardcore Violet with her and just fake smile through everything. I'm going to end up being the unstable one that cries in the privacy of her own bathroom because she so desperately wants to risk her life to turn off the pain, but made a promise to the only person she cares about that she would try not to do that anymore.

And I don't want to be here.

But really, I do, otherwise I'd have given up already.

Grunting in frustration at myself, I turn down the sidewalk for the Humanities building to go to class. I started going yesterday and am continuing today, which feels like a step in the right direction, whatever that direction may be. I spot a news van on my way there, so I take the long way, going behind the building where there's a wall of trees blocking their view of me. The media has this fascination with me dating Luke, the son of the woman who's being charged with involvement in my parents' murders. There have been reporters showing up at the university and at my home. I usually give them my best go-fuck-yourself attitude, but what I really want to say is: how the hell can I answer your question about what's going on with me, when I can't even figure that out for myself?

Yes, I like Luke.

To the point that it's actually starting to hurt when he's gone.

And my heart leaps when he's near.

But there's also this pain.

This pain linked with the idea of losing him.

But I want to be the person I know I can be when I'm with him. A new person maybe.

I think a lot, honestly.

Maybe it's because I have one less thing to think about. All that time spent thinking about Mira and now I don't have to worry about her anymore. So much time now to think about what I want.

What do I want?

I just want to be happy.

But happiness isn't something that comes easy to me and I think I'm going to have to learn how to let it in. But do I let something in that I'm not sure I've ever had?

Later that day, my mind is teeter-tottering somewhere between bored as hell and bummed out. I have count-less assignments scattered around me on the bed, some make-up assignments a few of my Professors who were kind enough to give me because of my 'condition'. As if having my parents' murder case plastered all over the place and a constant herd of reporters trying to get some insight into my head is the same as having an illness. Still, I'm glad I'm getting a second chance, although I did have to drop two classes, but it's my own stupid fault.

That's not what's making me bummed out, though. I took the box out again today, the one with my parents' stuff, for reasons that are unknown – maybe it was therapy or this dire need to torture myself. I did manage to flip through a few pages of the notebook and discovered that that's all it was. I guess my mother was trying to start a diary but stopped doing so a few days later, because she died.

I ended up throwing the box under the bed, hearing the contents spill, but not daring to clean them up. Out of sight, out of mind. That's what I keep telling myself. Then I buried myself into my homework, trying to use it as a healthy distraction instead of what I really want to do, which is wander up to the roof, or maybe knock back something strong and numbing.

'What are you doing in there?' Luke strolls into the room and shuts the door behind him. I have some grungy music blasting from my laptop, totally adding to my begrudging mood. I'm holding a marker in my hand and using it as a doodle tool to draw on my purple cast instead of working on my assignments. My hair's braided to the side, no makeup on, and I'm wearing a tank top, hoodie and boxer shorts, a real hot mess.

I reach over and turn the music down. 'Well, I was working on a Calculus assignment, but I started seeing numbers everywhere, so I took a break.' I lift my cast that's covered in drawings, some my own, others from Greyson and Seth who have took it upon themselves to turn my arm décor into art. 'I really do hate math.'

He closes the door behind him and slips off a shoe. It's late in the evening and from his sporty attire – drawstring shorts, a tank top and running shoes – I'm guessing he's just gotten back from the gym. 'Then why did you take Calculus? You know it's not a requirement for a General Studies major, right?'

'Yeah, but I had nothing better to take and I like a challenge.' I recline against the headboard and stretch my legs over the mess of textbooks and assignments, frowning at the Calculus book. 'It's not like it's hard, just not fun.'

He laughs as he kicks off his other shoe. 'Math never is . . . although, can I point out that most of your classes are higher course levels than most sophomores take, and they come easy to you, so not only are you smart, but you might want to rethink that General Studies major and do something else, like Physics or something.'

'Physics? Really?' I question with skepticism. 'That's what you see me doing?'

He shrugs as he removes his wallet and some spare change out of his pocket and drops them on the nightstand. 'You're good at science and math.'

'You are too, so maybe you should major in it.' I kneel up on the bed and slip the hoodie off that I was wearing because the bedroom is getting too warm for jackets. 'And how do you know I'm good at science?'

'Because I took Chemistry with you,' Luke replies as I throw the jacket on the bedpost, adding more chaos to the room. Luke and I used to be so neat and orderly but we've gotten kind of turned into slobs over the last month, too busy with other things I guess.

'That was before we were dating, though,' I say. 'Were you watching me or something?'

He pauses, then clears his throat several times, confirming my accusation. 'Maybe, but that's not how I know you got an A. It was because the Professor posted finals on the door.'

'Just because I got an A, doesn't mean I'm smart. I could have cheated.'

'Yeah, you could of.' He positions himself in front of the edge of the bed with his hands in his pockets. 'But you're smart enough that you don't have to.'

'So are you . . . And stop calling me smart.' I'm getting uncomfortable with the compliments about my allegedly wonderful mind. In the past there's only negativity when people brought it up. Crazy. Erratic. Unstable. Disturbed. Psychotic. That's what I'm used to and it makes it harder to listen to the positive. It occurs to me then that Lana might have been onto something today and I'm not sure how I feel about that.

Not wanting to think about that stuff and how it makes me feel, I aim for a joke. 'If you keep giving me compliments, I'm going to start glowing.'

His mouth curves to a smile as he chuckles. 'Oh really? Is that what happens?'

I nod, sitting down and bending my legs so I can rest my arms on my knees. 'All compliments and no negativity makes Violet a glowing girl.' I wink at him, all suave.

He laughs even harder, wrapping his arm around his taut stomach, and I can't help but let a smile grace my lips.

Then his elation fades and unexpectedly he's leaning toward me. 'It's good to see you smile,' he says, grazing his finger across my cheek and letting his fingertips linger at the corner of my lips.

I keep on smiling, but it's becoming complicated with the feel-goods that he's giving me and I don't know how to deal with those except for panic and run. I grow quiet, battling to keep myself calm and not bolt out the door. Try to be different. Try not to be that girl, the one he asked me to be in the truck.

Moving away from me, Luke tugs his shirt over his head and tosses it on the floor, fleetingly veering me away from my thoughts and toward his muscular abs and chest painted with symbols, sketching, and beautiful sayings. 'You look more muscly lately,' I admire absentmindedly.

Unbuttoning his jeans, he cocks a brow. 'Does it turn you on?'

I thrum my finger on my lips and pretend to think about it really hard as he slips off his jeans. 'That's a really tough question to answer. I may need to see more to come to an accurate conclusion.'

He chucks his jeans at me and they hit me in the face. I playfully throw them back at him, but he ducks and I end up missing him and knock over an empty soda can on the dresser. He laughs while I flip him the middle finger.

'I'm more muscly because I've been taking care of myself and working out more with Kayden,' he says and as if proving his point that he is indeed taking better care of himself, he picks up his case that carries his stuff for his diabetes to check his blood sugar level.

'I know you have been.' I collect a pen from the bed and lie back down on my stomach, trying not to think about how easy this conversation is. How simple. *It's been so long.* 'It's good that you are.'

After pricking his finger, he wanders to the dresser to get some clean clothes, but pauses and turns to look at me. 'You should come with me sometime.'

My gaze flicks up from one of my literature papers. 'To the *gym*?' When he nods, I snort a laugh. 'Yeah, that's not going to happen. I'm not athletic. At all.'

He grabs a pair of pajama bottoms from the dresser and then flops down on the bed with me. 'You don't have to be athletic . . . Callie comes with Kayden a lot.'

'Good for Callie.' I flip the page of my textbook. 'If I went to the gym, I wouldn't even know what to do with myself.'

'It would get you out of the house.' He slides my books out of the way so he can scoot closer to me then slips his fingers through mine, causing me to drop my pen. 'I worry about you . . . you haven't really left the house since . . . Well, since you went to the station a couple of weeks ago, nor have you talked about it . . . and I'm worried.'

'You've said that twice,' I say then give a heavy sigh. 'And it's hard when there's a mob always waiting around for me.'

He rotates onto his side and combs his fingers through my hair around his finger, gazing off with great contemplation. 'You can't let them control your life. And besides, I'll punch them in the face if they come too close.' The corners of his lips tease upward.

But I frown. 'No punching anyone in the face. I don't need you going to jail.'

'Please just come with me.'

Clearly this is important to him, although I don't know why. And if I'm being true to myself about trying to get my act together, heal all my brokenness besides the bones, I need to start attempting to make up to him for everything I've been taking lately. 'If I go, I'm just going to sit there.'

'You can do whatever you want.' He inches closer and his body heat engulfs me and puts me into this temporary state of high where I swear to God I'm floating. 'Although there is a kickboxing area. Seems like something right up your alley. You could take out your anger aggression on it.'

'Anger aggression?' I narrow my eyes at him, but it's more playful than annoyed. 'Are you saying I have anger problems?'

'Maybe . . . I mean, you have every right to be angry, but I think it would be good for you to try finding a healthy outlet.' He glances down at my cast then I catch his gaze flicking to the other wrist where there's a mark on my flesh hidden beneath a leather bracelet; a mark I put there when I cut my own skin hoping that maybe if I made myself bleed, my emotions would bleed out with the blood.

There's also a questioning in his eyes, and I get what he wants to know – needs to know.

'I haven't done anything since that day.' I fidget with the leather band self-consciously. 'I've been trying not to.' But it's been a rollercoaster of difficultness. Up and down. That's what I've felt like every second of every hour of every day.

'I know you have,' he says. 'I just want you to find something that might help, so maybe you won't have to do it anymore . . . so maybe it won't be so hard not to try.'

It's crazy how much he gets it and how much I want to stop for him and kind of for myself. But if I'm being honest, I can't picture my life without my reckless behavior and that makes me wonder how long I can go on like this. It's been so long that it doesn't even feel possible; even though I never want to have that helpless feeling I had in the water again. And I don't for one second believe that going to the gym is going to help get rid of my problem, but he's looking at me with hope in his eyes, so I agree.

'Fine, I'll go.' I force a smile.

He grins from ear-to-ear and it makes agreeing worth it, despite the fact I'm going to look like a dumbass trying to beat up a bag. 'Good, we start tomorrow at seven o'clock,' he says.

'In the morning?' I give him a disgusted look. 'What the hell. I don't get up that early.'

He laughs at me then gives me a kiss on the forehead before sitting up. 'Yeah, it's early but I have to pick up my dad and Trevor from the airport at noon and then we're going to dinner later, remember?'

Honestly, through all the stuff going on the past couple of weeks, I'd forgotten about it. 'I kinda forgot they were coming,' I admit, sitting up and reaching for my Calculus book.

'That's understandable.' He heads for the door with the pajama bottoms in his hand. 'You've been under a lot of stress lately.'

'You've been sounding like a psychologist lately. So either Seth's been wearing on you or maybe that's what you should major in.'

He releases a cynical laugh. 'Yeah, that'll be the day. Me sitting behind a desk, listening to other people's problems and trying to fix them.'

'You're better at it than you think.' My words carry more meaning than meets the ear.

Luke gives me a thankful smile that chips at my ice-cold heart just a bit, but his happiness quickly turns to hesitancy. 'So how was the therapy thing today?' he asks as indifferently as possible, but I can tell he's worried about asking me.

I shrug, not wanting to talk about the fact that my head is officially being examined. 'Not too bad I guess.'

'Do you have to see them again?' he wonders, his fingers wrapping around the doorknob.

I nod, wondering if I'm going to go through with it – keep going and let Lana dissect me. 'Yeah, next week.'

'Until when?'

'Until the unforeseeable future.' I shrug, then shrug again, not sure what else to say. Lana never mentioned how much I'd have to go there. What if it's a really long time? Sitting in that chair, talking about stuff I always avoid no matter what the costs. Can I handle it?

'Oh, okay.' Luke drops the subject and opens the door.

All this talk about our futures, I'm reminded of who I am. Like me, Luke has no declared major, but he still plays football and has hobbies so he's at least got that, unlike me. I don't have any hobbies, other than my extreme lack of people skills and my adrenaline junkie addiction. I have nothing really.

Maybe Luke's right. Maybe I do need to declare a major, get out of the house, do something. But I don't even know where to start. All my life, I've felt like I was drifting, drifting through homes, jobs, even classes, passing them but never really getting into anything I was being taught.

Drifting.

That's all I did – do. My thoughts always stuck in the past.

But now the past might get its justice – my parents might get their justice. And that leaves me with facing the future, whether I'm ready to or not.

Chapter 14

Violet

Later that night, I ride with Luke to work. We rarely have the same shifts, but tonight's an exception, which is both good and bad. Good, because I've been enjoying his nearness lately and bad because . . . well, because his enjoyable nearness is a distraction. Every time I pass the bar area with a tray in my hand Luke grins at me from behind the counter and gives me that look – the one that makes my skin tingle and my heart race. I damn near run straight into the wall one time and almost spill the cups of water on the tray, but luckily just bash my elbow against the doorframe. Thankfully, I recover without a mishap, but I head over to Luke to have a talk. 'Would you stop looking at me like that?' I ask, as I set the tray down on the countertop. 'I'm going to end up breaking my other arm if you don't.'

He twists the cap off a bottle of tequila and gives me a confused look. 'What are you talking about?' The corners of his lips quirk.

'Oh you know.' I point a finger at him. 'Otherwise you wouldn't be smiling like that.'

There are five shot glasses lined up on the bar, for the group of guys sitting at the end of it, I'm guessing. Luke tips the bottle of tequila and with fluid movements guides the bottle across the top of each glass, filling them up. Then he sets the bottle down on the counter and puts the lid back on. 'Oh you mean this look,' he says, his gaze lifting to mine, his brown eyes blazing with enough intensity to nearly light the damn shots on fire.

Someone from the back yells, 'Violet, order up!'

'You're asking for it,' I warn as I pick up the tray and head to the back to get the next order. After I deliver it, I go back through the bar again. Luke is getting drinks from the beer tap, a little distracted by the people flooding in. But I don't care. I want to get the upper hand, so on my way around, I 'accidentally' drop the empty tray I'm carrying near the corner of the bar, where only the people working behind the counter can see. The only person there right now is Luke and when he looks up at me, I bend over in a not-so-ladylike way to pick it up. I'm wearing a short black dress and by the breeze I feel hitting my ass cheeks, I know I'm giving him a good view.

I hear him let out a choke sound and then I stand up and give him my most innocent smile, mouthing, *I win.*

Pressing back a grin, he carries my gaze until a guy walks up to order and he has to look away, but not before adjusting himself.

I'm feeling pretty good about myself as I go back into the kitchen, set the tray down, and tell Tina, the other waitress working tonight, that I'm taking a break. Then I slip my jacket on and head outside, not to smoke, but to get some fresh air that doesn't smell like fries. I plop myself down on the steps and stare up at the stars, enjoying the night sky, when my phone goes off from inside my pocket. A shiver goes up my spine, but that always happens whenever I get a text. But the icy-cold feeling only amplifies when I see it's from an unknown number.

Unknown: I'm surprised at u Violet. I thought you'd try to figure this out.

I'm about to forward the message to Detective Stephner when another text comes through.

Unknown: Come on. Ask me why I do it.

My fingers tighten on the phone. Things have been going so well and then this shit starts up, reminding me that at any moment things can take a turn for the worse.

Another one goes through.

Unknown: I'll give u a hint. It's not because I'm in love with u. Like anyone ever could.

It triggers a nerve and I find myself texting back.

Me: Go fuck yourself.

Unknown: And there u r. Knew that'd get to u.

Me: Don't pretend like u know me.

Unknown: But I do know u. You're the girl who desperately wants to be loved, even though you'll never admit it.

Me: Go to hell.

Unknown: It's ok to want to be loved, Violet. I know u wanted love from me. And I was ok with it. Got me some nice head . . . u can really suck dick well.

I'm fuming. How dare he bring that crap up again and remind me of all the stuff I allowed to happen between the two of us. I'd been doing so well with it the last few weeks and I don't want to go back there. So I stop texting, because it's the only thing I can do.

But right before I put my phone away, one more text comes through.

Unknown: U and I are both parentless. U know that. We actually share a lot in common. Just something to think about.

I don't know what he means by it and I want to respond by asking. But then I'd be choosing to fall back into this, which might be exactly what he wants. So instead I forward the messages then put my phone away. Telling myself that he's wrong. That Preston and I have nothing in common, but in all actuality I don't know how true that is. Because I know very little about Preston.

And that makes me feel very vulnerable at the moment because I have a feeling he might know a lot about me, maybe even more than I know about myself.

Chapter 15

Violet

It takes me a while to fall asleep that night, Preston's text weighing on my mind. Finally, I manage to doze off, but I swear it's only seconds later that I'm pulling away from my nightmares with the sound of a voice.

'I saw you, Violet. Saw you in the water.' A voice floats from somewhere in the dark house. 'You were pretending you wanted to hurt yourself, but I know you didn't really want to. See, I do know more about you than you think.'

Did it come from the bedroom? I'm not sure, but they sound so close . . . wait, where am I?

I'm startled from my sleep then smothered by the darkness around me. It feels so heavy, so crushing that I can't breathe.

I'm alone.

Alone.

Alone.

Alone.

In the dark house.

Only I'm not alone.

A stranger is here with me.

'Wake up.'

This time I know I heard something for sure and I reach for Luke and feel his warmth beside me. 'Luke, wake up.' I give him a hard shake, my eyes frantically scanning the room. But there's no one there. 'I think I hear someone . . . out in the living room.'

It takes him a second to come out of his sleep, still dreary eyed as he flips on the lamp and looks at the clock. 'It's two in the morning . . . what's going on?'

'I hear someone in the living room,' I hiss, sitting up and straining to hear the noise as I grip tightly onto the blanket.

This can't be happening.

Not again.

No.

No one is here.

Thud . . . thud . . . thud . . .

A second later, Luke is out of bed and on his feet,

chucking me the phone. 'Get ready to call the police.'

I grab his arm as he cracks the bedroom door open. 'Don't go out there.' I dig my nails into his flesh, clutching onto him like a terrified child.

'I need to go check and see if someone's in the house.' He slips his arm from mine and walks out of the room in his boxers with no weapon, nothing to protect him.

Panic flares through me like a wildfire and images of that night blaze through my mind.

Darkness.

The Voices.

The noises.

The singing.

The blood.

The fear.

Jumping from the bed, I grip onto the phone and rush after him into the hallway, not wanting to let him out of my sight. Letting him out of my sight means that I may never see him again.

'Violet, get back in the room,' Luke hisses, putting his arm out and shoving me back.

I shake my head, my entire body trembling as I hear voices and see lights flashing from outside. The night when my parents died there were fireworks being let off and I thought the gunshots were firecrackers. It's happening now.

It's happening again.

'Are those fireworks?' My voice doesn't even sound like my own, lost in a traumatizing memory I've been thrown back into.

Luke shakes his head. 'No . . . it's the police I think . . . Violet, go back to the room. *Please,*' he begs.

I shake my head again, hugging the phone to my chest. Rattled, rattled, rattled – my insides are rattled and I can't think straight. *It's so dark. It's so loud. I'm so scared.* 'I can't . . . I can't leave you . . . I don't want to be alone.'

I can't see his face, but I feel his fingers lace through mine and hold on tight as he peeks around the corner into the living room. 'I promise I'll be right back,' he says then his fingers slip away from mine.

I start to cry.

Bawl like a little baby as I collapse to the floor.

I'm not going to see him again.

It's the most painful thought I've ever had, aching in my bones, muscles, veins, heart – everything. I never want this to happen – can't live without him. The fear consumes me, feels like it's burying me alive. I need to get it out of me. Need to go somewhere – do something. I've never felt this much pain before and I can't even begin to think about what it means, because I know that going there will kill me right now.

No, God, no. This can't be happening.

Moments later, the living room light flips on and I'm no longer in the dark. It makes it easier to breathe, but my heart is still slamming violently against my chest until finally Luke returns to me.

He appears frazzled and unnerved. 'I want you to stay inside.'

Hot tears stream down my eyes and all I want to do is grab him and hug him. 'Where are you going?'

He pretends to be calm, but I can see right through him – he's worried. 'The sliding glass door was open and the police are outside with their siren on. Someone's at the door. I need to step outside and talk with him.' He crouches down eyelevel with me. 'Violet, listen to me. I'm not going anywhere.' He cups my cheek. 'I promise.'

I nod my head up and down, stunned by what's happening inside me. Something's different, something's changing and it both scares the living daylights out of me and excites me in the most fearful way ever.

I let Luke steer me back to the room and into bed. I sit on the edge as he pulls a shirt on then disappears out of the room again. I watch the clock tick. Listen to the wind outside. Watch the blue and red lights flash outside. It feels like an eternity passes by before finally Luke returns to our bedroom.

'What was it?' I ask, the phone still in my hand.

He takes the phone from me, sets it aside on the nightstand, then climbs in bed beside me. His arms encircle me then he pulls me close and lies us down on the mattress.

Safe.

I feel so safe.

'Someone came into the house . . . the police saw him . . . turned on their lights.' His muscles go taut, his embrace so tight I feel like I'm being pressed into him. 'They think it scared whoever it was off. They're searching around but can't find them.'

I swallow the lump in my throat. 'It was him.' I'm afraid, yet I'm not. Because this time I'm not alone.

I'm not alone?

'Violet, it wasn't . . .' He trails off because he knows I'm right. It was Preston. Preston was inside my house. And I don't think it was the first time.

157

Chapter 16

Luke

Everything had been going so well. I'd gotten her to agree to go to the gym, get out of the house, hoping that maybe she could discover another way to release her pain and anger. But then a very terrified Violet wakes me from my sleep.

As soon as I saw that damn sliding door open, I knew someone had been in our apartment. We haven't been that careful about locking it, since we're on the second floor, but apparently we should have been. I'm getting a fucking alarm system – I can't take it anymore. This helpless feeling that I'm going to wake up and find Violet hurt by that fucking piece of shit.

The fact that he scared the shit out of her was enough to make me want to beat the shit out of him.

If he would have still been in the apartment when I walked out there, I'd have lost it. I could tell she was thinking of that night her parents were murdered, could see the fear in her green eyes. She thought something was going to happen to me and that she'd never see me again. It fucking hurts, seeing that in her eyes, makes me want to do anything to take the pain and fear away from her. But again, all I feel is helpless.

I watch her sleep for the rest of the night and finally fall asleep around five in the morning. About an hour later, I'm woke right back up by a knock on the door. The sun is starting to rise and the light is shining through the window, making it feel a little safer, but I still have a hard time leaving Violet in the bed alone, even if it's just to answer the door.

It ends up being the cops, wanting to tell me that they didn't find the person, but that they filled out a report.

'A report.' I lean against the doorframe and give them a cold, hard stare. 'Yeah, that's going to help a lot.'

'It's better than nothing,' the taller of the two male police officers replies agitatedly while the other one jots something down on a clipboard.

'No, it'd be better if you would have caught him

before he came into the house.' I clench my hands into fists, feeling that rage that lives inside me, the one that rises whenever I think of my mother. But this time it's about Preston. *I want to fucking beat the shit out of him so badly I can't stand it.*

'Kid, lose the attitude,' the shorter officer says as he scrawls something else on the paper. 'We're doing the best that we can.'

'Clearly that's not enough,' I snap. 'Since he made it into the fucking apartment before you realized something was up.'

They look just as annoyed as I felt, but continue on with their bullshit protocol. They show me this silver bracelet they found on the lawn, asking me if I can identify it. It's Violet's, the one that belonged to her parents and that she was confused about wearing or not. When I tell them that, they explain to me that they have to hang on to it for evidence, but will return it when they can. Then they give me a rundown of how they plan on upping security, but it's all bullshit. This is the second, maybe third time Preston has been here and he's getting braver. The annoying thing is, I'm not sure what he wants. To torture Violet? No, I think there's more to it than that. The thing that really gets to me is I don't think it'll stop until the police catch him. I know how sick and twisted people work, having lived with it for years.

When I get back to the room, Violet is still asleep. She looks peaceful, always does when she sleeps, until she wakes up screaming. I wish I could see her like that when she was awake, wish I could find a way to just give her peace in her life for all the peace my mother took from her.

'Who was that?' she murmurs, half out of it as I climb back into bed.

'Just the police,' I whisper as I pull the blankets over us and scoot toward her. I think about informing her of the bracelet, but decide to wait until she's fully awake.

'Did they . . . find him . . .' she asks, although clearly she's out of it.

'No, but you're safe.' I kiss her head, shut my eyes, and inhale her scent. 'I promise I won't let anything happen to you.'

'I know you won't,' she murmurs, nuzzling against me. 'But Luke . . .'

'Yeah?'

'I think Preston . . . I thought I heard him say he was there that day . . . that I almost . . . drowned . . . I think he really did put the bracelet on me which means he's been in the apartment before.'

Every muscle in my body winds tight like a knotted rope. Not just because he was there the day she went into the water, but that he's been in our apartment before. Fuck, I'm so angry and tense right now, I'm about to ram my fist through the wall just to make myself feel better, but then Violet scoots closer to me and it reminds me that I've got to be more stable than that right now. I'll try to let it out at the gym or something tomorrow, at least as much as I can.

'Thank you.' Violet says, pressing a kiss to my chest.

The fire in my chest simmers down. 'For what?'

'For . . .' She yawns as she traces a circle on my chest, right over where my heart is beating. 'For not leaving me.'

My heart clenches in my chest as I smooth her hair back and study her face, the way her eyelids keep fluttering, the way the sunlight hits the studded diamond in her nose, the way her lips are slightly parted. So fucking beautiful and so fucking tough, whether she realizes it or not. She's a survivor of so much shit that a lot of people will never even begin to comprehend – the lucky ones.

Only when I know she's fast asleep do I dare whisper the truth. 'I would never leave you,' I whisper. 'Because I love you.'

Chapter 17

Violet

The next day I wake up from the strangest nightmare, if you can even call it that. I'm not even sure what the hell it is or means. In it was my mom. She was standing in front of her grave with her arm outstretched to me and I was frozen at the edge of the cemetery, unable to step foot on the grass and go to her.

'I can't,' I'd cried. 'I just can't.'

She'd finally lowered her hand and smiled at me. 'I's okay, Violet my baby girl. You can do it. Just let me go.'

That's when I'd awoken, gasping for air, not necessarily terrified but confused. A confusion that's still whirling around inside me. And that confusion amplified when I remembered last night's events.

I still agree to go to the gym the next day, even though Luke gives me an out, saying that either we can stay home if I want or that I don't have to come after what happened last night. I can tell that he wants me to go with him, though, and honestly I don't want to stay in the apartment after what happened. The worst part about this whole thing is I don't even know why Preston is doing this or what he wants from me. In the past, I'd always know – deal drugs for him and sexual favors. But now it feels like he's playing some sort of game with me where I'm left wondering what the hell will happen next. It's been so quiet lately too that I'd started to let my guard down and almost forgot he was still lurking around. I can't do that, but I also don't want to live my life in fear anymore.

I want to be fearless.

I want to be free.

I just want to be me.

Trying to shake thoughts of Preston the best that I can, I get dressed to go to the gym, putting on a pair of tight shorts and a tank top topped with a hoodie. Then pull my hair up, the entire time pretending everything's okay, that I wasn't shaken to the core last night.

I feel exhausted, but Luke looks even worse than I do. When I ask him if he slept at all, he says, 'enough', but the dark circles under his eyes contradict his words.

We're headed out the door when Greyson comes bouncing up to me from the kitchen with way too much energy for six thirty in the morning. 'Happy Halloween!' He offers me a cupcake in the shape of a pumpkin. He's dressed in shorts, a t-shirt, and tennis shoes, ready to hit the gym. How the hell he manages to get ready and cook cupcakes already is beyond me.

'Thanks.' I take the cupcake with great appreciation, then lick a huge mouthful of orange frosting, savoring the sugar rush I get.

'We're heading out,' Luke tells him, slinging his bag over his shoulder. 'You and Seth coming?'

Greyson nods, returning to the kitchen and starts putting away the rest of the cupcakes he cooked. 'I am for sure. We'll see about sleeping beauty. He hates exercise.'

'Sounds like a brilliant man to me.' I bite the cupcake and nearly have a foodgasm, the buttery frosting and cake melting the moment it touches my tongue. 'Jesus, this is good.'

Luke watches me with a lustful look as if watching me lick frosting is the sexiest thing he's ever seen. 'Yeah, I can see that.' It takes him a moment, but he manages to blink his gaze off my mouth. 'Just tell him he can hang with Violet,' he says to Greyson. 'She's not too into it, just coming to keep me company.'

'Okay, that might get him to be more agreeable.' Greyson pops the lid on the case he put the cupcakes in then rounds the kitchen with another cupcake in his hand. 'One for the road?'

'What do I look like? A sugar junkie?' I ask, but then take the cupcake anyway. 'Thanks.'

Greyson shakes his head at me with a smile touching his lips. 'See you in a bit, sugar junkie.'

I wave goodbye to him then follow Luke out to the truck, feeling my guard go up the moment I step out the door as last night's events race through my mind. As if Luke senses my panic, he threads his fingers through mine and holds onto me tightly until we're safely in his truck.

He drives down the road as I munch on the cupcake, staring at the houses and stores lining the roads. Everything is splashed in oranges, blacks, and purples. Fake witches and skeletons and cobwebs cover the inside and outside of buildings.

'I've never been into holidays,' I divulge to Luke as I take another bite full of frosting.

'Really?' he asks me, although he doesn't seem too surprised.

I shrug, peeling the paper of the cupcake down lower. 'It's probably because I've never celebrated them. I never had costumes for Halloween, unless I wanted to make them on my own, which I never did because I never had anyone to take me out to get candy. I did the Thanksgiving a few times, but family dinners were usually awkward for the outcast and nonmember of the family clan. Then Christmas . . . I hate Christmas. There was nothing jolly about it all when I was younger . . . I mean after my parents . . .' I swallow hard as I pick at the cupcake and emotions well inside me, so I have to clear my throat. 'Yeah, but I can remember getting a single present one time from one of the families, that actually seemed great when I opened it. A pretty silver ring ornament with a violet stone that was surrounded by these little onyx gems. It was so beautiful and was perfect for the fourteen year old gothic version of me.'

That gets Luke to smile. 'I can totally picture you all dressed in black and covered in studs.'

'Yeah, I pulled it off pretty well. The ring would have looked totally kick ass too, but yeah, about five minutes after I got the ring, Mrs Fairly informed me that she'd given me the wrong present, took it away, and gave the ring to her daughter. My real present ended up being new socks.' I stop talking, my heart knocking inside my very long confessional. 'Yeah, sorry about the sad, pity party story. I don't know what got into me.' I glance down at the cupcake. What the hell did Greyson put in this thing? Truth serum?

Luke's continues to drive down the road, mulling over something. 'I hate holidays too,' he admits, flipping his blinker on to turn off the main road. 'We never really celebrated them right. For Halloween, we'd usually clean the house, although Kayden and I did go out trick or treating a few times. For Thanksgiving, if I was lucky, she'd let me and Amy cook a good meal or I'd get invited to one of my friends', but that's when I was older. And Christmas . . .' His mouth snaps shut, his knuckles turning white as he grips the steering wheel. 'Let's just say that Christmases were the worst.'

I feel like he's giving me something in return for sharing my story, even if I really didn't mean to. Stuffing the rest of the cupcake into my mouth, I slide across the seat toward him and hold my pinkie up. 'You know what we should do? We should make a promise not to make a big deal of holidays.'

He considers what I said, glancing from my pinkie to my face. 'You've never dressed up for Halloween and gone out trick or treating ever?'

I shake my head. 'I'm sure I did when I was still with my parents, but the memories are too foggy to remember it – most of them are anyway,' I say, my heart constricting in my chest at the painful reminder.

Instead of giving me a look of pity, determination fills his expression. 'Then how about this? How about we celebrate the shit out of all the holidays? Every single Goddamn one. Every single year.' When he stops at a stop sign, he turns to face me in the seat and lifts his pinkie in front of me. 'What do you say? Are you in?'

I know his words have much bigger meaning than just celebrate a few holidays, but I'm not sure if I'm promising them to the full. Still, what he's proposing sounds like something I've always wanted, but never let myself want, since I was about five years old. So I hook my pinkie with his and decide to give it a try. 'Okay, Mr Stoically Aloof, I'm in.'

Chapter 18

Violet

'Oh my God, I think I'm going to die.' I breathe through my nose because the smell of the mat I'm lying on is more pungent than spoiled eggs left out in the sun on a hot, muggy day. Seth is lying next to me, something he did after he declared he wasn't a gym person either. Greyson, however, is, at least the kind that loves to run on treadmills, but I'm not too surprised, considering how cheery he was this morning about going.

Seth and I are hanging out on the mats, lying on our backs, staring up at the ceiling, the sound of clanking and grunting surrounding us. Callie's doing some sort of kickboxing class, and Greyson's on the bikes. There's this super poppy song, with an upbeat

beat and lyrics playing, and it makes me want to find the stereo and break it.

Nope, I'm not a morning person, something I've known for a while, but it's been made clear to everyone that is graced with my presence today.

'Give me some of your coffee,' Seth playfully demands, reaching over me to steal my iced-latte.

I swat his arm. 'No way. Get your own damn coffee.'

He lets out a frustrated grunt as he lies back down on the mat. 'Greyson wouldn't let us stop to get one. He said we were running late and that it was my fault therefore I had to go without coffee.'

'Dude, he's so hardcore,' I joke, because Greyson is anything but that.

'Totally,' Seth agrees sarcastically.

Sighing, I sit up and offer him a sip of my coffee. 'But don't drink it all or I'll have to kick your ass.'

He shoots me a doubtful look as he takes the coffee from my hand. 'I highly doubt that. You may act a badass, but you're so not.'

I eye him over purposefully. He's wearing a plaid shirt with the sleeves fashionably rolled up to the elbows, dark jeans, and his hair is tousled and has these blondish highlights that look like he spent some time in a salon to get. But now I live with him I know that's not the case, that they're a-la-natural. He looks very Hipster, which would be fine except we're at the gym. 'Look who's talking. You look like you're getting ready to go to a concert instead of going to the gym.'

'Oh, speaking of concerts.' Seth takes a long drink of the coffee then hands it back to me. 'There's an awesome one playing tonight at The Silver Moon Grill. No one huge or anything, but there's a pretty good lineup. Plus, it's freaking Halloween and it has a theme and everything. You should come.'

I look at him suspiciously. 'Did Luke tell you to invite me?' He seemed so set on getting me out of the house more that I have to wonder.

He looks lost. 'No . . . I haven't even told him about it.' He pauses. 'Why would you ask that?'

I shrug, sipping on my coffee. 'It's not like you invite me to hang out or anything. You only started talking to me civilly a couple of months ago.' I wonder if it's because he pities me with all the shit going on, although Seth doesn't seem like a person who pities people a lot. He's actually pretty blunt, which I can handle, but this morning he's been tiptoeing around me, probably with what happened last night. If I were them I'd think about moving out with the girl who attracts the crazy.

It's not like I want them to; it just seems like it'd be safer and easier for them.

'And vice-versa.' He leans back against the wall and stretches out his legs in front of him. 'You're just as much of a drama mama as me, honey.'

I sip my coffee then set it down on the mat. 'I prefer the term interesting and never boring.'

'That is not the same.'

'Yeah, you're probably right.' I pause. 'Why are you nice to me now, though?'

He shrugs again, staring at his shoes. 'When I first met you, it seemed like you were a real bitch to Callie and kind of a whore, but after learning who you are, I realize my first observation was wrong.'

I am curious what he thinks of me now, but not enough to ask him. Deciding to change the subject, I put my legs out, doing a lame attempt at the splits, figuring I can at least pretend like I'm getting warmed up to do something. I'm wearing tight shorts and an old t-shirt and my hair's pulled up in a ponytail. 'Fine, if you really want me to go to the concert, I will,' I tell him. 'As long as it's after dinner with Luke's dad and Trevor and Luke can come with me.' I'm sure he will want to, since we promised to celebrate the shit out of holidays only a half an hour ago.

'It doesn't start till nine,' he tells me. 'And *duh*, I assumed you'd bring Luke with you. You two are attached at the hips now.'

Even though it's true, his observation still catches me off guard. Lost in my thoughts, I stretch again, leaning forward into this awkward position. 'God, why do people do this – my face is pretty much level with my vagina.'

Seth laughs. 'Well, you're choosing to do it, so maybe you're enjoying it.'

I flip him the middle finger without lifting my head. 'Ha ha, you caught me.' I stay in the same position, putting my hands on my legs, fingers wrapping around my thighs. 'You know, I think I'm going to get a tat on the side of my thigh,' I say more to myself than anything. 'Something new.' Yes, new would be good. Everything is old right now, connected to the past.

A shadow casts across me and then I hear Luke say, 'What are you two doing?' He sounds like he's out of breath.

'Oh just watching Violet touch herself,' Seth answers amusedly. 'And listening to her talk about self-infliction.'

'Huh?' Puzzlement floods Luke's voice.

I roll my eyes at Seth as I sit up and Seth reciprocates

my gesture with a smirk. 'Nothing,' I say, glancing up at a very shirtless, sweaty, and I'll admit, sexy Luke. 'I was just talking about getting a tattoo. That's all.'

'Oh yeah, where would you get it?' he asks curiously, still trying to catch his breath from the workout. I trace my finger up the side of my thigh, all the way up to my hip. His breathing grows quiet, maybe even stops as he tracks the path my finger made. 'That'd be a nice spot.' His voice is low, husky.

'You think so?' I ask, totally enjoying the fact that he's turned on by this. That and the fact that it's a normal moment right now. It's been a while and seems to be coming from nowhere, but I'm going to take it and grasp onto it with all the strength that I have.

Luke nods, finally jerking his attention away from my hip and focusing on my eyes. 'Definitely. And I'll come with you when you get it.'

'I don't need my hand held.' I bring my knees into my chest. 'I know what's up – it's my fourth one.'

'Oh, I'm not going to hold your hand.' His gaze is sweltering to the point where I swear to God my skin starts to melt, but I can't seem to look away. 'That would be sexy as hell to watch,' he says, his eyes dropping to my thigh again.

I want to tell him about every tattoo I plan on

getting, just to keep that skin-melting look he's giving me on his face.

But apparently Seth doesn't agree. 'Jesus, would you two let up with the eye-fucking.'

Luke gives Seth a harsh look and then shakes his head. 'Anyway, I just came to see what you two were up to and that if everything was okay.' There's an underlying meaning in his tone – he's worried about how I acted last night and wants to see if I'm okay.

I nod, letting him know that I'm fine, but really I have no clue what I'm feeling. Usually in these types of situations, I'd run to the nearest window and picture myself falling. Right before I hit the ground, I'd take my last breath. I want to really, really want to do it. Dreamt about it last night. Thought about the images repeatedly this morning, but between my choice to live in the water and making Luke a promise that I'd try to stop, I'm not going to.

He releases a stressed breath then nods. 'Okay, but if you need me, come get me.' He hitches a finger over his shoulder and points at one of the rooms. 'Kayden and I are switching rooms.'

I frown as I get to my feet. 'You're not done yet?'

He finds me amusing. 'We've been here for a half of an hour.'

I fold my arms across my chest. 'That's a half of an hour too long if you ask me.'

That gets him to laugh, even though I was being serious. 'You're cute.' Then he gives me a kiss on the cheek and a pat on the ass before walking off.

I turn to Seth and raise my eyebrow. 'What am I? One of his football buddies now?'

Seth looks up at me with this funny look on his face. 'I think you're pretty much the opposite for him.'

'And what the hell's the opposite of a football buddy?'

'I don't know . . . his lover.' He shoots me a devious grin and waggles his eyebrows.

That strikes a nerve as I think about a couple of weeks ago and how Luke said he loved me and I realized that I have no idea what the fuck love is and how I felt bad that I couldn't say it back to him. I want to at least understand it, but I have yet to figure out how to do so.

My expression immediately plummets and Seth notices that it does. He sits up quickly, eagerness written all over his face. 'Holy shit, he said it to you, hasn't he?' He scurries to his feet, eager to hear the gossip.

'I don't want to talk about this,' I say uncomfortably, scanning the workout room, searching for a diversion. But machines that look like torture devices and sweaty people I don't know surround me.

'Talk about what?' Greyson joins us from seemingly out of nowhere, sweat on his brow and in his hair. His shirt has some on it too, yet he looks content with his tired sweatiness.

'Nothing, hence why I said I don't want to talk about it,' I tell him, picking up my coffee, ready to bail. I'll tell Luke I had to run somewhere. Lie. Problem is, after last night, he'll freak out I'm sure and I don't want to do that to him.

'Luke told Violet he loves her,' Seth announces and I shoot him a dirty glare as he slaps his hand over his mouth. 'Sorry. I'm a terrible liar though.'

'What?' Greyson sounds more hurt than excited. He steps in front, blocking my path out of here. 'When did that happen?'

I pick at my purple fingernail polish. 'I don't know, like a couple of weeks ago.'

The hurt in his eyes magnifies. 'Why didn't you tell me?'

I shrug, guilt burning in my chest. 'Because there wasn't much to tell.'

There's a pause then he grabs my good arm and tugs me to the corner of the gym that smells worse than the mat. Seth calls out to him, but he ignores him.

'What happened?' Greyson asks, standing in front

of me, so I'm kind of trapped in the corner. A cornered cat, that's what I am. And one that wants to run.

'He said,' I make air quotes. '"I love you" . . . I couldn't say it back.'

'Yeah, okay.' A slow breath escapes his lips as he nods at something he must be thinking inside his head. 'Couldn't because you don't love him? Or couldn't because you just couldn't say it back yet?'

I wish I could say the latter, that I was the kind of person capable of love and just needed more time, but I honestly don't know. 'I'm not sure which one.'

He gives me a sad look. 'Violet, I know love can be scary and everything, but it's scary in the amazing, steal your breath, feels like you're flying kind of way. You shouldn't be afraid of it.'

'I'm not afraid of it.' My heart begins to do a panicked dance inside my chest as emotions surge through my veins. 'Just confused what it is.'

I don't want to have to say it – that I don't even know what love is. That the last time I felt loved and truly loved someone was when I was five and my parents were still alive. Greyson knows enough about my past that he can perhaps figure this out on his own. *Please, please figure this out on your own so I don't have to say it aloud.*

I don't know if he figures it out or not, but he steps back and drops it.

We head back to the mat when suddenly his eyes light up. 'I have an idea,' he says, his sullen mood vanishing.

My mind is swimming with too many emotions. I've been trying not to do it, to run off and seek some sort of dangerous thrill in order to calm myself the fuck down. But it's been two weeks, two weeks of piled up emotions, heavy, painful emotions. 'Oh yeah . . .'

He nods then motions at me. 'Follow me.'

I don't want to follow him. I want to run out the door – the door that I can see, so close, I just need to step toward it. But what happens when I get outside? What happens when I decide to dive into the water this time and I don't make it out? Or what if I make it out and Preston is there and this time a crowd doesn't show up?

'Hey, Violet.' The sound of a female voice greeting me forces me to turn my head away from the door. I've reached the mat area in my daze and Seth, Greyson and Callie are all standing near me, like we're at camp and attempting to form some sort of friendship circle. I feel like we should be holding hands and singing. Seriously.

I give Callie a tight smile. It's not that I don't like Callie. It's just that things are a little weird between her and me since we shared a dorm freshman year and she thought I was a prostitute. Really I was selling drugs, but I let her believe that I was a whore because I never really cared what people thought of me – still don't. But I was kind of mean to her sometimes; although my argument is it wasn't just her I was rude to, but everyone.

I'm about to bail, figuring I'll let them do their thing and I can go do mine when Greyson says, 'Callie, you should show Violet some of your kickboxing moves. I think it'd be good for her to let a little steam out.' It seems funny to me, Callie teaching me to kickbox. She's about four or five inches shorter than me, brown hair, blue eyes, thin – basically a little tiny thing. Yeah, I'm thin myself, but I look rough around the edges. But looks can be deceiving and I'm guessing from the way everyone is acting, she's got some hidden badass kicking skills.

'Why does everyone think I have anger issues?' I ask, fixing my hair tie, wondering if they all know about my twisted past and the issues going on between Luke and me. Just the news alone will give them details about the case so I'm guessing they at least know my history. Maybe that's why they think I have anger issues. Either that or Luke told them something, but I doubt he'd do that to me, especially when he has his own secrets I'm pretty sure he doesn't share with them.

'Um, because you do,' Seth says with an eye roll.

Callie shoots him a warning look. 'Don't be rude,' she says like I'm something precious and can't handle a little bluntness.

I almost laugh at the idea, but restrain it, thinking about how I couldn't handle it at therapy the other day. 'Yeah, well you do too,' I tell Seth in a lame attempt to get the attention off of me. Besides, I've seen Seth angry before, many, many times.

Seth rolls his eyes again. 'Honey, I have the exact opposite of anger issues.'

I cross my arms and give him a conniving look. 'Oh yeah, tell that to the *Silver Linings Playbook* DVD.'

Greyson looks at him aghast then points a finger at him. 'That was you.'

Seth aims me a dirty look and I smile innocently back at him. 'Hey, it was a total accident.' But he sighs as soon as he says it. 'Okay, that's a lie. But the damn thing wouldn't play.'

'That was one of my favorites.' Greyson shakes his head. 'And you broke it in half.'

'I'll buy you a new one today. I promise,' Seth says and Greyson nods and lets it go. Then Seth turns to me. 'You are paying for half of that for ratting me out,' he hisses, not really mad, just being a drama mama as he put it earlier.

'No freaking way,' I retort. 'I didn't break the DVD. You did.'

'I'll tell you what,' Seth replies. 'If you kick the bag a few times, I'll let it go. But they have to be badass ninja kicks.'

'Why does everyone keep pushing me to do this?' I ask. 'Yeah, I have anger issues. So what? Kicking some damn bag is not going to do anything for me.'

'Oh, but it will,' Seth assures me while Greyson wanders back to this large boxing bag dangling from the ceiling over the center of the mat. 'I know these things. I took a psych class.'

'I've taken three different ones,' I tell him. 'And that wasn't mentioned in any of them.'

'Three different classes?' Seth gapes at me. 'Really.'

I shrug as Greyson calls out, 'Violet's a badass when it comes to classes. Don't let her looks and attitude fool you, she's a smart girl.'

Wanting to get off that subject of me, I sidestep around Seth and walk up to the bag. 'Fine, I will kick this damn thing a few times, but only if we can stop talking about me, my brain, and my anger issues.'

'Deal.' Greyson moves behind the bag and puts his hand on it to hold it in place. I don't know why. Damn bag is big as hell. I'm sure I'm not going to be able to make it budge.

'So what do I do exactly?' I ask. 'Just kick it?'

'Yeah, but kind of turn to the side to begin with.' Callie comes up to me and surprises me by putting her hands on my hips and forcing me to shift to the side. Then she gives my hip a pat. 'Pivot your hip and bring your leg up. You can also use these.' She grabs my arms and positions them in front of me. 'You can even punch the bag, but probably not with this hand.' She taps my cast then steps back, giving me space. 'Go ahead. Trust me, you're going to feel a whole lot better.' She has this look on her face like she understands her words very well. Hell, maybe she does. Maybe hidden in that tiny body is a person who is raging with anger. Perhaps she has a messed up past too. God, maybe everyone does in their own way.

Giving them what they want, I do exactly what Callie said, pivot my hip and bring my leg up, slamming my foot against the bag. It doesn't move, but I also barely kicked it.

'Oh, come on,' Greyson says disappointedly. 'Show us that tough girl kick.'

I tolerate them, giving it a good hard kick. For the briefest moment, when my shoe collides with the bag, I do feel a twinge of relief from the emotional overload I was experiencing. I decide to kick it a couple of times more and the feeling gets more intense.

I finally stop, breathing pretty hard. I don't say anything, wiping the sweat from my brow, but Greyson gives me this *I told you so* look.

'You should do it with the other leg now,' Callie encourages. 'And this time, try to think about something that will give you fuel.'

I arch my brows at her. 'Fuel?'

'Yeah, you know, for the kicking,' she says simply, leaning down to grab her bottle of water beside her feet.

Figuring it won't hurt anything, I turn to the other side and try to figure out what the hell she meant by fuel. Then something snaps inside me and I start kicking the crap out of that goddamn bag. Last night, two weeks ago, fifteen years ago, none of it feels so heavy inside me. Control. That's what it is. I feel like I have more control over myself. Right now, in this moment, there is only me and this bag and this bag is everything – all my foster parents, Mira, Preston, all the guys who've copped a feel, everyone who's taken something from me.

When I finally stop, I'm gasping for air, my skin is drenched with sweat, and my heart is hammering inside my chest.

'I'm so tired,' I say, hunching over as I catch my breath.

'It's called exercise,' Greyson teases me with a grin.

I'm too tired to retort with a good comeback, so I turn and smile tiredly. But it's a real one, not my shiny, fake one I used on him the first few conversations we had. The same smile I used when I went to parties and dealt. The smile I used on everyone almost my entire life.

No, this one is real because at the moment I feel like myself.

I feel like the real Violet.

Chapter 19

Luke

She's been sleeping for a couple of hours. I'd worry she was depressed, but not only did she get up way too early for her, she also exerted herself with kickboxing, so I figure she has a reason to be sleeping.

It's rounding toward eleven in the afternoon. I have to pick up my dad and Trevor at the airport in like an hour. They'd offered to take a cab from the airport and I had to explain to them that Laramie wasn't like San Diego and that getting a cab means calling and waiting at least an hour for one. They said they could rent a car, but I'd insisted.

Yeah, I Luke Price insisted that I'd pick up my father. Never thought that'd fucking happen and I'm still uncertain how I feel about it.

I'm borrowing Seth's Camry to go pick them up so we don't have to crowd into my truck. Violet was going to go with me, but she looks so peaceful sleeping on her side, her hair splayed over the pillow, her legs tangled in the sheets that I almost don't want to wake her up.

Sitting down on the edge of the bed I brush her hair back out of her face and then graze my finger up and down her cheekbone. She sucks in a soft breath and then her eyelids flutter open, her green eyes glazed with exhaustion.

A few confused blinks later, she's sitting up. 'What time is it?' She yawns, arching her back like a cat as she stretches her arms above her head.

'Eleven.' My eyes skim over her nearly naked body. She'd stripped off her sweaty workout outfit the moment we'd gotten home, left her panties and bra on, collapsed into bed and fell asleep about thirty seconds later. 'You can stay here and sleep if you need to. Seth and Greyson said they'd be here until tonight so you won't have to be home.'

'No, I want to go with you,' she says, swinging her legs over the edge of the bed then standing up.

I don't argue with her, glad she wants to go with me. I sit down on the bed and watch her pull a t-shirt on and a pair of black jeans.

'I have to shower when we get back though,' she says, sniffing herself. 'I have gym scent.'

'Gym scent?'

She pulls a repulsed face. 'Yeah, those mats in there smell like they haven't been washed in years.' She runs her hands over her arms. 'I swear I can feel the smell on me.'

I chuckle at her as she grabs her boots and bends over to put them on. 'Well, you look good.'

She peers up at me as she's tying her boot. 'I look like shit, but thanks.' She stands up and combs her fingers through her red streaked hair then adds some glossy shit to her lips.

I stand up and cross the room to her, kicking dirty clothes out of the way. 'You look beautiful,' I tell her, brushing the pad of my thumb over her bottom lip. 'You always do.'

She looks like she's about to tease me for being sappy, but then decides against it and bites down on her lip. 'You seem in a good mood.' Her eyes carry a question.

'Just happy that you seem happy.' I trace my thumb back and forth over her lips, mesmerized by the softness of them. 'That shiny stuff you just put on them makes them look so tasty.'

With a wicked look in her eye, she opens those soft lips and bites down on my finger. It's gentle but still sexy as hell. 'Wow, did you used to use those kinds of lines on women? I know you and I haven't really dated,' she says. 'So I'm not sure what your moves are.'

'Hate to break it to you, but we've dated. A lot.'

'Not really. We went out on a couple of dates in the beginning, but even before that, things were different between us. I mean, it's not like you met me and wanted to fuck me right away. I just kind of forced myself into your life, or well destiny did anyway.'

There are a million things wrong with what she just said. 'First of all, I've always wanted to fuck you, even before we met. It just got way worse when we met.' I pause. 'Remember the party when we danced.'

That gets her to laugh, her green eyes sparkling. 'And you told me I was beautiful and that we should go back to one of the rooms – I remember.'

'Yeah, it was an awesome line, right?' I joke as I put my hands on her hips and pull her closer. 'The one that won you over?'

Her expression falls, her skin turning white as she gives me a guilty look. 'Actually, if we're being honest, I freaked out, ran out of the house, and jumped into the lake.' She sighs but continues before I can make a remark. 'I'm sorry, but you were making me feel things I wasn't ready for.'

'That's okay. I was pretty freaked out too by what I said to you – about what I was feeling.'

She gazes off over my shoulder, lost in her thoughts. 'It just feels like almost all the memories of the time we've spent together are like that.' Her attention snaps in my direction. 'Don't get me wrong. I love spending time with you . . . It's just that . . .' She bites down on her bottom lip and gives me an apologetic look.

'It's just that what?' I'm worried where she's going with this.

She lets her lip pop free and her expression conveys uncertainty. 'It's just that I think maybe we should try to change that. You know, not have a bad memory connected to every semi-normal one . . . So I was thinking that maybe we could try tonight, to do something normal, I mean. After we have dinner with your dad and Trevor, like go to a concert. Seth says there's a good one in town and I told him I'd try to go.' She's talking really fast like she's nervous.

It makes me smile, fucking grin like the stupidest, most happy idiot in the world. 'Oh, you're asking me out.'

Her brows dip. 'Why are you smiling like that?' I

191

can't help it – I bust up laughing at her. She swats me with her good arm. 'Luke, seriously, what the hell is so funny?'

Shaking my head, I try to settle my laughter. 'I'm sorry, it's just that you looked so nervous I was seriously expecting you to say something really bad, like you thought we needed to take a break or something.' She playfully slaps my arm again and I cover the area with my hand. 'Hey, what the hell was that for?'

'For laughing at me. You know, I've never asked a guy out, right?'

'And I've never really used lines on a girl either. Trust me, for the most part I was a fucking asshole.'

She rolls her eyes. 'Jesus, what is wrong with the female population? Treat them like shit and they want you even more.'

'Not all of them.' I trace the path of her jawline, loving the way her eyelids flutter from my touch. As far as I know, she's the only woman who's ever reacted to my touch that way and that's because she's the only woman I've paid enough attention to, to notice her reactions in that much detail. 'That's one of the first things that attracted me to you – because my shit didn't work on you.' I give her a half-smile. 'I was drawn to the fact that I seemed to annoy the shit out of you whenever I opened my mouth. Well, that and the fact that you were so fucking sexy and I couldn't stop thinking about fucking the shit out of you.' I give her a full smile now as she rolls her eyes. 'See those are my lines. Not too impressive, right?'

She shakes her head, but then wraps her arms around me and presses her lips to mine, giving me a quick, but deep kiss. I nip on her lip as she pulls away.

'We better get going.' She looks at the clock on the nightstand. 'Or we'll be late picking up your dad and Trevor.'

'Yeah, you're right.' I collect my wallet from the nightstand then start toward the door, but she grabs my hand and draws me back to her.

'Are you going to be okay with this?' she asks. 'With them being here. I mean, I know we spent that time at their house, but this feels a little different.'

No, not at all. 'Yeah, I'm good.'

She's right. This is different. When Violet and I went to their house, it was to hideout. Yeah, my dad and I talked and everything, but most of my time was spent on taking care of Violet. This is just a plain and simple visit, to hang out, chat, have dinner, spend time together. It's strange and unnatural and something I'm completely not used to. But all I can do is cross my fingers that it'll be okay.

That everything will be okay.

We're about fifteen minutes late picking them up, but my dad seems happy with me just showing up, like he expected me not to. When I pull up to the curb, park and get out, he comes up and gives me this awkward hug while Violet helps Trevor put the suitcases in the trunk. After they're finished, my dad pulls away, giving me this strange, almost choked up look and I can't help but think: *fuck, is he going to cry?* Thankfully, he doesn't and steps back to give me a good look.

'I swear you've grown taller,' he says to me with a smile. My dad is about four or five inches shorter than me, medium build, with thinning brown hair. He likes to wear a lot of jeans and t-shirts, nothing business-like, something I learned when we were in San Diego.

'I'm twenty years old,' I tell him. 'I stopped growing like five years ago.'

His smile falters, but he quickly recovers and steps back to let Trevor give me a handshake. 'It's good to see you again, Luke,' he says. Trevor is closer to my height with blond hair and he likes to wear a lot of button down shirts, so pretty much the opposite of my father.

'You too.' I really don't know what to say. Trevor and I don't know each other very well at all. We've only met the one time and he was working a lot, so we maybe had like ten conversations tops.

Trevor releases my hand and steps back, opening his mouth to say something when my father walks up to Violet and pulls her in for a hug. I can tell it startles the shit out of her by the way she goes tense as a board. She manages to pull herself together enough, though, to give him a one-handed hug.

'It's so good to see you,' my dad says as he frees Violet from the hug. 'Both of you.'

Violet shuffles back from him toward the curb and starts fidgeting with her cast, scratching her fingernails up and down on it, staring off at the doors of the airport. There's not much to look at, though, hardly any people coming in and out since it's a small airport and it's in the middle of the afternoon. I'm guessing there's some sort of emotion building in her and she's trying to keep it together.

'Yeah, good to see you too.' I give Violet's hand a squeeze. She doesn't look at me, but she does inch closer. 'Should we hit the road?' I ask.

My father nods then opens the back door of Seth's Camry. While they're climbing in, I open the passenger side door for Violet and when she starts to duck in to climb inside, I place my hand on the small of her back, stopping her. Putting my lips beside her ear, I whisper, 'Everything okay?'

She nods then lowers herself into the seat. 'Yeah, everything's fine.'

I don't believe her, but now's not the time to press. I round the car, get in and drive down the road toward the center of town where Trevor and my father are staying for the next three nights. They keep making comments about how small and quaint the town is, but Laramie is anything but quaint. Yes it's low in population, but it doesn't have that old-fashioned, homey look to it. And the wind blows like a mother-fucker; the winter's cold enough to freeze your balls off if you stayed outdoors for too long.

Violet barely says anything the entire drive, staring out the window like the sights are fascinating, like she hasn't seen them a thousand times. Once we drop my father and Trevor off, I head back to the apartment until we head out for dinner in a few hours.

Finally, her silence gets to be too much and I turn down the volume of the stereo. 'What are you thinking about?'

'The many complications and complexities that make

up my life,' she responds without so much as a glance in my direction.

'Was it the hug?' I ask. 'Did it get to you?'

She breathes heavy enough that it fogs the window in front of her face. 'I don't want to have a pity party.' She turns her head toward me. 'Or feel sorry for myself.'

'You have every right to feel bad over stuff,' I tell her, slowing the car down to a stop at a red light.

She shakes her head. 'No, I need to get over it. I want to, you know.'

'Want to what?'

'Get over getting worked up over everything.' She slumps back in the seat and props her boots up on the dashboard, looking straight ahead. 'Stop getting worked up over simple things like getting a flipping hug . . . it's just that it's been a while, you know . . .' Her head slants to the side as she dazes off, her hair curtain around her face. 'Since someone's hugged me. I mean, I know you do, but . . .' she shrugs. 'I honestly have no idea what my point is. I guess I'm just rambling.' She waves it off, wanting to dismiss the conversation. 'Ignore me.'

I had the exact opposite problem, forced to spend hours being hugged by my mother in a way that felt unnatural and caused me to be ill to my stomach.

I'd always thought things would have been better if I'd never been hugged, but Violet is contradicting this theory. Maybe if the hugs had come from a sane person, if my dad hadn't bailed out, then I'd think differently.

I sweep her hair out of her face, knowing she's trying to hide whatever expression she has, but I care too much about her to let her conceal her pain anymore. 'I'm not going to ignore you. Not when you say something like that.'

She shakes her head, glancing at me. I swear I can see every infliction, every invisible scar. 'Please, can we just drop it?'

I start to lean over the console toward her. 'Violet, we're not going to—'

'Light's green,' she interrupts, waving me forward while the person behind me honks their horn.

I drive in silence the rest of the way home. As soon as I park the car under the carport, Violet opens the door and hops out. I follow her eager exit, turn off the engine, hop out and meet her around the front. Before she can move past me, I catch her in my arms and yank her against me.

'Luke, I said I was okay,' she protests. She works to get her good hand between us, then attempts to shove me back. But she's not strong enough to get me anywhere, no matter what she believes.

'If it was possible, I'd hug you every hour of every minute of every second of every day.' I pull her closer to me, disregarding the fact that she hasn't put her arms around me yet.

We stand that way for a while, me giving her everything and her afraid to take it as the wind surrounds us and the grey sky begins to rumble. It takes her a snap or two of lightning to get there, but finally she relaxes.

'We'd look pretty ridiculous walking around like this all the time,' she whispers, her arms sliding around my waist. She tucks her good hand into the back pocket of my jeans and rests her head against my shoulder. 'Although I'd love to see the looks on people's faces as we attempted it.' She sighs, surrendering. 'Sorry I freaked out on you.'

'You don't need to apologize.'

'No, I need to . . .' She tips her chin up and looks up at me. 'I need to get my shit together. I'm just trying to figure out how to do it.' The wind blows her hair into her face and she plucks strands from her mouth. 'Maybe this whole therapy thing will help . . . I don't know though. I'm still skeptical.'

I'm not sure if I entirely disagree with that idea either. 'Why?'

'I don't know . . . I guess I don't trust adults very well. They can be nasty, disloyal people.'

'Baby, we're technically adults.'

'I know that, but sometimes I forget that we are,' she says, saddened. 'Maybe it'll work out though. Maybe they'll be able to fix all the cracks and ugliness inside my head.'

I press my lips to her forehead. 'This thing is anything but ugly.'

'Yeah, yeah, we'll see if that's the case after they crack me apart and see what's inside.' She makes a mock scary voice then makes a ghostly sound.

My brow curves upward. 'What's up with the Halloween sounds?'

'We made a promise to celebrate the shit out of holidays, remember.' She glances over at the main building of the apartment complex, which is decked out with hay bales and a scarecrow. 'I need a costume if we're going to do this.'

'I can help you find one,' I offer, even though it's probably the last thing I want to do. Stores. Crazy ass people rushing around to get last minute things.

She shakes her head and looks back at me. 'It's not

really a you and me thing. I think I'll ask Seth.'

'Really?' I can't hide my shock.

She shrugs. 'We've been getting along okay and I know he likes to shop.'

'He'll probably want to invite Callie,' I tell her, not because I think it's bad that Callie and her hang out. It's just that the two of them have an iffy past. Plus, Violet tends to scare other girls with her I-don't-give-a-shit attitude.

'That's okay.' She nods her head, like she's convincing herself that her words are true. 'Everything's going to work out. I can feel it.'

But right as she says it, a van with the security alarm logo on it pulls into the parking lot, reminding the both of us that everything can't be okay until Preston is put away. Until he is, we'll always be looking over our shoulders, sleeping less, listening for sounds in the night. It pisses me off, thinking about it makes my blood curl, especially when Violet gives me that look, the one that lets me know she's suddenly been reminded of everything and that it's secretly terrifying her.

I need to find a way to take away that look.

But the only way that's going to happen is when Preston is behind bars.

Chapter 20

Violet

It seems like the last few conversations between Luke and me feel more like therapy sessions. I don't know what's wrong with me, but the less time I spend standing on top of roofs, jumping in raging waters, cutting my wrists, popping pills, getting drunk, the more time I talk. And it's like I don't have any control over my mouth anymore, words spilling out without any thought. So I'm a bit relieved to have some time away from Luke to shop for a costume, hoping I can clear my head and pull myself together before I spook him – or myself.

'So Halloween's the slutty holiday, right?' I ask Seth as we stroll through the nearly empty racks of the closest Halloween store we could find. I pull a face at what's left: clowns, a dinosaur, there's even a sexy giraffe costume – not sure how the hell they consider it sexy but whatever.

Seth nods, searching through the racks with a disgusted look on his face. 'Yeah, that would kind of be the point.' He glances over at Callie, who's looking at the cape section of the store. 'Unless you're Miss Callie over there. Then you go with the traditional but flawlessly beautiful kind of costume.'

Her cheeks flush as if what he's said is extremely embarrassing. 'I go with what I'm comfortable with.'

Seth nods as she moves over to a section that has masks. 'I know you do,' he says.

I wander to the next rack and sift through the limited selection. 'I don't want to be sexy or traditionally, flawlessly beautiful though.'

Seth glances around at the pathetically empty room that's supposed to be a store. 'Then what do you want to be?'

I give a nonchalant shrug. 'Something edgy, gothic, different.'

His eyes scroll over my outfit I'm wearing now, black jeans and a matching shirt, dressed up with my studded boots. 'So basically what you have now.'

'I have an idea,' Callie says in her quiet voice as she

walks over to us. She looks me over from head to toe. 'A really good one actually, for what you said, I mean.'

'Really?' I don't mean to sound as doubtful as I do.

She nods then motions at us to follow her as she heads out of the sad store. 'Yep, follow me.'

Callie was right. Her idea was a good one for me and I end up with the perfect costume, if you can even call it that. I definitely can't wear it to dinner tonight, especially when Luke informed me of his father and Trevor's plans to eat out at this fancy five-star restaurant. Yeah, I'm a burger and fries kind of girl, but tell myself to suck it up and go eat some fancy food. I leave my wavy hair down and put on this thin strapped black dress that has flowers on it, probably one of the most girly items I've ever worn. Then I top it off with my leather jacket, boots, red lipstick and kohl eyeliner because I still want to be myself. They make me check my jacket, though, and I get some looks as we're seated at a table, but they're snooty waiters and I'm sure overpaying costumers can go fuck themselves.

'This place is insane,' I whisper to Luke as the waiter drops the cloth napkin onto my lap – *what the hell?* The table has the cleanest white tablecloth I've ever seen, and the plates and silverware – don't even get me started on those. They are so shiny it's ridiculous.

Luke sweeps my hair to the side and leans in, lowering his voice. 'I know, but I think they wanted to do something nice for us,' he says while his father is telling the waiter something about wanting sparkling water – water should never sparkle. I open the menu while Luke places a kiss on my bare shoulder, momentarily shutting his eyes as if relishing my scent. 'You look beautiful, though.'

'Thanks,' I say, then joke, 'but my uncanny beauty isn't going to help me understand this menu.'

Chuckling under his breath, Luke leans over my shoulder and glances at the menu even though he's got one of his own. I don't mind, though, the scent of him is absolutely amazing, like soap and cologne with just the barest hit of cigarette smoke.

His face scrunches up as he sees what I'm talking about. 'What is it?' he whispers. 'Written in French or something?'

I scrunch my nose up. 'Either that or it's just food we've never heard of.'

Sighing, Luke sits back in his chair and studies the menu in front of him. I take the time to study him, figuring there's no point in looking over the food selection since I have no idea what any of it is. He looks extra good tonight in a plaid shirt with the sleeves rolled off. He's got a pair of dark jeans on, his boots, and I think he gave his hair a trim because it's shorter, the perfect length. There's nothing different about his lips, but I stare at them the longest. Those lips have explored almost every inch of me and right now, I'd way rather be back at our place, dressed in my 'Halloween costume' with his mouth all over me, than getting ready to fill my stomach full of food I can't even pronounce the names of.

'Enjoying the view?' Luke cocks his head at me with a huge ass grin on his face. I realize I've spaced out, put my elbow on the table and rested my chin in my hand. Probably not the best etiquette and the waiter seems to be annoyed as he fills up our glasses with water that fizzes.

'Maybe.' I bite my lip as I sit up straight.

We're interrupted by Luke's father chuckling and Trevor saying, 'You two are simply adorable.'

Luke and I exchange a doubtful, almost repulsed look then Luke turns to his dad. 'I'm not sure adorable describes us correctly.'

Trevor takes a sip of his water. 'Okay, then what does describe you two?'

I contemplate what he said. 'How about Stoically

Aloof and Mysteriously Awesome.' I combine my nickname for him with one I make up for myself.

'Mysteriously Awesome isn't your nickname,' Luke says as he reaches for his glass.

'Yeah, you're right. I'm more . . .' I trail off, racking my brain for what the hell I am. I think of all the names I was called while growing up, but there's no way in hell I'm going to bring them up at a nice dinner.

'How about wildly beautiful, ridiculously smart and a never-ending surprise?' Intensity burns from his eyes, his lips quirking, half serious, half teasing me. I'm verging toward blushing, which never, ever happens and I refuse to let it happen now.

I'm trying to think of some comeback, something witty to take the upper hand. But Luke's father interrupts and I'm grateful for it.

'I think we should make a toast to that,' he says, raising his glass in the air. 'Or to you guys anyway.'

I glance at Luke and give him an *is he for real* look. Luke shrugs then raises his glass, going along with it and I have no choice but to follow or look like a bitch. But Jesus, I didn't think people actually did this. Then again, I haven't spent much time eating dinner with people.

'To Luke and Violet,' Luke's father says. 'May you

always find happiness in each other even in the darkest of times.'

Okay, so his words weren't that bad. Kind of poetic and fitting actually.

We clink glasses and then I move mine to take a sip like everyone else does. But the sparkling water tastes wrong and the fizz on my tongue causes me to spit it back into the glass.

'Sorry,' I cough, setting the glass down. 'But that tasted like shit.'

There's a pause and then they bust off laughing, like full on belly laughter, faces red and everything. Luke's not laughing as hard, but he looks totally amused as he sets his glass down without sipping from it then winks at me. 'Thanks for the blunt warning.'

The rest of the night goes smoothly, at least for the conversation part. The food is awful and I mean straight up awful. Even high I wouldn't have enjoyed it. Luke's on the same page as me, thankfully, and we come up with this system where we ever so discreetly hide as much as we can in the napkins on our laps whenever Trevor and his father are chatting with each other and not paying attention to us. We're acting ridiculous, giggling like little kids who have a secret. But it's the most fun I've had in a long time. There's even live entertainment when some dude decides to propose to his girlfriend right there in the middle of a restaurant with a hundred strangers to share the experience.

'Wow, way to lack originality,' I remark, pulling a face at what I think is supposed to be chicken but it's covered in this weird looking sauce.

'Awe, I think it's sweet,' Trevor says. 'Albeit a little clichéd.' His gaze slides to Mr Price and he gets this goofy love-induced grin on his face. 'Definitely not a candlelit dinner in my favorite art gallery, but still sweet.'

'Is that how he proposed to you?' I wonder, taking a sip of my Coke, the one and only thing I recognized on the menu.

Trevor nods, tearing his attention away from Mr Price and taking a bite of his salad. 'So tell me, Violet, in your opinion, is there really a non-clichéd way to propose?'

Luke clears his throat several times while I squirm in my chair. His question seems to be packed with this alternative meaning, like he's wondering if I ever think about marriage. Yeah, right. I can barely think about the next breath I need to take, let alone five years down the road and if I'll be making promises to be together forever with someone. Another thought occurs to me then that Luke kind of already did this when he started rambling about being with me forever and loving me. It makes me panic, my mind racing with an answer to give Trevor, so he'll leave me alone because I can't think about this right now, not when I'm doing so good. 'Out in the middle of nowhere with nothing but truck headlights for lighting and the sounds of crazy animals.'

'That actually does kind of sound nice.' Trevor smiles with that dazed look again. 'Out in the mountains, under the stars. Only instead of the crazy animals, your favorite song would be playing from the stereo.'

He's making my lame scenario sound kind of good. Dammit, I need a subject change. I want to look at Luke for help, but am scared shitless of what I might see in his expression. '"The River", by Manchester Orchestra.'

They give me a confused look. 'What is that exactly?'

'One of my favorite songs,' I say over the applause of the crowd as the girlfriend says yes. 'And trust me, it wouldn't be romantic – none of my favorite songs are. They are tragic, depressing, and angsty.'

'Still, it would be a beautiful way to get engaged.' Trevor must get the hint, though, because he lets the subject go. 'So what are you kids up to tonight? I remember when I was your age, always doing something crazy on Halloween.'

'We're going to a concert,' Luke says, the first words he's uttered since the uncomfortable marriage thing. He reaches for his water and takes a few long gulps. 'You guys can come too, if you want.'

His dad appears apprehensive as he dabs his face with his napkin while he speaks across the table to Luke. 'Are you sure you're going to be okay with going to a concert, considering . . . well, there will be alcohol.'

'We actually won't be drinking,' I tell him truthfully. Seth informed me that despite the epic fun the night will hold, The Silver Moon Grill is super strict with their fake IDs and that we should probably just chill in the twenty-one and under section, especially since Luke will be there. It was actually a really nice gesture, especially coming from Seth, the King of Drinking. 'The place we're going is too hard to get alcohol from.'

Luke's father gives me a grateful look, like he's thanking me for this, even though I didn't do anything. 'Good. I'm glad.'

'It wouldn't matter anyway,' Luke says as he picks at one of his side dishes that looks like some sort of soup. 'I've been doing good — been sober for almost two months.'

'I know you have,' Mr Price says. 'But it doesn't mean I don't still worry . . . you're not even going to meetings.'

'That's because I don't have time,' Luke replies in a tight voice. 'Nor do I need to – I'm doing fine on my own.' This isn't just about the drinking anymore and I decide I should intervene before things get really ugly.

'We actually really need to get going.' I glance at my phone to check the time. 'The doors open in an hour and we still need to go home and change.'

Luke nods, but is still tense. His father looks upset and Trevor appears to be as uneasy as I am. He flags down the waiter for the check, then we leave the restaurant and hopefully the tension behind. But the silence of the drive proves otherwise.

'So tomorrow's the game then?' Trevor asks as we're pulling up to the hotel to drop them off, the first words anyone has uttered since we got into the car.

'Yeah, it starts at six,' Luke mutters, shoving the car into park. He doesn't look at his father, staring ahead. 'But you guys don't need to come if you don't want to. We can meet up afterwards or beforehand.'

'I already told you I want to come.' His father scoots forward in the seat, dithering before reaching forward and placing a hand on Luke's shoulder. 'I know it's not even a start, but I want to attempt to make up for all the things I missed while you were growing.'

I can tell Luke's fighting to stay mad at his dad, the big softy that he is, despite the fact that he'll never admit it. 'Fine. Okay. See you there then.'

'Do you want to ride with us?' Trevor asks me as he opens the door to get out.

I've never actually been to a game before – not really my thing. 'Oh, I . . .' I trail off, not wanting to say that I don't go, even though it's the truth.

'We'll pick you up at, say, seven?' Trevor says even though I didn't even answer his question.

Not knowing what else to do, I nod. They get out and shut the doors and Luke pulls away and onto the road. He's quiet as we drive toward our apartment, the streetlights reflecting in his brown eyes and giving them the similar glow the stars hold. I'm assuming his silence has to do with his father and what he said at dinner, so he startles me when he asks, 'So are you really coming to my game?'

'Um . . . yeah, I guess I'm going.' I chew on my fingernail. 'I've never really been to one. Not my thing, but I guess I can pop that cherry.'

The corners of his lips twitch, probably because he's

thinking about the first time we had sex, which was my first time ever. 'Yeah, I guess it's about time then.' He gives me a sidelong glance. 'But you don't have to go if you don't want to.'

But I can tell he wants me to. Not sure how, but I do.

'No, I want to go, but I'm not going to dress up in the school colours and prance around clapping my hands and yelling "Go, team, go!"' I make this cheer-leader motion with my arms and it gets him to laugh.

'Fine by me,' he says, with a smile threatening at his lips. 'Not really into that shit anyway.'

I smile back. 'Good, otherwise I'd wonder what the hell you were doing with me.'

He continues to perk up for the rest of the drive and his worries about his father fade into the night, and into costume and concert time. After we get back to the apartment, I go get dressed in the outfit I bought earlier today. I'd actually bought it at a gothic store that Callie knew about – not sure how. A leather dress, these stockings with black stripes on them, a lace-up arm warmer for my good wrist, and boots that have these gadgets on them, making them totally look steam-punk. I'm not even calling myself anything, though, just basking in the fact that I get to dress up.

I put my hair up in this curly braid style then stain my lips with dark lipstick, trace my eyes with black liner, then look in the mirror and totally admire my handiwork. 'Okay, project Celebrating Holidays. I think I'm liking Halloween.'

'Who are you talking to?' Luke asks as he opens the door and enters the bedroom. He makes it about two steps in when he actually sees me and stops dead in his tracks.

'Pretty awesome, right?' I ask, turning away from the mirror and to him with my hands on my hips.

He lazily scrolls my body, from my boots to my chest, finally residing on my eyes. 'You look like a dominatrix.'

I glance down at my leather outfit and knee-high boots. 'Well, that wasn't what I was going for, or anything really – just having fun,' I say. 'But I guess you can call me that for the night if you want.'

'Can I?' He says it absentmindedly, severely preoccupied by my legs, half concealed by the lace-up boots I'm wearing. He scratches at the back of his neck, then jerks his attention off of my legs. 'So what am I then?'

'Well, if I'm a dominatrix then wouldn't that make you my bitch?' I give him my best sexy wink and he chokes on his laughter.

'Yeah, I'm not sure I could give up that much control for you,' he says, when he stops laughing. 'Sorry.'

'I don't think I could be that mean to you,' I reply then head over to his closet. 'But I have an idea of what you could be.' I rummage around until I find it, tucked in the back of his closet – a faded leather jacket I've never seen him wear before. 'How about you wear this?' I step out of the closet, holding up the jacket in front of me.

He seems hesitant. 'That was actually my dad's.' He steps toward me with his hands stuffed in his pockets. 'It was one of the few things he left behind when he took off.' He touches the front of it then winces as if the fabric – or the memory – has scalded him. 'I'm not even sure why I still have it.'

'Oh, never mind then.' I lower the jacket and move back toward the closet to put it away, but his finger on my arm stops me.

'Let me try it on,' he mumbles, then takes the jacket from my hands. Summoning a deep breath, he slips it on and the leather fabric fits his build perfectly. He glances down to look at himself as he moves up to the mirror to get a better look.

I join him, standing to his side. 'We look like

badasses,' I state, staring at our reflections. 'Hey, that's what we could be.'

He smiles softly, then slides his arm around my back and pulls me closer. 'We look good together.'

We really do. I'm not even sure how that happened. When I'd first met Luke, I thought of him as a popular, brooding jock. It was absurd, and very stereotypical and judgmental of me, and very untrue. My opinion changed about him when I got to know him and honestly I'm starting to wonder if my opinion has changed about myself as well. Luke brought out this other side of me and even though I lost it for a while, when I found out about Mira, I feel like it's coming back again, only it's different now.

Something's different.

He stares at me through the mirror for a few more moments, then he turns to me and leans in, his voice husky as he whispers, 'The things I want to do to you right now.' His lips collide with mine, the roughness mismatching with the softness of his voice. But I meet his passion with equal eagerness, kissing him back with everything I have in me, pouring out of me. I grip onto him, pulling him closer, seeking air, yet forgetting to breathe. I'm desperate for more of his touches, kissing, closeness – I'm desperate for everything. I'm under no control of my own anymore. I'm not sure anything I do when it comes to Luke anymore is in my control anymore. Because I'm falling.

Falling.

Falling.

Falling.

Only this time it's different. I still don't know where I'm going to end up and when, but for once it feels like maybe there's something to land on.

Chapter 21

Luke

After kissing Violet for ten minutes, we finally part when Seth bangs on the door and tells us it's time to go. Her kisses have made me feel better, but I'm still stirring over some of the shit at dinner, when I get the call. A Goddamn call that I was kind of expecting, but it still somehow blindsided me. It's from the attorney representing my mother, wanting to talk to me.

I had to step into the bathroom – I was so shocked – and I didn't want Violet hearing either.

'I'd like to meet you in person, just to talk,' the douche attorney said and I almost rammed my fist through the wall, which would have pissed the shit out of Seth since I've done it before and he wasn't happy about it.

'I don't want anything to do with this,' I'd snapped at him. 'And if you knew better, you wouldn't be asking me to do so.'

'Your mother thinks otherwise,' he'd replied. 'I'd really like to—'

'My mother's a fucking psycho who deserves to be behind bars.' I was practically shaking, gripping onto the counter for support and to keep my hand from doing any damage.

'Yeah, we'll see,' he'd said and that's when I'd hung up on him and almost threw my phone against the wall.

Regardless of the shitty, depressing call, I'm determined to have a fun night sober. Violet and I made a promise to celebrate the shit out of the holidays and fuck if I'm not going to go through with it. The problem is, I'm all worked up and the only thing that ever calms me down when I'm like this is booze. I can't drink, though. No, I won't let myself. I avoid it at work all the time and I can sure as hell do it now.

But it's harder tonight. Between the call about my mother and the fact that my father got me all worked up at dinner. All that talk about worrying about me and then trying to make stuff up to me – it had pushed me toward the edge, and now the phone call has me teetering somewhere mid-fall. And then there's Violet and her reaction to Trevor's question about marriage and how she made it clear that she was against it and for some crazy ass reason that got under my skin – not sure why the fuck it did, but it did. It's not like I want to get married, at least not in this decade, but the fact that she seemed so against it – against being with someone forever – made me start to wonder how long she was planning on sticking around. And that reminded me of how I said I love her and how she clearly doesn't reciprocate the feeling. So what am I to her? I have no idea.

I'm riled up on the inside, letting things get under my skin too much and pretending to be okay on the outside, just like I used to all the time. Thankfully, my friends decided to choose the lower section of the place where alcohol isn't served, otherwise I'd have caved the moment we walk in. It makes it easier to stay away from it and I have a good distraction – Violet and her Goddamn leather dress. The thing barely covers her ass making her long legs look nearly endless. And those boots with those heels . . . Jesus fucking Christ, she's sexy as hell. The music's good too for the most part, plus it's nice to hang out with Kayden, Callie, Seth, Greyson and Violet all at one time.

The whole place screams edgy Halloween theme with black lights, mist, and spray paint covering the walls and almost everyone is dressed up in some sort of costume. There's this neon effect going on and everything with bright colors and in white glows. Violet would blend in with the darkness, but Seth, Callie and her decided to take this weird lipstick-looking thing and draw all over the skin showing, which means Violet is glowing with designs and patterns on almost every inch of her body.

Yes, fucking ridiculously sexy.

'I'm going to dance. Who wants to save seats?' Violet rises from her chair. We've secured a table as close to the dance floor and stage as possible, so losing the seats would suck.

Seth and Greyson both jump from their barstools. 'Not it,' Seth calls out, then grabs Callie's hand and pulls both Greyson and her toward the dance floor before anyone can protest.

Violet looks at me and I give her the best smile I can muster. 'Go ahead. I'll sit this one out.'

She hesitates. 'You sure?'

I nod and force my smile to be more cheery – more fake. 'Yes, go.' I wave at her to get a move on.

She whirls toward the dancing area and I feel this

instantaneous urge to follow her, remembering how sexy Violet is when she dances. But I'm not sure I'm in the mood, nor do I want to bail and leave Kayden sitting solo, so I keep my ass planted in the chair.

'I have a fucking headache,' I mutter and take a sip of my Coke, wondering if maybe my blood sugar's low or if I'm just really stressed.

'You look like you haven't slept in a while,' Kayden states, glancing at his cellphone screen. 'We probably shouldn't stay out too long considering we have a game tomorrow.'

'Yeah, probably.' I'm distracted as a waitress with a tray full of shot glasses walks by. *I thought they don't serve alcohol here?* I watch her as she pushes her way through the crowd heading for a spiral staircase. She struggles to balance the tray as she maneuvers her way up the stairs and to the top area – the twenty-one and over area. I have a fake ID and even though this place is notorious for being able to identify fake ID's, I think about going up there. Honestly, if I wanted to, I could wait for the waitress to come back and charm her until she gives me one. I don't want to, but I just keep thinking about how things would be so much easier to deal with tonight if I could have just one sip.

Just one.

'I think I'm going to see how long Callie wants to stay,' Kayden gets out of the chair. 'You can ride back with us if you want.'

I nod, my gaze drifting back and forth between the stairway and him. 'Yeah, if Violet's ready to go . . . then okay.'

He wavers, tucking his phone into the back pocket of his jeans. 'You gonna be okay here alone for a few minutes?'

'What? Are we babysitting each other now?' I question, when really I probably do need babysitting right now.

He seems torn, glancing over his shoulder at the staircase, in the direction I keep glancing in. It's clear what I'm looking at and it's clear he's going to stick around if I don't reassure him that I'm not going to go chasing down my addiction.

'It's fine,' I say, signaling for him to go. 'I'll sit here and save the table.'

He wavers then nods before disappearing into the crowd of dancing, sweaty people. I'd like to say that it takes me a few minutes to get up and head over, but it's really only about ten seconds, getting to my feet the moment Kayden's out of sight. I have every intention of doing it, tracking down the waitress and coaxing her into giving me a shot. I don't like myself for needing to do it, but old habits – addictions – are hard to break. I just want to feel my body burn into numbness, just one more time. *One more time,* I keep telling myself.

I'm halfway there when I spot Violet in the center of the crowd. I don't even know how I see her, since there's so many damn people packed in a small space. Yet she manages to appear, the throng parting for the slightest moment, just enough to give me a glimpse of her dancing and laughing, so free at that moment, so beautiful. Violet's always talking about destiny and I've never been too sure on where I lie on the whole concept that maybe we're not in complete control of our lives, but right now I'm wondering if maybe it does exist and that maybe my destiny is in her.

What am I doing?

Seriously, what the fuck am I doing, fucking this up?

I don't want this – want to be that person again.

I don't want to lose what I have.

Just like that, I'm pulled toward her, magnetized by an unseen force that I'll never be able to explain. I move away from the stairway, the waitress, the alcohol and push my way through the crowd, my eyes fixed on where I saw her. Every once in a while, there's enough of a gap in the sea of bodies that I get a glimpse of her green eyes, red and black hair, and that fucking sexy as hell leather dress she's wearing. It keeps me traveling in the right direction and farther away from the wrong. The music is throbbing as I move up behind her. She doesn't see me first, only feels the touch of my hands as I put them on her waist. She must sense it's me, because she sinks into the touch without saying a word.

Then she peeks over her shoulder with a wicked grin on her face. 'Glad you could join me.' She winks then starts to really dance.

I'd almost forgotten how amazing the way she moves is, not too much or too little, the perfect amount of rhythm and sway of her hips that makes her ass brush up against my cock just the right amount. I go rock hard within just a few moments as I move with her, allowing my hands to travel up and down her hips, her sides, her breasts. There are people everywhere – Seth, Greyson, Kayden and Callie included. But as far as I care, it's just Violet and me out there. The rest of the room is just a blur.

We dance this way forever, through the entire concert, becoming sweaty, breathless, and fucking turned on more than I ever have been. Neither of us seems in any rush to stop, our bodies welded together, refusing to break this strange, destiny induced bond we've stumbled upon. Kayden and Callie bail out pretty early, while Greyson and Seth stick around with Violet and me. Eventually the large throng of people starts to dwindle into a small crowd. Before I know it, we're pretty much the only ones left on the dance floor. Still, we don't stop moving, lost in some sort of moment where only the two of us exist.

Eventually Greyson announces that it's time to go. 'It's getting late,' he says, checking the time on his phone.

Seth frowns as he continues to dance but then gives in. 'Fine, you win this one.'

Violet and I dance for a little bit longer then holding hands, follow them to the front door and hang with the rest of the loiterers while Seth goes to get the car. The air feels electric, like there's a lightning storm nearby, except the sky is clear, full of stars and the moon shining brightly.

A minute or two of waiting and my hands are all over Violet again, unable to stop myself from touching her. Somewhere between touching her hips and sucking on her neck, she turns around and presses her lips to mine. I grab her ass and pull her against me as her fingers slide up my chest, loop around the back of my neck. She lets out a groan as I give her hair a gentle tug to tip her head back and then my tongue slips deeply into her mouth, moaning at the taste of her. With each touch, each brush of our tongues, each moan, the crappy thoughts I was trying to sort through earlier dissipates into nothing. Nothing else matters. All my focus is on her, the amazing taste of her, the incredible scent of her skin and feel of the heat of her body. And the little sound she makes as I spin us around and back us up against the building is enough for me to verge on losing it, right here on the side of the road.

But I manage to keep myself contained, pulling her closer, kissing her with everything I have in me. *This is what I want. This is where I want to be.*

'Luke.' She gasps between kisses, her legs moving restlessly around as if she can't figure out what to do with them. Finally, she hitches one over my hip and grinds her hips against mine. I respond with the same movement, pressing up against her as I move my mouth away from hers to place kisses down her jawline, her neck, to the base of her throat where I lick a path toward her breasts.

'Um, guys.' I hear Greyson clear his throat from

somewhere behind us, but I disregard him as my hand travels up Violet's thigh to the bottom of her dress.

Beep. Beep. Beep.

'Hello, as much as everyone's enjoying the live porn show, it's time to go!' Seth hollers.

I'm not one to get embarrassed. Neither is Violet. Which is why it takes us a few more touches and kisses before we reluctantly break apart. I don't move too far away from her, slipping my fingers through hers as we head toward the Camry parked near the curb.

'Jesus,' Greyson says after we've all gotten in the car. 'I thought they were going to fuck right there on the street.'

Seth glances at me in the rearview mirror and gives me this knowing look. Seth has known me since my man-whore days and knows that I've never acted this way before with a woman, so uncontrolled. A little while ago, his insinuating looks would have pissed me off, but now I shrug them. This is the freest Violet and I have ever been. Usually there's this distance between us, even when we're close. But right now, that look in her eyes I've seen so many times – the look that means she's using sex and kissing me as a distraction – is gone. Instead all I see is want.

Desire.

Need.

Lust.

It almost matches how I'm feeling, except for maybe one more thing on my part, something I don't dare utter, not wanting to fuck up and scare the shit out of her again. So I keep my undying and eternally devoted thoughts to myself and go back to kissing Violet in the backseat, glad with the choices I made tonight.

Glad I chose her over everything else.

Chapter 22

Violet

He's all over me, his hands touching every inch on my body, his lips struggling not to follow since we're in the back of a car with Seth and Greyson in the front seat. But once we get into our room, all bets are off as the little lust we've been holding inside us combusts. He rips my dress off immediately, then yanks my boots and tears my tights off, so I'm lying in the bed with nothing but a lacy black bra and panties on. The lamp is on so I can see the look in his eyes as he stares down at me. It's a look of pure lust, want, and something else. Something that makes me extremely uncomfortable and makes me want to run to the tallest building I can find.

Like I'm something he wants to keep.

Savor.

Love.

Keep safe.

For a second, I feel all those things, like he's wrapped me in his emotions and they become part of me. It sends a jolt of undiluted terror through my body and makes my eyes dart to the door.

Run, Violet, run!

I quickly forget all about running though as he slips out of his jacket and shirt then covers my body with his. His warmth is like a blanket, the kind that makes me feel safe and protected and so much more. The warmth only grows as he kicks his jeans and boxers off and slips inside me. I don't even know what's happening, but every rock of his hips, brush of his hands, how he seems to be touching every inch of me at once, makes me feel like I'm shattering inside, in a way that I don't quite understand. And when he looks at me, I swear I feel whole again, like he picked up all the pieces that just shattered and mended them together again.

I feel breathless.

I feel raw.

I feel like I'm falling and all I can do is hold onto him and never let go as he pushes me toward the edge of oblivion. And we continue to move with each other, grasping onto one another, breathless, afraid.

Afraid of letting go completely.

Afraid of what I feel.

But I can't stop myself and I lose it as I feel myself veering toward the end of the fall. He kisses me through it, holds on tight while I break apart and in the middle of it all, I swear I hear him whisper, 'I love you.' But it's so faint and I'm so far lost in my fall that I can't be certain. Still, it overwhelms me that maybe he does care for me that much, that maybe he does love me. The idea that someone could causes tears to sting the corner of my eyes as I finally crash and shatter all over again. But I manage to suck them back before Luke notices, his breathing hot against my neck as he lies still inside me.

I hear him sigh, even though I don't think I was meant to hear it, then he pushes back, sweeps my hair away from my damp forehead, and looks me directly in the eye.

'Tonight was amazing,' he says then gives me a soft but meaningful kiss.

I'm trying to stay calm, but I'm losing my shit. Something is going on inside me and I don't know what it is. Or maybe I do and that's what's really scaring me.

'Such a softy,' I tease, but my voice sounds all wrong, all ragged and breathless.

He smiles, but there's confusion in his eyes as he senses my off tone.

'I had fun too,' I quickly add then kiss him before he can ask questions. If he asks, then I might tell the truth and I'm not ready for the truth yet.

Still looking lost, he slips out of me, then rolls over to the pillow. 'Jesus, it's almost two o'clock,' he mutters when he picks up his phone.

'You should get some sleep,' I say. 'Big game tomorrow.'

He nods, but he's looking at me like he can read me like an open book. 'Are you still coming to that?'

I shift on the pillow. 'Of course.'

He gives me a weary, but content smile, then yawns and moments later he's passed out in dreamland. About an hour later, I'm still wide-awake and my mind is racing so fast and so wildly it feels like I'm on crack or something. Everything's all jumbled in my head and I can barely make sense of it, but what I do make sense of strikes me to the core.

Love.

Love.

Love.

It's an echo in my head, programmed on repeat, a hauntingly beautiful melody I can't get rid of. I saw it in Luke's eyes tonight, but that's not what's scaring me. I already knew he felt this way, although I don't think I took in the full meaning until now. Understood what it – I – meant to him. But what was really terrifying is that for the briefest, heart-splitting, air ripped from my lungs, can't think, breathe, or process anything, moment, I swear my eyes reflected what was in his. It happened so quickly that my mind is still trying to catch up with it. Either that or I'm in denial.

I watch Luke sleep for the longest time, listening to his soft breathing. The longer I observe him, the more I'm convinced that I've either finally lost my goddamn mind or I'm stupidly and foolishly in love with this guy lying next to me.

'No, it's not possible,' I mutter to myself, rubbing my chest as emotions stir inside me, powerful, potent, *too much*. 'I'm not supposed to fall in love. I don't even know what the fuck it is.' I throw the blankets off me and climb out of bed. I have no initial plans of where I'm going – out is as far as I've gotten – when I spot one of the photos from the box sticking out from under the bed. I'd made a mess the last time I put it under there and never cleaned it up. Bending down, I pick it up, then find myself smiling. It's of my mother and father, her in his arms, wearing her wedding dress. She looks so happy and I feel kind of happy seeing her like that. I'd always had this thought that looking at these photos was going to tear what little of my heart was left and I was going to bleed dry. But that's not what's happening at the moment. No, I feel strangely calm.

Instead of going out of the room, like I'd planned on doing, I get back in bed with the photo in my hand. I don't snuggle up to Luke like I usually do, not wanting to bring the emotions that I've managed to lullaby to sleep out again without harming myself. I trace each line, each shade, every aspect of their happy faces in the picture, engraining the image of them into my mind.

'This is what I wish I could remember you like,' I whisper to myself as I grasp the photo over my beating heart. I visualize the picture in my head, hoping that when I shut my eyes this is how I will see them, instead of the last time that I saw them. That for once my dreams might be filled with happiness instead of sheer terror.

It's the first time I've tried it.

Tried to change things.

Let things go.

I wonder if it's possible.

Chapter 23

Luke

I wake up to the sound of a quiet house and the sunlight blinding me as it shines through the window. It takes me a bit to come out of my disoriented state and let go of the dream I was having where everyone was watching me play the game tonight and I fucked up epically. I didn't really think I'd ever worry about that shit, but then again, I've never actually had people in the stands for me.

After I'm fully awake, I roll onto my side and spot Violet sitting on the floor wearing one of my t-shirts, her hair in a messy bun. She's hovering over what looks like a Calculus book, tapping a pen against the pages. The fact that she's doing her homework this early alone is shocking, but what's really getting to me is the fact that I didn't hear her wake up. I always hear Violet wake up, her gasping ritual too loud to sleep through. Was I that tired? Did I manage to sleep through it finally?

I sit up in bed and glance around, like the mystery of what's going on lies somewhere in the garbage and clutter around our narrow room and the dirty laundry on the floor. 'How long have you been awake?' I ask, but she doesn't respond, bobbing her head up and down to a tune only she seems to hear.

Climbing out of bed, I notice she has earbuds in. She looks totally into her assignment, too, her hand moving ridiculously fast. I almost don't want to interrupt her, but I also want to get to the bottom of what's going on. So I grab a pair of boxers, slip them on, then settle on the floor beside her. My sudden appearance startles her and she jumps, pressing her hand to her heart.

'Fuck, you scared me,' she says really loudly, dropping her hand into her lap.

I reach for the earbud cord and give it a little tug, causing them to fall out of her ears.

'Oh,' she says then scratches her head. 'I almost forgot I had those in.'

I toss the earbuds aside. 'How long have you been awake?'

Her eyes rise to the ceiling as she thinks about it. 'I don't know . . . maybe like an hour.'

I glance over my shoulder and look at the time. A quarter after nine. 'You woke up voluntarily before ten o'clock? Seriously?'

She sets the pen down on the open book and rubs her eyes. 'Yeah, I slept well. Guess my body wakes up earlier when it gets rest.'

She's avoiding eye contact with me, her head tucked down, strands of her hair hanging into her face. I should just let it go. Clearly whatever's going on, she wants to keep it to herself. But I can't fucking help it – I need to know.

'So you slept well?' I run my hand over my cropped brown hair. 'Really?'

She shrugs. 'Better than I have in a really long time.'

I pause. *Don't say it.* 'Any nightmares?' Fuck, why can't I just keep my dumb mouth shut?

There's an elongated pause and then she gives her head the softest shake. 'No,' she whispers, almost sounding like she's in pain. I see a tear roll down her cheek, but she swiftly wipes it away with her hand.

'How long has it been since that happened?' I ask, treading with caution. Another tear escapes her eyes and this time I wipe it away from her cheek myself. I leave my hand there and she relaxes into my touch.

She squeezes her eyes closed then inhales deeply. 'Since I was five.'

This is a huge moment for her, one that she should be celebrating, so her tears are confusing to me. 'Can you . . . Can I ask . . . why you're upset?' I know I'm treading on thin ice. An emotional Violet usually means instability and the risk of her doing something to herself, but I need to figure out what's going on, how I can help take the pain away.

She sucks in another sharp breath. 'Because I'm afraid of why they stopped.'

'Do you know why?'

'Maybe.'

I waver, unsure what the right thing to say is. 'Do you want to talk about it?'

She quickly shakes her head. 'No, not right now.'

I'm not sure what to do, what to say to her, what the hell is going on in her head. Maybe it's because I can't see her eyes – they usually give me a sliver of insight into what she's keeping trapped inside her.

I fix my finger under her chin and tip it up so I can have a better look at her. Her green eyes are massive, swimming with powerful emotions and glossed with tears. For a brief instant, I'm struck speechless by the sight.

'Please . . . just tell me what I can do.' Because I need to do something otherwise I'm going to go crazy worrying about her.

Her eyes search mine. The longer she studies me, the more the tears subside. 'You could take me for coffee.'

I'm thrown for a turn by her simple response. 'Really? That's what you need right now?'

She nods, more at ease. 'Caffeine seems like the best thing ever right now.' She gets to her feet and heads for the closet to get some clothes. 'And a healthy addiction for the most part.'

It's like she's trying to tell me something without actually saying the words aloud. I'm pretty sure I know what it is and the pressure that I've had in my chest deflates the slightest bit. I don't want to get my hopes up, don't want to just assume that maybe she's finally going to try and get over her adrenaline addiction, but she's never actually looked like she means it, like she does right now.

'Alright, let's go get you some coffee, then,' I say, for once feeling like maybe through all this shit, through everything, just maybe things might be okay.

Violet and I will be okay.

Chapter 24

Violet

Luke is nervous before the game and I find it adorable. Mr Tough Guy all distracted and unable to focus because his dad is coming to watch him play. Plus, it's a good distraction from what's going on in my own life. Last night I had a dream, not a nightmare. The dream was fairly simplistic, Luke and I sitting on this hill, staring at this view I had to have made up myself because it was so bright with colors and sunshine, straight out of a gorgeous painting, that there's no way it could be real. It was the cemetery my parents are buried in, yet it wasn't – couldn't be – because I was too at peace with being so close to it. And my heart understood why. Luke was there with me, my safety net. We weren't even talking, just sitting and enjoying the quiet. Then I'd slipped my hand into his and that's when I'd woken up and I was oddly enough holding Luke's hand. And I'd woken up quietly, soft breathing, slightly disoriented, but in a slumbering way. It'd definitely freaked me out, but instead of doing something irrational, I'd gotten out of bed and thrown all of my concentration into my homework. And surprisingly it helped settle me down.

'So you'll be okay going up to the stands by yourself, right?' he asks as he gets ready to leave the apartment. He's got to go to the stadium quite a bit earlier so I'm going to go with Seth and Greyson later and meet up with Luke's father and Trevor.

I roll my eyes as I sit on the bed, watching as a scatter-brained Luke wanders around, throwing stuff to take to the game in a duffel bag. 'Yes, Luke. I promise I'm competent enough to find my way to the massive stadium that takes up half a block.'

'Okay. Okay.' He pats his shorts like he's checking the pockets, even though he doesn't have pockets. 'I should get going then.' He swings his bag over his shoulder and focuses on me, then his brows furrow. 'Why are you looking at me that way?'

I shrug, pressing my lips together to contain my amusement. 'What way?'

'Like I'm being funny or something.'

'Maybe because you are.'

His eyes narrow. 'What's going on?'

My amused smile breaks through. 'It's nothing. You just are so nervous and I'm finding it amusing.'

'Well, I'm glad my uneasiness is making you amused.' He gives me a cold stare, clearly not in a joking mood.

'I'm sorry.' I kneel up on the bed and inch toward the edge of it, closing the space between us. 'It's just that I've never seen you act this way before.'

The hardness in his features softens. 'Sorry.' He drops his bag on the floor and huffs out a breath as he rakes his fingers through his hair and starts pacing the floor. 'I'm just freaking out and I have no idea why. It's not like this is some special game or anything. It's the same one I've been playing since my junior year, yet it feels like the first one.'

'It's because your dad's coming,' I say. 'At least that's my two cents.'

'Yeah . . . And you, too.' He massages the back of his neck tensely as he stops in front of the bed.

I point at myself, stunned by his confession. 'Why do I make you nervous?'

'Why wouldn't you,' he says, his gaze locked on mine, his hand still cupping the back of his neck. 'You mean more to me than him.' He shrugs as if we're discussing something as casual as what movie we want to see. 'More than anyone really.'

Deep breaths, Violet. Do not freak out. You can do this. 'Well, I guess you're in trouble then, because there's going to be a whole lot of people there cheering you on.' I put my hands on his shoulders and look him directly in the eye. My fingers are quivering because I'm fighting back the compulsion to simmer down the emotions inside me the old way and I'm sure Luke can feel the tremor. 'Should I give you a pep talk? I could even pat your ass before you walk out. That's what football players do, right? To get all pumped up and ready to win.' My voice comes out light and I silent breathe in the relief. *I did it. Holy shit.*

He relaxes a little. 'No, I'm good. My nerves will settle before the game starts I'm sure.' He picks up his bag then pauses, a naughty look dancing in his eyes. 'You can slap my ass if you want to though.'

That gets me to grin and then we lean in to kiss each other goodbye. As he turns to leave, I extend my arm out and slap his ass, laughing as I pull back my hand. He flashes me a grin, one that I swear only belongs to me, before he walks out the door.

I exhale loudly then get out of bed to get ready for

my therapy session. I'm nervous about going again, more than I was the first time, because I know what to expect. I'm all over the place right now, battling a demon I've been carrying inside me for fifteen years and Lana just might set that demon free, let someone see it other than Luke. But if I'm being honest with myself, I'm half worried and half hoping that it'll happen. Maybe she can give me some sort of words of wisdom to help me cope with the freaked-out mode I get every time I feel an emotion.

After bundling up in a coat, boots and gloves I head out the front door with Greyson at my side, since I promised Luke I wouldn't go to the university – or anywhere really – alone.

'How long do you think you'll be?' Greyson asks as he drives down the street. There's a drizzle of rain falling from the clouds and the windshield wipers are on, the heater cranked.

'I'm not sure,' I reply. 'Last time it was only for half an hour, but today might take longer.'

He nods as he makes a right onto a busier street in town. 'Okay, so do you just want to text me when you're done? I have to run a few errands anyway.'

'That works for me.' I thrum my fingers on the sides of my legs, nervous.

'Can I ask what's got you so restless?' Greyson asks, noticing my anxiousness.

'Just this whole visit with the therapist thing,' I lie, stilling my fingers.

'Okay.' It's clear from his skepticism that he doesn't believe me.

'Luke's got me worried too,' I blurt out, scaring the bejesus out of myself because I swear my mind just took on a mind of its own. When he gives me this interrogative sidelong glance, I add, 'He's just nervous over the game.'

'And that makes you nervous?'

'No.'

Rain splatters against the window as he stares at me. 'Okay, I'm so confused.'

'So am I,' I admit, rubbing my hand over my face. 'These last few weeks I've been nothing but confused.'

He downshifts to turn. 'Over?'

'Mira being in prison,' I say. 'Preston; wanting to move on from that ordeal . . . how I can't move on until he decides to let me.'

'The police will find him, Violet.' He reaches over and gives my leg a pat. 'And until they do, you're safe. You've got a lot of people looking out for you.'

'I know.' I bite at my fingernails. 'Can I ask you a question?'

He nods. 'You know you can ask me anything.'

'Okay, but I need you to promise that you won't tease me or get all excited and overanalyze it. And that you'll drop it when I say so.'

'Okay, now you've got me nervous.'

'I've got myself nervous,' I tell him, tracing one of the heart drawings Seth put on my cast. 'But I feel like I'm going to explode if I don't figure out what the hell is going on inside my head.'

He turns the car down one of the side streets that lead to the university. The shedding trees that canopy the road are evidence that winter is just around the corner. 'Okay, I promise not to do any of those things. Now spill what's on your mind.'

I'm not sure where to start. I blow out a breath and just let it out of me. 'So I've been having these thoughts.'

'Mmm hmm.' He's choosing his responses carefully.

'About my . . . feelings.' The word feels so foreign.

His grip tightens on the steering wheel. Greyson knows me well enough to understand that me talking about feelings is a huge deal. 'Okay, what feelings exactly?'

I itch at my wrist where the cut used to be, but now is just a thin, fading scar. 'About life and . . .'

'Yeah . . .'

'Luke.' I wince as I say it, because letting it out into the world makes it that much more real, and also bluntly obvious that something is unquestionably going on inside me.

He turns into the parking lot of the university and parks as close as he can. He leaves the engine running and turns in the seat to face me. 'Do I dare ask what feelings we're talking about?'

'I honestly can't answer that because I don't know.' I pause, my mouth opening and closing repeatedly.

'Violet, this is a safe zone,' Greyson says, putting a hand on mine. 'You can say whatever you want without judgment.'

I hate that I have to be reassured, that I've become that kind of person, but it is what it is. 'What's love like?' I blurt out like a madwoman.

It's clear I've shocked him and that this wasn't the question he was expecting me to ask. As he takes in the entire meaning of what I just said, his eyes fill with sadness. I half expect him to say something about being so sorry that I don't know the answer to this, but he doesn't and it makes me like him that much more.

'It's like falling and flying at the same time.' He shakes his head and then waves it off. 'Sorry, that was a bad analogy. Let me try that again.' He mulls over it for a minute, gazing off, a smile forming before he clears his throat and returns his concentration to me. 'You know I can actually remember that exact moment I did fall in love. It was so crazy too, because it was like one second I was in the really-like phase and then suddenly I was fucking in love, like super, crazy, out-of-my mind in love.'

'So it just happened?' I ask skeptically. 'There was no warning at all.'

He shrugs. 'Maybe for some people there's a warning, but not me.'

I bring my knee up and rest my chin on it. 'Were you scared?'

His eyes widen and he nods. 'Heck, yeah, I was terrified out of my mind, but in this really good way, you know. But that's because Seth made me feel good. Every time I was with him I was the best version of me and I was happy and felt so fucking content in life. More than I ever had.' He pauses, growing reluctant. 'Can I ask why you're asking this?'

'I'm not sure yet.' I glance at the clock on the dashboard and ignore the voice inside my head that's telling me that I do know why I'm asking this. 'I should get going.' I grab my bag and open the door, about to climb out into the rain, but then pause. 'Thanks for sharing your story, though,' I tell him. I'm not sure if it was hard for him or not, but I want him to know that I'm grateful.

He smiles as he sits back in his seat. 'Any time. It's fun to remember anyway. It was a good moment in my life that should never be forgotten.'

His smile is contagious and I end up stepping out into the rain looking so happy that people I pass by probably think I'm high. And I try to carry the feeling with me as I make my way to Lana's office, knowing I'm probably going to need it when I get there.

Two hours later, I'm in the backseat of Seth's car with him, Greyson and Callie, headed to the game, but my thoughts are elsewhere. The therapy session went okay. We didn't get into anything too deep, just talked about my life now and how I feel about it, albeit the feeling part was hard and I didn't verbalize it so great. Then we chatted a little about my parents, mostly just remembering what little things I could, which made me both sad and happy. The only thing that was really hard to deal with was when I told her about the dreams I've been having about the cemetery. When she asked me if I'd ever been to visit them, I'd shook my head and then she'd suggested that maybe one day I go. As if it was as simple as plucking a leaf off a tree. I told her I'd think about it, which I am, but not in the calming way she suggested. My mind is all over the place, thoughts floating around in my head like ping pong balls. My parents. The cemetery. My feelings. Luke. My parents. My feelings.

I swear my brain is about to short-circuit. The thing that pulls me back to reality is when my phone starts ringing from inside the pocket of my leather jacket. I take it out and see an unknown number, which makes me hesitate before I answer. I'm guessing it's either a reporter or Preston, and plan on hanging up right away, but it's not. It's Detective Stephner.

'So I have some good news and some maybe bad news, depending on how you look at it,' he says after I answer.

I glance around the car, glad to see that Seth, Greyson and Callie appear to be engaging in a very intense conversation about football. 'Okay, I'm listening.'

'Well the trial is going to be starting soon,' he says. 'Which means things are moving forward.'

I face the window, trying to keep the conversation

as private as I can. 'But she still hasn't said who the other person was?'

'No, not yet, but I wanted to give you a heads up that, for one, there's a chance that her lawyer might try to plead insanity.'

'For some reason, I'm not surprised,' I mutter, then sigh, not sure how I feel about it. 'Was that the good or bad news?'

'I'm not sure,' he replies, then sighs to himself. 'I don't know, maybe I just have so-so news.'

I frown. 'So what's the rest of it?'

'That if we go to trial they might call you up on stand,' he explains. 'And Mira will be there when it happens.'

I glance down at my cast, which will be off in two more weeks. 'I'm not sure I can do that. My arm's still in a freaking cast, for God sakes.'

'Violet, we already talked about this,' he says. 'It'll be easier than the first time, seeing her, I mean. She'll be under more control.'

'How is that easier?' I snap. 'She'll still be there.'

'You're a strong girl, Violet Hayes,' he tells me, not really answering my question. 'I know you can do this if needed.'

'A lot of people would disagree with that statement.'

'I'm a detective. I see more than most people.'

I'm not sure what to do with this or if there's anything I can do but accept it. I close my eyes and picture the photo I found last night. *That's what I'm doing this for, right?* 'Okay, I'll do it if I need to.'

'Good girl.' He pauses and I open my eyes. 'Have you talked to Luke at all?'

'I talk to him every day,' I say, warily. 'Why? You going somewhere with this or just being your annoying self?'

'Maybe I'm going somewhere with this.' He's speaking in code.

I catch Greyson glancing over his shoulder at me with an inquisitive look so I turn toward the door as much as the seatbelt will let me. 'Just spit it out, whatever it is.'

'Watch it, Violet,' the detective warns. 'Remember who you're talking to.'

'Yeah, the guy who wears Christmas ties on Halloween,' I reply dryly. 'Clearly I need to be careful.'

He sighs and I know he's going to drop it. 'Look, I just wanted to say that you should probably make sure you and Luke are communicating since I'm guessing he's going to be called in too – he might have already.'

'He has?' I ask. Well that's news to me.

'Maybe . . .' One, two, three seconds tick by. 'It might have been a call to defend.'

I rest my head against the cool glass and shut my eyes as my chest constricts and sucks the air out of my lungs. *Why didn't he tell me?* 'Did he agree?'

'I'm not sure. I'm just telling you things so you won't be surprised if he says something about it to you.' I hear someone saying something in the background. 'But look, I have to go. I just wanted to give you a heads up.'

'Thanks,' I mumble, then hang up the phone, leaving my forehead pressed against the window. *There's no way Luke would do that. He hates his mother. And he said he loves me.* But all those years of being passed around through foster families are making me doubt this so called thing known as love. All the foster mothers and fathers who took me in, to take care of me, but then got sick of me and booted me to the door.

'Violet, we're here.' Greyson's voice rips me from my daze and when I look around I realize we've arrived at the stadium. It's absolutely insane how many cars are parked there and how many people are walking around decked out in the school colors.

'Holy balls,' I say, not sure if I'm disgusted or impressed.

Callie, Seth, and Greyson all laugh at my reaction then hop out of the car. I follow them, the loudness of their enthusiasm slamming me in the chest as I get out. The sun is peeking through the clouds and drying up the puddles on the asphalt, but the air is still ice cold.

As we make our way through the chaos and toward the shiny steel stadium, Greyson links arms with me and Seth, then Seth links his through Callie, so we're kind of this human chain. I don't even know what to make of it. Never in a million years would I have ever thought that I'd be doing this with three other people. But here I am, going to a freaking football game. I get lost in the atmosphere, the buzzing enthusiasm, the amount of people that we have to maze our way through.

Just when I think it can't get any more chaotic, we enter the stadium. My jaw just about drops; at the massive size of it, how packed it is, and how glowing and amped up everyone seems to be.

'Jesus, it's like a bubble full of enthusiasm, isn't it?' I say with wide eyes, wondering if I should back away because I clearly don't belong here.

Greyson must feel me trying to slink back from him because he tightens his grip and shakes his head. 'No way. You are so doing this. If nothing else, for Luke.'

Okay, he's got me there. 'Fine. You're right.'

'Aw, I know your soft spot now.' He grins at me and I flip him off as I follow him to our seat, our arms still linked so it makes it super awkward and pretty annoying for the people passing us, which makes it entertaining for me. Every time someone huffs in frustration when they have to either wait for us to pass or squeeze by us, it makes my grin grow bigger.

'See.' Greyson waggles his eyebrows at me from over his shoulder. 'Fun, right?'

I shrug, but there's a smile tugging at my lips. 'Perhaps.'

He rolls his eyes, but then grins as he continues up the stairs. 'I'll tell you what. If you promise to try and have fun, I will bake you an entire batch of cupcakes for yourself.'

'How old do you think I am?' I say, as we drop down in our seats, which are about halfway up the bleachers, giving us a decent view of the field and team benches down below. Callie and Seth are sitting on the other side of Greyson and I have two vacant seats beside me for Luke's dad and Trevor.

He gives me an accusing look as he reaches into his pocket and takes out a pair of gloves. 'So you're saying that you don't want them?'

I think about what he said, but not for very long. 'Will you make them look like turkeys?'

He slips on a glove. 'What?'

I zip up my coat. 'For Thanksgiving.'

He chuckles as he puts the other glove on. 'Sure, I think I can do that.'

'Fine, then I will try to have fun.' I draw my hood over my head to keep my ears warm.

Smiling, we both turn and look in the direction of the field, tucking our chins and mouths under the collars of our jackets to protect our skin from the cold. We've got a decent view, but Seth still brought binoculars and Callie brought a camera. While we're waiting for it to start, Seth and Callie make a snack run and that's when Luke's father and Trevor join us. They sit to the side of me and I make introductions.

'Greyson, this is Trevor and Mr Price.' I gesture back and forth between them.

'Please, call me James,' Mr Price says as he shakes Greyson's hand. 'And you too, Violet. None of this Mr Price stuff.'

I nod and then Seth and Callie return with their hands full of popcorn, soda and candy bars, so I have to introduce them as well. Seth gives James's hand a shake then gives me a bag of M&Ms, which I'm thankful for, before he plops into his seat and starts giggling with Callie about something.

'You know, I'm going to risk looking stupid here, but I totally don't get football,' Trevor says almost shamefully as he buttons up his jacket.

'Me neither,' I reply, way less ashamed.

James grins proudly as he takes a sip of the coffee he brought up with him. 'Well, then, you two are in luck, because I just happen to know a ton about it.'

Trevor nudges him with his elbow. 'Maybe that's because you played in high school.'

James laughs and goes into this big speech about the rules and stuff, talking animatedly with his hands, seeming to enjoy the topic. I don't understand ninety-nine percent of it, but smile and pretend I'm listening. He stops talking, though, when the team comes out and starts clapping and cheering with the rest of the crowd, yelling at the top of his lungs, his breath foggy in the air, but everyone is, really. I'm totally not into it, not understanding what the big deal is, until I spot Luke amongst the players. It's not like I become some sort of football junkie or anything the moment I see him, but it still causes my heart to do this little flutter inside my chest that's only happened a couple of times. I must be grinning or something too, because Greyson pokes me in the side and gives me this big cheesy grin.

'See, not so bad, right?' he says, still clapping while Callie and Seth jump up and down, laughing.

'It's alright,' I say, but my lips have become traitors and can't seem to stop grinning like a ridiculous idiot. And as silly as it seems, for the first time in a while, I sit back and momentarily enjoy life without worrying about anything, really.

I end up waiting for Luke after the game with Callie. I wasn't going to but I guess it's a thing or something. After every game, Callie waits for Kayden, and I guess now that I'm with Luke and am coming to games, I'm expected to wait for Luke with Callie, at least that's Greyson's theory. When I don't agree at first he threatens me with cupcakes, so I stay behind, but deep down it's not really about the cupcakes.

Trevor and James tell me that they're going to go back to the hotel and warm up for a while, that California people were not made for this kind of weather. But they say to have Luke call them when he's ready and we'll go out and get something to eat.

'And you guys can pick the place,' Trevor says through his chattering, then laughs. 'Since you weren't a fan of the restaurant we picked.'

'Was it that obvious?' I ask, tucking my hands into my jacket pockets.

Trevor laughs again. 'It was kind of a dead giveaway when you spat out the water.' He walks over to the edge of the canopy we're standing under, heading toward the parking lot.

James doesn't follow him right away, instead pulling me in for another awkward hug like he did at the airport. 'It was good to spend time with you,' he says as I give him a pat on the back, feeling edgy and tense. He pulls away, seeming happy, then waves as he follows after Trevor, shivering the entire way. 'See you at dinner,' he calls out.

I wave, then just stand there, under the canopy, staring up at the stars, trying to figure out how I got to this point in my life where people make me cupcakes, make me laugh, give me awkward-as-hell hugs, and invite me to dinner.

I don't get it.

I really don't.

But I like it.

My last thought gets to me because I'm accepting it – this life. Which means I'm accepting the possibility that I could lose it. It's hard to admit this to myself, that I'm taking that chance, something I haven't done since my parents died.

'They played a good game, didn't they?' Callie says and I startle – I'd almost forgotten she was standing there with me.

I put on a smile as I turn to look at her. 'Yeah, I guess. Although, I really don't know. Not a football fan. But I'm guessing it's good because they won.'

She's leaning against the wall across from the door Luke and Kayden are supposed to be coming out of. The hood of her jacket is pulled over the top of her head and she has a scarf on. 'Yeah, it was a good game. You should come to the next one with Seth, Greyson, and me.'

I shrug as I recline back against the wall. 'Maybe.'

'It gets easier to understand,' she says. 'And it makes it more fun.'

I kick the tip of my boot against the ground. I've never been good at chatting with girls, and Callie and I don't have the best history, so I feel a little awkward. 'You seem to know a lot about it.'

'My dad's a high school coach,' she explains. 'He was actually Luke and Kayden's coach when they were in high school.'

'That's cool. It must have been fun to watch them play back then.'

She smiles but it doesn't quite reach her eyes. It

makes me wonder what it was like for her in high school; I wonder if she hated it like I did. 'So I was thinking that maybe you and I could do some more kickboxing. You seemed to have fun the other day.'

'Not necessarily fun,' I say. 'It was just a little therapeutic.'

She turns to face me. 'It's that way for me too, at least it was when I first started it. Now it's more for fun. I go at least twice a week. Seth usually goes too. You could ride with him.'

I'm not sure about the idea, but don't just want to throw it away. 'I'll think about it,' I tell her, surprised I actually mean it. It did feel good kicking the shit out of something, even if it was just a bag. I open my mouth to ask her how she got into it, when Jonah Malforten walks up to me and interrupts our conversation.

'Violet, long time no see.' He grins his stoned grin as he nudges my boot with his foot. Jonah is a guy I used to deal with and seeing him standing here, near the stadium while I'm talking to Callie, feels like the past is mingling with my present. I find myself not liking it, especially the reminder of my life with Preston.

'What do you want, Jonah.' I turn my bitchy attitude

on, but this is nothing new to Jonah because back when he knew me, this is how I always was.

'I think you know what I want.' He winks at me as he adjusts his beanie farther over his head, the stench of pot reeking off of him and his bloodshot eyes full of hope that I'm going to deal to him.

I glance over at Callie, who is looking in the other direction, as if she's deeply preoccupied by a poster of the upcoming Winter Ball. As far I know, Callie thinks I'm a prostitute, at least that's what she used to think I was, but maybe she knows the truth now.

'Look, I don't do that shit anymore, okay?' I keep my voice low, but firm. 'So take your stoned ass to someone else.'

'You're mean,' he says, pouting in a way that I think he thinks is sexy, but is just plain annoying. 'But you've always been mean. Sexy as hell, but mean. No wonder Preston has you doing his dirty work.'

My muscles ravel into frayed knots about to snap. '*Had* me do his dirty work. Past tense. Now get the fuck out of my face.' When he keeps grinning at me, I give him a little shove. 'I'm serious, you dipshit. I don't deal anymore nor do I have any connection with Preston.'

He scratches the back of his neck, seeming lost.

'Weird . . . I just saw him and he said to hit you up, that he was dry but that you'd help me out.'

The knots in my muscles wind so tight it hurts and I frantically scan the area around me, searching for his face in the dwindling crowd and the remaining cars still parked in the lot on my right. 'You saw Preston here?'

He tips his head to the side, still confounded. 'No . . . not here. At Garyford's, down on Elm, earlier today.'

My heart skips a beat but I tell it to settle down – don't get too excited yet. 'The bar?'

Jonah nods. 'Yeah, he's always down there trying to sell. But today he was just chilling. Said I'd need to find you if I wanted anything . . . I think he was super drunk or something. Said if I found ya to tell you that he was looking for you.'

Fucking asshole! God dammit, what the hell is the point of this? To drive me mad. 'Thanks, Jonah.' I pat his arm then push him toward the exit. 'It's been super fun talking to you, but time for you to go.'

'What about the stuff I need?' He stumbles over his feet as I push him.

'Preston lied. I have nothing.' I retrieve my phone from my pocket and press Detective Stephner's number.

Jonah is mumbling about something as he wanders away and Callie is giving me this worried look. But I disregard them both as I move to the outside of the canopy with the phone against my ear. As soon as Detective Stephner answers, I blurt out everything that just happened.

'Violet, calm down,' he says. 'I can barely understand you.'

I take a breath, realizing I was getting no oxygen in with my words. 'I just ran into someone who told me that Preston hangs out at Garyford's on Elm every day. You know the bar where college kids like to hang out.'

'Okay, I'm on it,' he says and I can hear him rustling around. 'But Violet, I want you to go home and wait to hear from me, okay? Stay indoors. I don't want anything happening.'

What the hell does he think's going to happen that hasn't already happened? 'Okay, I wasn't planning on going anywhere, just dinner with Luke and his dad.'

'No, stay indoors,' he says. 'Promise me, Violet. Just go home and wait this out.'

'Why does it matter?'

'Dammit, Violet, just listen for once, okay?'

'Okay, Dad,' I say sarcastically but then realize I'm acting like a brat. 'Sorry, I promise I'll stay in.'

'Good.' He breathes a breath of relief. Something's off. He's acting more worried than he normally does.

'What aren't you telling me?' I ask suspiciously, watching a group of people closely as they walk by. What if Jonah lied and Preston is out there watching me right now?

'A lot,' Detective Stephner replies. 'There's a lot of stuff I can't tell you.'

That's news to me and by the time I hang up, my mind's racing with a million different ideas. I shut it down though when Luke finally walks through the doors. He's wearing jeans and a hoodie, his hair damp, probably because he just showered. At least he smells like he did, the fresh scent of soap surrounding me as he pulls me in for a hug. He does it without so much as a hesitation, as if it's the most natural thing in the world. It's starting to feel that way for me too.

'So what did you think?' he whispers in my ear, still holding onto me.

'Those were some super tight pants,' I try to tease, but my voice sounds off pitch.

He pulls back, concern evident all over his face. 'What's wrong?'

I look over at Callie who's smiling at Kayden as he

walks out of the door Luke's just emerged from. 'Can I tell you in the truck?'

He glances over his shoulder at Callie hugging Kayden and then nods. 'Okay, yeah, let's go.' He moves back, but doesn't go too far, sliding his arm around my back. 'Hey guys, we're going to head out,' he calls out to Kayden. 'See ya later.'

Kayden waves, but he's distracted by Callie, who's smiling as she tells him something which creates this big goofy grin on his face. I wonder what she thinks about what just happened. I wonder why I care so much.

Luke and I head across the parking lot to the truck in silence, the sounds of our hurried footsteps adding to the tension around us. He's parked toward the back so it takes a while but finally we reach it. He opens the door for me then once I'm settled in the seat he shuts the door and gets into the driver's seat. His truck makes this gurgling noise as he starts the engine and then backfires. He curses then tries again, this time pumping the gas. Once it's on and clearly going to stay running, he cranks the heat and turns to face me.

'Okay, what the hell has got that look on your face?' he asks, scooting toward me.

I slip my gloves off and unzip my jacket as what

happened barrels out of me. I explain to him how I ran into Jonah and what he told me about Preston. I also tell him how I called Detective Stephner and how he told me to stay in our apartment tonight and how he seemed to be acting strange.

'I'm sure he just wants to make sure you're safe.' Luke reaches for my hand when I'm done telling him and traces the folds in my fingers. 'It's what we all want.'

I'm not sure who he means by *we*, but I don't ask. 'Yeah, maybe. But I talked to him earlier today when we were headed to the game and he seemed fine.'

'He called you today?' he asks, turning my hand upward and stroking the inside of my wrist. *God that feels so good.* 'About what?'

Through all of this, I'd spaced off the conversation the detective and I had earlier and how I never did come to a conclusion on whether Luke would agree to help Mira. Although being here with him now, his touch bringing me so much calm, I'm starting to wonder why I doubted him to begin with. 'About the case . . . and you?'

His fingers pause on my palm. 'Me?'

I nod. 'He said he thinks you got a call from the person defending your mother in court.'

He suddenly looks like he's in pain, his grip on my hands tightening. 'Yeah, the other day I did.'

'Why didn't you tell me?' I ask. 'When it happened?'

'Because I was confused . . . and pissed off.' He sighs, defeated, as he laces our fingers together. 'Sorry, that's no excuse. I should have told you right when it happened.'

I press my lips together, attempting to hold back the words, knowing I shouldn't ask, but I can't help it and they force their way up. 'What did you say?'

A pucker forms at his brows. 'About what?'

'When they asked you to testify,' I say. 'What did you say?'

He looks like I've wounded him, his expression mixed with hurt and disappointment. 'I told them they could go fuck themselves and that she deserves to be behind bars.' He lets go of my hand and slides away, looking a bit angry. 'What the hell else would I say, Violet?'

I stare down at my hands because the hurt look in his eyes is too great to endure. 'I'm sorry I asked, but I needed to hear you say it . . . I don't know why. I was pretty sure I knew your answer.'

He shakes his head, huffing a breath of frustration as he stares ahead at the window. 'I would never, ever do that. Not only because it'd be wrong – she deserves to go to prison – but I could never, ever hurt you like that.' It's like he's fighting to breathe, his solid chest rising and falling heavily with each breath he takes. 'You have to start trusting me.'

'I do trust you. Too much,' I whisper, shutting my eyes. 'You could crush my heart if you wanted to.' The silence that follows is maddening. *Did I just say that aloud?*

One . . .

Two . . .

Three . . .

Time feels endless as I wait for what comes next. I hear him shift on the seat, feeling him scoot closer.

'Violet, open your eyes.' His breath dusts my cheeks.

I swiftly shake my head, smashing my lips together. 'I can't.' But I find myself opening my eyes anyway and he's so close, only inches away from me.

'I would never, *ever* hurt you,' he promises, his hand gently cupping the back of my neck, fingers spreading across my skin. His touch sends a shot of tingles across my flesh and causes me to shiver as he guides me toward his lips. But I'm already leaning in, an invisible current pulling me toward him, like two magnets about to collide. When we do crash into one another, it's dangerously intoxicating, stealing the air from my lungs, sending my heart slamming into my chest. I'm already falling again to that place where I feel helpless, yet safe. Emotions press their way to the surface, this time too strong to ignore. It hits me like lightning, an electric current surging through my body, overwhelming heat that both brings me alive and kills me at the same time.

I think it's then that I know what I'm feeling. The thing I've been trying to avoid for days now, and I'm both terrified out of my mind and alarmingly at peace.

Our kiss is slower than normal, but equally if not more intense. Every sensual sweep of his tongue, soft nibble of his teeth, it's like he's memorizing my lips. His hands are exploring my body, leaving blazing trails of heat wherever they brush, my body so warm I swear I'm on fire. And I'm moaning, God am I moaning, as the stuff I've felt so confused about burns under my skin and pours out through my lips as I devour him with my kisses. I just want to keep doing this forever, never move again, but eventually Luke breaks the connection, putting a sliver of space between our lips.

I whimper a protest and he crooks a pleased smile. 'I promise we will pick this up later. I promise,' he says. 'But I think we need to get you home.'

I nod, my swollen lips unable to form words. So I

turn and face forward in my seat, buckling my seatbelt, my mind turning right back on the moment we pull away from the stadium. Only this time it's thinking about something entirely different, the realization I had while we were kissing. I'm not sure I want to accept it, but honestly it might not be about what I want anymore. Like Greyson says, when it happens it just sort of happens out of nowhere. There is no control, no ignoring, no putting on fake smiles to get around it. Nope, this is out of my control, no matter how much it terrifies me.

Love.

Love.

Love.

I think I might be in love with Luke.

Chapter 25

Luke

I was pretty overwhelmed before the game, thinking about everyone there watching me. Yeah, I'm used to shitloads of people watching me play, but this was different. My father and Trevor were there.

And Violet.

She was making me the most nervous and it took me forever to figure out why. Because someone I love was going to be there. Once I got past the mind-boggling moment though, I was pretty okay with it. Excited, even. I played an awesome game too, so that made my mood better. Then the thing with Preston happened and I'm trying not to get too worked up about it, but if they manage to catch him, then there would be this huge opening for Violet and I to have a semi-normal life, maybe.

And really, that's all I want right now. Just her and me, and the normalcy that we've been having for the last few weeks. I've never had that before and now that I've gotten a taste for it, I want it more than anything.

Once I get Violet home, I call my dad and tell him we can't make it to dinner. When I explain to him why, he suggests that they can bring over a pizza and we can eat at my place. When I tell him I can't pick him up, he says they'll see if the hotel can get them a taxi. Seth and Greyson are out for the night, so we have the place to ourselves. I agree to my dad's offer. He tells me he'll text me back in five, letting me know if they can manage to get a taxi. Five minutes on the dot later, he sends me a message that they'll be there in about an hour or so. I grab two sodas from the fridge then head over to Violet.

She's biting on her fingernails, a habit she's developed over the last couple of weeks whenever she gets nervous. She has the television on, some infomercial playing, so it's pretty clear she's not paying attention to it.

'What's bothering you?' I set the sodas down on the coffee table, sit down beside her on the sofa, and brush her hair off her shoulder. She's wearing a black tank top and her hair's up, so I can see her tattoos peeking out on her neck. 'Is it Preston?'

'What?' She blinks at me, completely out of it.

I take her hand and move it away from her mouth so she can no longer bite her nails. 'It's going to be okay.'

Her body stiffens. 'What is?'

'The thing with Preston.' I sketch my finger along the lines of her star tattoos. 'He can't hide forever.'

'Oh.' Her body unstiffens and she fixes her attention on the television. 'That's not what I'm worried about.'

'Then what are you worried about?' My hand moves from her neck down to her shoulder, then to her side. I urge her to turn and look at me instead of staring at the television, but she fights it, shaking her head.

'I can't yet,' she says quietly.

'Can't what?'

'Talk to you just yet.'

That one stings a little. 'Okay . . . we don't have to talk if you don't want to.'

She nods her head up and down way too swiftly. There's a pause where she fights to breathe then suddenly she's turning toward me, kissing me in desperation. It's not the first time she's done this, used me to distract herself from whatever's she's battling internally, but it's harder to deal with after the other night, when we kissed, danced and had sex just for us, nothing else. I feel like we're stepping backwards and I don't want that. I want to keep going forward, away from the person I used to be and that shitty life I used to live, full of booze, gambling and meaningless sex.

I'm fighting between what's right and wrong, while continuing to kiss her, when she suddenly pulls away, gasping for air. I open my mouth to ask her to please for the love of God explain to me what's going on in that head of hers but then she starts to cry.

'I don't know what's happening to me,' she says, blinking through a veil of tears as she looks everywhere but at me. 'I don't think I can do this anymore.'

My heart plummets inside my chest, my lips still hovering over hers, my hands on her waist. 'Do what anymore?' I don't want the answer, don't want to hear what follows my question, don't want to lose her.

'Fight it.' Tears are still flowing from her eyes, but I think she's stopped crying. She sucks in several breaths and when she looks at me, her eyes are clearer than I anticipated. She's scared shitless – that's clear – but it's like she's stopped fighting the fear, giving in to it instead.

Her lips part and I almost stop whatever she's about

to say, silence her with my lips, but I don't, forcing myself to hear, needing to know what's got her all worked up.

'I think I'm in love with you,' she says, her chest heaving with every ravenous breath she takes, yet her voice is astonishingly even and she manages to maintain my gaze.

My voice however is the exact opposite of even, coming out all high pitched like I'm thirteen years old and going through puberty all over again. 'What?'

She sucks in a breath, then releases it slowly, the fear in her eyes subsiding, as if she's just won it. 'I think I'm in love with you . . .' She bites on her lips and shakes her head. 'No . . . I don't think. I know.'

I gradually process her words and the full extent of what she's saying. I think I'd honestly believed that she might never say them, that this love thing was going to be a one-way street. Hearing her say it . . . I don't even know how to describe it. It's like my entire life I've associated the word with hatred. Every time my mother said it, it felt like she was trying to take something from me and it made me hate her and myself – love equaled hate for me. But hearing it from Violet's lips, seeing that look in her eyes, the one I've never seen from anyone, is so different. She's not taking something from me right now, she's giving me something.

She's giving me everything.

I can't control myself. I smash my lips against hers, probably too roughly. But she doesn't seem to mind, kissing me back just as intensely, her fingers tugging through my hair as she pulls me closer, consuming me with her lips as her body lifts to meet mine. It's like she needs every part of her touching me, but it's not enough. Nothing feels like it could ever be close enough.

As her legs fasten around mine, I grip tightly onto her and stand up, carrying her with me as I head back to the room. Our lips stay sealed, only parting so she can yank my shirt off when we reach the hallway. We bump into walls, slam into tables, knock over the lamp on our way into the room, but we laugh against each other's lips, never parting. When I reach the bed, I fall blindly onto it, catching us with my hands. I take the opportunity to pull her shirt off and unclasp her bra. Then I lean back and take in the sight of her, every speck of flesh, every freckle, every line of ink she has. So fucking gorgeous I can't stand it. I feel like I'm about to combust. I want her so badly that my body is throbbing, my veins pulsating with desire and need.

The need to be with her.

Forever.

And ever.

And ever.

And when I open my mouth to say it, this time it's different – this time it means more than the first time I said it, because I know that I can say it and it'll be welcomed not feared.

'I love you too, Violet Hayes,' I whisper then my lips crash against hers showing her with my mouth just how much I mean it.

God, do I fucking mean it. More than anything else in my life.

Chapter 26

Violet

So this is what making love feels like? That was the last coherent thought I had.

I wasn't planning on telling him that I loved him. I was having an internal argument over the many reasons why I should keep it to myself, that I should just go back to my old ways and deal with it in my own way. That Luke was Mira Price's son and that should matter, right? But then I started thinking about how I didn't want to go back to my old ways, how I hated that life even though I wouldn't admit it at the time, and how he really isn't Mira's son. Yes, he shares her blood but everything about him is the opposite of what that woman is. He's so much more than that.

So, so much more.

He's the guy who helped me to class when I jumped out the window and hurt my foot.

He's the guy who beat the shit out of Preston when he hit me.

He's the guy who protected me.

Who gave me a roof over my head with no stipulations.

The guy who taught me that kissing wasn't just lips and tongue it was emotions and intensity and passion.

The guy who would do anything for me.

The guy who has done anything for me.

The guy who loved me when I thought no one ever would.

He's the guy who made me understand love enough that I could feel it myself, and he should know that, how much he means to me.

'I think I'm in love with you.'

Once I said it aloud, everything changed – I changed in so many ways it's almost too much to take at once. Then again maybe I started changing a while ago and am just accepting it now. Honestly, I don't really care at the moment what it is. I'm too focused on Luke and what his mouth is doing to me, paths of kisses up and down my stomach, across my breasts, up my legs. *Everywhere.*

It's almost too much to take. My mind is so in tune with everything he's doing, my body on the verge of combusting with each brush of his lip and taste of his tongue. Finally I can't take it anymore. I grab at his face and pull his lips up to mine as I lift my hips, needing him inside me. He gladly gives me what I want, slipping deep inside me. I let out the loudest groan, the feeling of him inside way more intense than it usually is, but in the best way possible.

We move with each other, kissing and touching, sweat beading our skin as we take our time, never wanting it to end. I can feel myself falling again and this time I don't fight it, only clutch onto Luke and hold on. Let the emotions take over me, let myself feel every single one of them, let them own me without fearing them.

Seconds later he joins me and we come undone together, my nails stabbing into the flesh of his shoulder blades, which elicits a groan from his lips then he bites down gently on my bottom lip.

Moments later, we start to still, but our lips keep moving, kissing each other until we're breathless and have to stop for air. He doesn't move out of me right away, instead pressing kisses to my neck while I stare up at the ceiling, feeling strangely content inside. All this fighting my emotions and now I wish I hadn't fought them so hard, not when I get to feel like this.

'I hate to say this,' Luke whispers against my ear, nibbling at my earlobe. 'But we need to get dressed before my dad and Trevor show up.'

'We could always just pretend we're out,' I joke, turning my head so I can kiss him.

'Yeah, but it's their last day here,' he says, breathless from the kiss. 'I'd feel bad for bailing.'

'Me too,' I say truthfully, but press my body to tease him, which causes him to groan in frustration. I smile my wicked smile. 'But after they leave, I say we pick this right back up.'

Nodding, he kisses me passionately. 'It's a deal.'

Grinning like two love-struck idiots we get out of bed and get dressed. I don't care though, that I keep grinning like a moron. I'm happy. Completely and utterly terrified but absolutely and positively happy, a place I haven't been in in years.

About five minutes after we're fully clothed, Trevor and James show up with a pizza. We laugh and chat well into the night and everything seems perfect. Then my phone starts to vibrate. It's late, so I know that there are only a few people it could be – Seth, Greyson or Detective Stephner, but he rarely texts me so I figure it's one of the first two. But to my shock, it's from the unknown number.

Unknown: So did u ever wonder how u ended up with me?

I'm guessing from the fact that I'm getting this text Detective Stephner hasn't found him yet.

Another message comes through before I can even get out of my messages.

Unknown: Kelley knew someone from social services who helped us get u into the house. It wasn't a coincidence u ended up with me Violet. I wanted u there.

I can't help it. I have to respond.

Me: Why, though? Why did u want me?

I'm afraid of the answer.

Unknown: At first I wasn't sure if it was because I hated you or because I felt sorry for u. It took me a little while to figure out that it was a love/ hate thing.

Me: U don't love me. U said so yourself.

Unknown: That was partially a lie. Sometimes I do, but I hate myself when I do, I hate that I'm so obsessed with u and can't seem to finish what I thought I wanted.

I stop breathing.

Me: And what do you want?
Unknown: Revenge.

'Give it to me.' Luke's stern voice causes my attention to flinch away from the screen and land on him. I realize he's been leaning over my shoulder, reading everything. He sticks out his hand while Trevor and James give us a strange look.

'Everything okay?' James asks.

Neither of us answers and I give the phone to Luke right as another text comes through.

Unknown: Did I scare u away? So easy to break, even though u pretend to be so tough.

Luke grinds his teeth as he types.

Luke: You're lucky I haven't found u yet, otherwise your hands wouldn't be working to type.

'Luke don't,' I protest, but he's already typing again.

Luke: If I ever find u, you're in for a fucking hell of a lot of pain.

Unknown: I'm guessing this isn't Violet anymore, but the fucking dumbass that follows her around like a lovesick puppy.

Luke: One of these days you're going to be found and you're going to pay.

Unknown: One of these days I'm going to decide to stop tormenting her and finish her off.

'I'm going to fucking kill him.' Luke tosses the phone onto the table and jumps up from the sofa, storming for the door.

'Wait, where are you going?' I ask, chasing after him.

He starts to open the door, but I get there and slam my hand against it, slamming it shut before he can walk out while Trevor and James start to get to their feet, worried.

'Get out of my way, Violet.' Veins bulge in his neck as he reaches for the doorknob again.

I shake my head and stand between the door and him. 'Not until you tell me where you're going.'

'To Garyford's,' he says, flexing his fingers as he tries to stay calm.

Fear slams through me. 'You can't go looking for him. It's too dangerous.'

'Like hell I can't.' He reaches for the doorknob again, but I snag his wrist and catch his gaze.

'It's not worth the risk. If you go, something could happen. And I can't deal with anything happening to you,' I say, my voice wobbly. 'Otherwise I'm going to break and I don't think I'll ever be able to fix myself, so please, for me, just stay here and wait with me to hear from Detective Stephner.'

He's struggling to control his breathing, his gaze moving back and forth between the doorknob and me, conflicted.

'Son.' James steps up behind him. 'I know it's hard, but Violet's right. It's better to let the police handle it.'

'The police have done nothing.' His voice is firm, but his gaze is softening, eyes on me, the anger chipping away. The bulging veins have settled and slowly the tension in his body follows.

James puts a hand on Luke's shoulder. 'I know it's hard and you feel helpless, but think of what it'll do to Violet – to me – if something did happen to you.'

His father's words make the rest of his anger dissolve. 'Fine,' he says, then even though I can tell it's hard for him, he walks back to the sofa and sits back down. 'I'll wait.'

James and I exchange a relieved look then we sit down too. Luke turns the movie back on, but it's kind of pointless, everyone too worried to focus on the screen. Then tension begins to build every time my phone vibrates. I don't check the messages and wish I could turn off my phone, but I'm worried I'll miss a call from Detective Stephner.

Finally, the texts stop coming and then after what feels like hours, the phone rings.

'Wait. Are you sure it's him?' Luke asks as I reach for my phone on the coffee table.

I check the screen then nod. 'Yeah.' Picking up my phone, I wander toward the hallway as I answer it, wanting to have a little bit of privacy.

'Hello?' I answer tentatively after I'm out of the view of the living room.

'Oh, good, you're awake,' he says, sounding relieved. 'I thought about calling you tomorrow, but wanted to let you know so that maybe you could sleep in just a little bit later.'

My heart leaps inside my chest. 'You caught him.'

I can hear the smile in his voice when he says, 'Yeah, we caught him.'

'And you can keep him in jail, right?'

'Yeah, we have him for a lot of things.' He's vague, but he usually is with this kind of stuff.

'Has he said anything about why he did it?' I wonder, resting my head against the wall. 'Because he was texting me earlier and said something about revenge.'

'Yeah, he said a little bit about it.' He proceeds with caution. 'Violet, I have to be honest with you. I've had my suspicions about Danny Huntersonly' – he refers to Preston by his real name – 'and his motives for what he's been doing to you.'

I suck in a sharp breath. 'Oh my God, he's the killer, isn't he?' My heart slams against my chest and I almost buckle to the ground.

'Not quite.'

'Not quite. How can he be a not-quite-killer?' I must be talking loud, because Luke rounds the corner with worry on his face. And the worry only magnifies when he see the shocked and horrified look on my face.

'What's wrong?' he whispers, but I hold up a finger, indicating him to be quiet, so instead he holds my hand and I clutch onto it for dear life.

The detective sighs. 'I've had a suspicion after digging into things that Danny might have been related to the killer. And after we arrested him today and questioned him, my suspicions are right. Danny Huntersonly is the son of Benny Huntersonly, the man who killed your mother and father, something Danny confessed.'

My grip tightens on Luke's hand, my palms starting to sweat. 'And where is this Benny Huntersonly now?'

'He's dead,' he replies solemnly and it's like a blow to the gut. 'He took his own life not too long after he killed your parents. Danny said he was doing drugs and not taking his medication when he broke into your parents' house with Mira Price to rob them. Not sure how much of that is true, but I'm working on it.'

'And what about me?' I ask. 'Why did Preston . . . I mean, Danny, do all this shit to me?'

'Revenge. Obsession. He's out of his mind. Honestly I don't know.'

I don't want to ask it, don't want to think of my mother this way, but I need to know. 'The robbery . . . it didn't have to do with my mom doing drugs, did it?'

He pauses. 'I'm not sure yet. Like I said, there's still a lot I don't know, nor can I share with you yet because it could ruin the case. I just wanted to call you because you deserve to know – deserve to be able to relax. I know you haven't done it in a while.'

'In years,' I whisper.

I can hear him rustling through papers and a phone ringing in the background, probably still at the station. 'Then right now you should just relax and get some sleep. It's probably been hard for the last couple of months.'

I start to smile and cry at the same time as waves of emotions ripple over me. Some of relief. Some of heartache. Some I don't even recognize. 'Okay, I will.'

Luke's freaking out – I can see it in his brown eyes,

so I give his hand a reassuring squeeze. *It's okay. I'm going to be okay.*

Either the detective can hear my thoughts or hear my tears because he says, 'Violet, it's going to be okay.'

It takes me a moment to answer, to process everything that he just told me. I'm not sure how I feel about Preston being the son of the man who took my parents' life. I feel sick to my stomach. Disgusted. Disappointed. Confused. There's a lot of history with Preston and I, a lot of things that I did, and all that stuff slams me in the chest at once. I almost fall.

Almost, but not quite.

I grasp tighter onto Luke's hand. I don't want to live in the past, let my guilt control me like that, let Preston control me like that.

It's still a lot to take in and I know there's something that can briefly take it all away, but that's the thing. It'll only be temporary and if I survive whatever crazy, erratic thing I do, everything will still be the same afterward and I'll still have to face it.

'I know it is,' I whisper through my tears and it feels like the truth. For once, it feels like everything's going to be okay. Yes, not everything turned out perfect. In fact, if I really analyze it, I can see all the ugliness and darkness that has come out of this. I could sink back into that dark hole and let it eat me up, like I did for years. But I've only just climbed out of that fucking hole and I don't want to go back. I want to be strong. I want to let myself be happy.

And let myself be in love.

Two things I never, ever thought were going to be possible, but then I had a taste of them and it was wonderful – I'm not ready to let the wonderful go. I know nothing will ever be perfect; things won't always turn out the way that I want. That's not how life works and perfect doesn't exist. But for the most part, everything will be okay if I just let it be. And I'm going to try my damn hardest; I'm going to go on living life, trying to get better instead of worse. And I have Luke by my side.

And really, that's all I need.

Chapter 27

One month later . . .

Violet

'Are you sure this is a good idea?' I ask, as I stare at the roundabout. It's barely December but winter has rolled in and has turned the entire park into a winter wonderland. Ice glazes everything and all of the swings glisten with frost.

Luke nods as he brushes some of the snow off the roundabout. 'Lana told you to do something childishly fun so here you go.'

I pull my coat tighter around myself, wishing I'd had time to shower before we came here. But Luke picked me up straight from the gym after my kickboxing thing with Callie and Seth, something I do at least twice a week. 'But it's freezing.'

He cocks an eyebrow at me as he brushes the snow off my gloves. 'Since when does snow make you back down from a challenge?'

Snow is falling from the sky even though the sun is peeking through the clouds. 'How did this become a challenge?'

'Because I'm making it a challenge,' he tells me cockily as he zips up the leather jacket he's wearing and waits for me to get on the frozen deathtrap.

Earlier this week, Lana had suggested that I do something fun, something that I missed out on when I was younger. Luke came up with this idea when I couldn't figure out one on my own. Said he played at the park sometimes when he was hiding from his mother.

'Oh fine.' I walk over to the thing that looks like a flying saucer with bars on the top of it and hop on. The chilled metal sinks through my clothes and freezes my skin as I sit down in the center and hold onto the bars. 'Now what?'

He gets this goofy grin on his face and I know I'm in trouble. 'Now you hang on.' Before I can say anything else, he takes off running, holding onto the bars so it causes the roundabout to spin. The faster he runs the faster the thing spins until everything around me is a blur of shapes and colors. Then he jumps on himself and joins me in the center.

I'm laughing my ass off as my eyes fight to focus on something around me, but I just get dizzy, so instead I focus on Luke's face.

'See, fun, right?' he asks, gripping onto the bar.

I nod, smiling as I stare up at the sky. 'It feels like I'm in the center of the world and everything around me is moving.'

He chuckles. 'There's that philosophy class showing again.'

'It's a fun class,' I admit, daring to let go of the bars and spin freely, feeling as though I'm flying. Luke's hands clamp down on my legs as if he's afraid the force is going to send me flying, which only makes my grin expand. 'I picked a major today.'

'Really?'

I nod.

He waits for me to explain but then grows impatient. 'Are you going to tell me what it is?'

My smile takes up my entire face. 'Physics.'

His grip tightens on my legs as the roundabout continues to spin. 'Are you being serious?'

I look away from the sky and to him, nodding. 'Someone told me I'd be good at it once.'

His lips quirk. 'Sounds like a smart person if you ask me.'

'Yeah, a real genius,' I say with a grin. 'We'll see how it goes, though. I still might change it.'

'I don't think you will,' he says as the roundabout starts to slow.

'We'll see.' I grow quiet as the spinning slows to a stop and suddenly it feels like we're grounded, but neither of us move. 'How's your job going?'

'Good.' Luke's been working at the gym for the last few weeks and he seems happy about not having to work at the bar anymore. 'I mean, I don't want to do it forever, but it'll get me through school.' He pauses, then sits up. 'Oh yeah, I forgot to tell you. I got a text from Ryler this morning.'

Ryler is Luke's mute cousin that I met once when we were in Vegas. His dad's an asshole and I felt kind of bad for him, especially since he also grew up in foster homes.

'Oh, yeah? What'd he say?'

'That he was thinking about starting next semester at the University of Wyoming and wondered if it'd be okay if he crashed with us for a few days when he got out here, until he found a place to live. I told him sure.'

'Good, I feel bad for him.'

'Because he can't talk?'

I shake my head. 'No, because he didn't have a real family growing up.'

Luke looks at me with empathy. 'Speaking of families, how have you been doing with all the trial stuff?'

I scoot closer to him as the wind starts to blow and snow flurries around us. 'You ask me that all the time.'

'I know, but I want to make sure you're okay all the time,' he says, brushing a snowflake off my cheek.

His touch warms me from my head to my toes to my soul. 'I'm still doing okay, although I'll be more okay when Preston starts trial.'

Luke shakes his head, anger flashing in his eyes, which happens every time we talk about Preston. 'I still can't believe he's saying he did all that stuff because he blamed your family for what his father did. Guy seriously has some bolts loose.'

'I know, but at least he's behind bars, right?' Although I wish he was being sentenced for more, that somehow he could be blamed for what his father did. I know it's kind of selfish of me to want it, and that really I know he doesn't deserve that, it's just hard sometimes thinking about how his father is dead and will never actually pay for what he did. 'How about you?'

He sucks in a slow breath. 'I'm doing fine, but I'm glad I got my part over with.'

Luke was called up last week and questioned. He was really nervous about doing it, but the important part is that he did; he conquered his fear of his mother and let the world know what a monster she is.

'Thank you for doing that.' I press my lips to his and give him a soft kiss.

'I'm not going to lie,' he says. 'I did partly do it for myself.'

'I'm still glad you did it.'

'Me too.'

We sit back and enjoy the quiet for a while until the wind kicks up, then he takes my hand and pulls me to my feet. 'Ready to do the rest of Lana's challenge?'

I instantly frown. The rest of the challenge is a lot harder than playing at the playground. 'I don't know if I can do it,' I admit.

'Yes, you can,' he encourages, taking both of my hands in his and guiding me off the roundabout.

I hop off with him and land in the snow. 'But what if you're wrong? What if we drive all the way out there and I freak out and can't do it?'

He offers me one of my favorite smiles. 'Then I guess I'll get to spend some time with you.'

'You spend all the time with me, pretty much, now.'

'Now I'll get more.' He tugs on my arm and pulls me through the snow toward his truck and I reluctantly drag my feet as I follow after him. When he feels the weight of my walk, he pauses and looks at me. 'Baby, you don't have to do it if you don't want to. I would never make you do anything you don't want to.'

'I know you wouldn't.' I stand there in the middle of the snow, holding his hand, terrified out of my mind. I've dealt with so much stuff lately I'm not sure if I'm ready for this. But then again, if I don't do it now then I'll just think about how I didn't do it and it'll drive me mad and I'll disappoint myself. 'No, I'm ready,' I say, then pull him toward the truck, so that I'm the one choosing to do this.

Because in the end, it has to be my choice.

Two hours, five *Eagles* songs, and one 'Songs that Remind me of Violet' mixed tape later, we're pulling up to the cemetery I've been dreading coming to. It's bad enough in my dreams, but seeing it in real life it's . . .

'It's so empty and quiet,' I whisper, as I press my

face to the window and stare out at the frosted ground dotted with headstones.

Luke puts the truck in park and leaves the engine running. 'Do you want me to come with you?' he asks.

I shake my head with hesitancy. 'No, this is something I have to do on my own.'

It takes me at least fifteen minutes to get out of the truck, but Luke waits patiently in my silence never questioning or pushing me, one of the things that I love about him. Finally, I get the door open and step out into the snow. It takes me another ten minutes before I actually make it through the gate and into the cemetery itself.

This is the first time I've ever stepped foot into a cemetery since I was five years old. The air is cold, the trees leafless, the headstones all a painful reminder of why I'm here – who I'm here to see. Lana told me that it would be good for me. That it'd be healthy to finally face this milestone in my life. That I've been doing so well and that maybe it's time, not necessarily to say goodbye to my parents, but to accept that they're gone and that I'm still alive and that that is okay.

I don't even know how I find their headstones so easily. Maybe it's my subconscious or maybe I just luck out, but it only takes me a few minutes of wandering around before I see two Hayes' tombstones, side by side.

I sit down in front of them, in the snow, even though it's freezing. I trace hearts patterns in the frost, avoid saying anything for the longest time, but then it all comes spilling out suddenly.

'I used to be so lost.' I pick at the frostbitten grass as the wind dances around me. 'In fact, I've been lost since you guys had to go, up until a month or so ago.

'It might sound weird, but I felt like if I let myself have direction, have purpose, let people into my life, care for them, that eventually it would all be taken away from me and I'd be left alone again, drowning in my pain. In the weather, the words of the people around me, in the eyes of others.' I scoop up a handful of snow and let it slowly slip from my fingertips. 'I used to be so good at masking off my emotions. I had these little tricks, ways to numb myself to the point that anything I was feeling inside was overpowered by an emotion much stronger than any other. Fear. The fear of death. Although, I worked a little different.'

I let the grass go in my hand, sit back and utter words I've never dared to truly say aloud before. 'Death wasn't so much a thrill as a panicking thrill to me. Was I terrified of dying?' I consider the question and admit the truth. 'I thought I wasn't – thought I was fearless. But it turns out I wasn't . . . turns out I didn't want to die. It took me a while and a lot of self-torture to realize that. That really what I wanted was what I was most afraid of.'

Tears sting my eyes as emotions prick inside me but I let them come because I know that eventually they calm down and I'll survive through it. 'Things haven't been so easy for me, mostly because of my own doing. I guess that's what I've learned over the last few months . . . Lana told me that's what I was supposed to do here,' I mutter. 'Admit what I've learned – how I've healed.' I pause, gathering all the strength I have in me. I have to glance over my shoulder at Luke in his truck and that gives me the extra boost I need. 'What I've learned is that I wasn't just pushing myself toward death. That I put a wall up around myself to keep me away from everyone, so I wouldn't have to feel anything because no one can hurt you if they don't know you, right? That was my motto in life. I think it partly came from being passed through foster family after foster family, but some of it stemmed from the fact that I experienced a loss so great that I never wanted to feel it again.'

I start to choke up and the letters on the headstone become blurry, beginning to melt away. 'But I'm getting better. I can't take all the credit, though. I've got some great friends and a boyfriend who help me every single day. I'm even going to a therapist. It's crazy, but for once things actually feel okay.' I raise my wrist and pull back my sleeve, showing that I have the bracelet with *Sempre* on it. 'I've been doing a little research and found out that you guys went to Italy for your honeymoon because Dad has a little bit of Italian in him. I'm not sure how Mom got the bracelet exactly, but I'd like to think that you gave it to her while you were there. It seems like such a nice story.' I lower my hand to my lap and let the tears pour out, knowing that my story will always be just a story, that I'll never know for sure, but that there's nothing I can do about that but accept it and hold onto what I do have – my life.

With tears still flowing from my eyes, I lean forward and press my hand to my mother's headstone. 'I do miss you . . . God, I miss you . . .' The tears flood my eyes, overpowering me. My initial reaction is to force them back, stop them, but it's why I'm here. Live and learn. I move my hand to my father's next and start to sob. 'I wish you could be here to meet everyone

. . . I wish a lot of things . . . but I guess that's another thing that I've learned. Wishes are just wishes. Destiny is just destiny. And neither really has control over your life. Shit happens, shapes our lives, but it doesn't have to shape who we are. And I'm trying now, to be a daughter you can both be proud of.' I suck in another breath and say the last thing I need to say. 'I love you both. I'll love you forever.'

I let myself cry until my tears become frozen to my eyes, until the sadness in my heart shifts to contentment, then I get up and make my way back to the truck, wiping the tears from my eyes.

'Are you okay?' Luke asks as I hop in and shut the door.

I give one last look at the cemetery and then turn to him. 'You know what, I really, really am.' I can't help myself. I lean over and kiss him because in the end, it's all I need. Just Luke and I, and the certainty of our future.

Epilogue

Two years and one month later . . .

Luke

'This scarf smells like cheese,' I say, biting back a laugh. 'Please, let me take it off before the smell gets stuck in my nostrils.'

'Still not taking it off,' he says, clearly amused with himself.

I've been cracking jokes left and right for the last hour to entertain myself, since Luke won't tell me where we're driving to. It's driving me crazy; Christmas day, a spontaneous trip for which I have to be blind-folded the entire time. What the hell? Yeah, that was pretty much my response when I opened my present and there was the little piece of paper which he'd put in the box with the scarf. It wasn't as good a present as last year, but I'm assuming it's because our whole 'seize the holiday' motto is starting to die down.

'Pretty please.' I clasp my hands together and give him my best begging look.

He chuckles. 'No way.'

Dammit. It's the eyes that always win him over. That's why this isn't working – because he can't see my eyes.

Sighing, I give up and sit back in the seat, enduring the last half an hour in eager anticipation, listening to a tape that I know is labeled with my name.

Finally the truck stops and I hear him put it in park. I wait for him to tell me to take off the blindfold, but instead all I hear is him switching tapes, then he gets out of the truck.

What the hell?

I reach to take my blindfold off as 'The River' by Manchester Orchestra starts playing through the stereo, really, really loud. A memory tickles at my mind and I throw off the blindfold. 'Oh my God.' My jaw instantly drops at the sight of the snowy mountains and trees before me, highlighted by the headlights of his truck.

Luke is waiting for me at the front of the truck,

kicking the tips of his boots against the snow with his hands in the pockets of his coat. It takes me a moment or two to get the courage to do so, knowing that once I step foot out the door everything is about to change. I have to really think about it. Do I want that change?

Yes, I do. God, do I want the change.

With a trembling heart and fingers, I push open the door and step outside, leaving the door open so the music can flow outside. Luke doesn't look up at me until I'm halfway around the truck, about to step up to him.

His eyes are filled with nerves and he's shivering either from the cold or from the fact that he's clearly nervous. 'Now, if you listen really quietly,' he says, cupping his ear as he leans toward the trees. 'You can hear the faintest sound of crazy animals.'

I press my lips together, trying not to smile at the fact that he remembers that almost two years ago I set up this scenario, when a guy proposed to a girl in a restaurant in what I thought was a very clichéd way.

I make my way over to him and he reaches into his pocket to take something out. I hold my breath in anticipation but then frown in confusion when he holds out the silver bracelet that belonged to my mother.

'I thought you should have this on when this

happened, so that your parents could be with you in a way.' I try not to cry as he puts the bracelet on my wrist, but a tear or two slips from my eyes. Then he steps back and pats his pockets before letting out a breath. 'Now, I know getting down on one knee is a little clichéd.' His smile is all nerves but it's ridiculously adorable. 'But I'm going to do it anyway.'

I suck in a deep breath as he drops down to his knee right there in the snow. Then he pulls out a small black box from his jacket and holds it up. 'Violet Hayes, will you marry me?'

He opens the box up and if I wasn't already going to say yes, I would have now. Because what's inside it is my ring – the purple one surrounded by onyx gems that I was once given as a Christmas present, before it was taken away. Of course it's not the exact same ring. It looks a bit smaller, but a bit shinier. It looks a bit more perfect.

I'm not going to cry, I tell myself. Because even though I let myself feel everything now, I don't want to be that girl that sobs like a baby because she's going to get married.

But I turn into that girl, tears pouring out of my eyes as I nod my head. Then getting back my dignity, I say, 'Hell yeah, I'll marry you.'

He laughs, but it looks like tears are staining his eyes too, the big softy that he is. Then he gets to his feet, puts the ring on my finger, and kisses me the way he's been kissing me every day for two years.

With passion.

With certainty.

With love.

Have you read the first book in the story of
Violet and Luke?

Find out how it all began in

The Destiny of Violet & Luke

Read on for an extract . . .

Prologue

Luke

(Eight years old)

I hate running, but it always seems like I'm doing it. Always running everywhere. Always trying to hide. I hide just as much as I run, but if I don't then bad things will happen. Like getting found. Or getting forced to do things that make me sick to my stomach. Getting forced to help *her*.

"Come out, come out wherever you are," my mom sing-songs as I run out the front door of my house. Her voice is slurred, which means she's been taking her medication again. She takes her medication a lot and it doesn't make any sense to me. I have to take medication sometimes, too, but because I get sick. Whenever she takes it, it seems to make her sicker.

She used to not be like this, well not as bad anyway. About a year ago, when my dad was still around she would act normal and not take medication. Now, though, she does it a lot and I think she might be going crazy. At least she seems that way compared to everyone else's moms. I see them picking up my friends from school and they always look happy and put together. My friends are always glad to see them and they don't run and hide from them, like I do all the time.

I race around to the back of the house, running away from the sound of her voice as she chases after me, looking for me. She's always looking for me and I hate when she does—hate her sometimes for always making me run and hide. And for finding me. I usually hide underneath the bed or in the closet or somewhere else in the house, but she's been finding me quicker lately, so today I decided to hide outside.

As I make it to the back porch stairs, I slam to a stop, panting to catch my breath. There's just enough room for me to duck down below the decaying boards and hide underneath. I pull my legs up against me and lower my head onto my knees. The sunlight sparkles through the cracks in the wood and down on me. I'm nervous because if the sun can see me, then maybe she might see me, too.

I scoot back, closer to the bottom step and out of the sunlight, and then I hold my breath as I hear the screen door hinges creak.

"Luke," my mom says from up on the top step. She shuffles across the wood in her slippers and the screen door bangs shut. "Luke, are you out here?"

I tuck my face into my arms, sucking back the tears, even though I want to cry—she'll hear me if I do. Then she'll probably want to hug me better and I don't like when she does that.

I don't like a lot of things she does and how wrong she makes my life feel.

"Luke Price," she warns, stepping down the stairs. I peek up at her through the cracks and see her pink furry slippers. The smoke from her cigarette makes my stomach burn. "If you're out here and you're ignoring me, you're going to be in trouble." She almost sings it, like it's a song to some game we're playing. Sometimes I think that's what this is to her. A game that I always lose.

The stairs creak as she slowly walks down to the bottom step. Ashes from her cigarette scatter across the ground and all over my head. A few land in my mouth, but I don't spit. I stay as still as I can, fighting to keep my heart from beating so loudly as my palms sweat.

Finally, after what seems like forever, she turns around and heads up the stairs back to the house. "Fine, have it your way, then," she says.

It's never my way and I know better than to think so. That's why I stay still even after the screen door shuts. I barely breathe as the wind blows and the sunlight dims. I wait until the sky is almost gray before I peek up through the cracks in the stairs. If I had my way I'd stay here forever, hiding under the stairs, but I'm hungry and tired.

I can't see or hear her anymore so I lean forward, poke my head out from under the stairs. The coast looks clear so I put my hands down on the dirt and crawl out onto the grass. I get to my feet and brush the dirt and the rocks off my torn jeans. Then, taking a deep breath, I run around to the side of the house and hurry quickly up the fence line until I make it to the front yard.

I've never liked where we live that much. Everyone's grass always looks yellow and all the houses look like they need to be repainted. My mom says it's because we're poor and this is all we can afford thanks to my dad leaving us and that he doesn't care and that's why he never comes to see me. I'm not sure I believe her since my mom's always telling lies. Like how she promises me time and time again that this will be the last time she makes me do things I don't want to do.

I stand in the front yard for a while, figuring out where to go. I could climb through my sister's bedroom window and hide out there until she gets home, then maybe she can help me. But she's been acting strange lately and gets annoyed whenever I talk to her. She's lucky because Mom never seems to notice her as much as she notices me. I don't know why. I do my best to blend in. I don't make messes, keeping the house clean and organized like she likes it. I keep quiet. I stay in my room a lot and organize my toys in categories, just the way she likes them, yet she's always calling for me. But Amy seems invisible to her.

She's so lucky. I wish I were invisible.

I decide to go for a walk down to the gas station at the corner where I can get a candy bar or something because my stomach hurts from hunger. But as my feet touch the sidewalk, I hear the front door swing open.

"Luke, get in here right now," she says in a frenzy, snapping her fingers and pointing to the ground below her feet. "I need you."

I freeze, wishing I were brave enough to take off running down the sidewalk. Just leave. Never come back. Sleep in a box because a box seems so much nicer than my sterilized house. But I'm not brave and I turn around and face her just like she wants me to. She's holding the door open, her hair pulled up messily on top of her head and she's wearing this purple tank top and plaid shorts that she always wears. It's pretty much like a uniform for her, except she doesn't have a job. Not a good one anyway where she has to wear a uniform. Instead, she sells her medicine to creepy men who are always staring at her or Amy when she walks out of her bedroom.

She crooks her finger at me. "Get in here."

An unsteady breath leaves my mouth as I trudge to the front door, a nauseating feeling rising in my stomach. It happens every time she needs me. I get sick to my stomach at the thoughts of what she's going to make me do creep inside my head.

When I reach the stairs, she moves back, not looking happy, but not looking sad either. She holds the door open for me, watching me with her brown eyes that remind me of the bag of marbles she made me throw away because they didn't look right. Once I'm inside, she closes the door and shoves the deadbolt over. She fastens the small chain and then clicks the lock on the doorknob before turning around.

The curtains are shut and there's a lit cigarette on a teal glass ashtray that's on the coffee table, filling the room with smoke. There's a sofa just behind the table and it's covered in plastic to keep "the dirty air from ruining the fabric," my mother told me once. She always thinks the dirt in the air is going to do something to either the house or her, which is why she rarely goes outside anymore.

"Why'd you run off?" she asks me as she walks over to the sofa and flops down in it. She picks up her cigarette and ashes it, before putting it into her mouth. She takes a deep inhale and seconds later a cloud of smoke circles around her sore-covered face. "Were you playing a game or something?"

I nod, because telling her I was playing a game is much better than telling her I was hiding from her. "Yes."

She takes another drag from the cigarette and then stares at the row of cat figurines on one of the shelves lining the living room walls. Each row on the shelf is organized with figurines, according to breed. She did it once when she was having one of her episodes from too much medication, the one that makes her stay awake for a long, long time, not the stuff that makes her pass out. The glass clinking together and her incoherent murmuring had woken me up when she was rearranging the figurines and when I'd walked out she was moving like crazy, frantically trying to get the animals into order or "something bad was going to happen." She knew it was—she could feel it in her bones. I think something bad already did happen, though. A lot of bad things actually.

"Luke, pay attention," my mom says. I tear my gaze away from the figurines, wishing I was one of them, so I could be up on the shelf, watching what's about to happen instead of taking part in it. She switches her cigarette to her other hand and then leans to the side, grabbing her small wooden "medication box." She sets it on her lap, puts the cigarette into her mouth one last time, and then places it down so she can turn on the lamp. "Now quit messing around and come here, would ya?"

My body gets really tight and I glance over my shoulder at the front door, crossing my fingers that Amy will come home and interrupt us long enough that I can find another place to hide. But she doesn't and I'm stuck out here. With her.

"Do I have to?" I utter quietly.

She nods with chaotic frenzy in her eyes. "You need to."

Shaking, I turn back around and trudge over to the sofa. I take a seat beside her and she pats me on the head several times like I'm her pet. She does that a lot and it makes me wonder how she sees me; if I'm kind of like a pet to her instead of her kid.

"You were a bad boy today," she says as her fingers continue to touch my hair. I hate it when she does that and it makes me want to shave my head bald so she won't be able to touch me. "You should have come when I called you."

"I'm sorry," I lie, because I'm only sorry I was found. I need to find better hiding spots and stay in them long enough that she'll stop looking for me, then maybe I can become invisible like Amy.

"It's okay." She strokes my cheek and then my neck before pulling her hand away. She places a kiss on my cheek and I shut my eyes, holding my breath, trapping in a scream because I want to shout: *Don't touch me!* "I know deep down you're a good boy."

No, I'm not. I'm terrible because I hate you. I really do. I hate you so much I wish you were gone.

She starts humming a song she made up as she removes the lid from the box and carefully sets it aside. I don't even have to look inside it to know what's in it. A spoon, a lighter, a small plastic baggie that holds this stuff that looks almost like brown sugar, a thin piece of cotton, a half a bottle of water, a big rubber band thing, and a needle and syringe that she probably stole from the stash I use to give myself insulin shots.

"Now you remember what to do?" she asks, and then starts humming again.

I nod, tears burning in the corners of my eyes because I don't want to do it—I don't want to do anything that she tells me. "Yes."

"Good." She pats my head again, this time a little rougher.

I don't watch her as she opens the baggie and puts some of the brown sugary stuff onto the metal spoon along with some water, but I can pretty much visualize her movements since I've seen her do this a lot, sometimes twice a day. It really depends on how much she's talking to herself. If it's a lot then she brings out the needle a lot. But sometimes, when she gets quieter, it's not so bad. I like the quieter days, ones where she's either focused on cleaning or stuck in her head. Or I'll even take her being passed out.

She heats the spoon with the lighter as she mutters lyrics under her breath. She actually has a beautiful voice, but the words she sings are frightening. After the spoon is heated enough, she ties the rubber band around her arm, I sit on the couch beside her, tapping my fingers on my leg, pretending I'm in there instead of here. Anywhere but here.

I hate her.

"All right, Luke, help me out, okay," she finally says after she's melted her medication into a pool of liquid and sucked some into the syringe.

I turn toward her, shaking nervously. Always shaking. Always nervous, all the time. Always so worried I'll do something wrong. Mess up. She instantly hands me the syringe and then extends her arm onto my lap. She has these purple marks and red dots all over her upper forearm from all the other times the needles have gone into her. Her veins are really dark on her skin and I don't like the sight of the needle going in just as much as she does like it. Like a routine, I point the needle toward her arm near where all the other dots on her skin are.

My hand quivers unsteadily. "Please don't make me do this," I whisper. "Please Mom." I don't know why I even try, though. She'll do anything to get her medication. And I mean anything. Dark things that normal people wouldn't do.

"Deep breaths, remember?" She ignores me as she wraps her free arm around the back of my neck. "Remember, don't miss the vein. You can mess up my arm or even kill me if you're not careful, okay?" She says it so sweetly like it's a nice thing to say and will make me less nervous.

But it makes things worse, especially because part of me wishes I'd miss the vein. I have to take a lot of breaths before I can settle down inside and get my thoughts from going to that dark place they always want to go, reminding myself that I don't want to hurt her. *I don't.*

When I get my nerves under control the best that I can, I sink the needle into her vein, like I've done hundreds of times. Each time it gets to me, like I'm sticking the needle in my own skin and feeling the sting. I wince as her muscles tense a little underneath the poke of the needle. As I push in the plunger, the medicine enters her veins and seconds later she lets out this weird noise, before sinking back on the couch, pulling me down with her. I hurry and pull the needle out before we fall down completely onto the couch cushions.

"Thank you, Luke," she says sleepily, patting my head with her hand as she holds me against her. Her throat makes this vibrating noise, like she's trying to hum again, but the noise is trapped like I am.

I press my lips together, staring at the wall across the room, barely breathing. After a while, her arm falls lifelessly to the side, her hand hitting the floor as her eyelids flutter shut and I'm temporarily freed from her hold.

I sit up, sucking the tears back, hating her for making me do this and hating myself for doing it and being secretly glad she's passed out. I toss the syringe down on the table, then I push to my feet. Using all my strength, I rotate her to her side because sometimes she throws up. I have a house full of quiet now, just how I like it. Yet, at the same time I don't like it because the emptiness gets to me. What I really want is what all the other kids have. The ones I see at the park playing on swings while their parents push them higher. They're always laughing and smiling. Everyone always seems to be, except for me. Every time I get close I always remember this feeling I have inside me right now, this vile, icky feeling, mixed with hatred and sadness that makes me sick all the time. It always wipes the smile right off my face and I don't even bother trying anymore. Happiness isn't real. It's make-believe.

I throw the syringe and spoon into the box, wondering if my life will always be this way. If I'll always carry so much sadness and hate inside me. I'm shaking by the time I get everything into the box and I feel like I need to flee somewhere—run again. I can't take this anymore. I can't take living here. With her.

"I can't take it!" I shout at the top of my lungs and ram my fist into the coffee table. My hand makes this popping sound and it hurts so bad tears sting at my eyes. I cry out in pain, sinking to the floor, but of course no one hears me.

No one ever does.

Violet

(Thirteen years old)

I hate moving. Not just from house to house, but from family to family. I hate moving my legs and arms, moving forward in my life, because it usually means I'm going to someplace new. If I had my way, I'd remain motionless, never moving forward, never going anywhere. The thing is I always have to, it's not a choice, and I never know exactly where I'm going or who I'll be stuck with. Sometimes the families are fine, but sometimes not. Drunks. Religious freaks. Haters. Wandering hands.

The family I'm staying with now always tells me everything I do is wrong and that I should be more like their daughter, Jennifer. I'm not sure why they took me in to begin with. They seem pretty content with the child they have and I'm just a decoration, a flashy object they can show off to their friends so they can get told how great they are for taking in such a messed-up child. I'm the unwanted orphan they took in, hoping to fix me and make their family appear wonderful.

"It was so nice of you to give her a home," a woman with fiery red hair tells Amelia, who's my mother at the moment. She's having one of her neighborhood shindigs, which she does a lot, then complains about them later to her husband. "These poor children really do need a roof over their head."

Amelia glances at me, sitting in a chair at the table where I was directed to stay the entire party. "Yes, but it's hard, you know." She's wearing this yellow sweater that reminds me of a canary that was a pet at one of my foster parents' homes that never stopped chattering. She arranges some crackers and sliced cheese onto a large flowery platter and then heads for the refrigerator. "She's kind of a problem child." She opens the fridge door and takes out a large pitcher of lemonade. She looks over at me again, then leans toward the redhead, lowering her voice. "She's so angry all the time and she broke this vase the other day because she couldn't find her shoes...but we're working on fixing her."

Angry all the time. That's what everyone seems to say; I'm so angry at the world and it's understandable considering what I've been through, yet no one wants to deal with it. That I probably have too much rage inside me. That I'm broken. Unstable. Maybe even dangerous. All the things that no adult wants in a child. They want smiles and laughter, children who will make them smile and laugh, too. I'm the dark, morbid side of childhood. I swear they're waiting around for me to do something that will give them an excuse to get rid of me and they can tell everyone they tried but I was just too messed up to be fixed.

"And her nightmares," Amelia continues. "She wakes up screaming every night and she wet the bed the other night. She even came running into our room, saying she was scared to sleep alone." Her eyes glide to the tattered purple teddy bear I'm hugging. "She's very immature and carries that stuffed animal around with her everywhere...it's strange."

I hate her. She doesn't understand what it's like to see things that most people can't even admit exist. The ugly truth, painted in red, stuck in my head, images I can't shake. Death. Cruelty. Terror. People taking other people's lives as if lives mean nothing. Then they leave me behind to carry the foul, rotting truth with me. Alone. *Why did they leave me behind?*

327

This teddy bear is all I have left of a time when ugly didn't consume my life.

I turn my head away from the sound of her voice and stare out the window at the sunlight reflecting against a lawn ornament shaped like a tulip, and hug the teddy bear against my chest, the one my dad gave me as an early birthday present the day before he died. There are little red, heart-shaped beads on the tulip and when they catch in the light they flicker and make dots dance against the concrete on the back porch. It's pretty to watch and I focus on them, shoving my anger down and bottling it up—trying to stay in control of my emotions. Otherwise all the feelings I've buried will escape and I'll have no choice but to find a way to shut it down—find my adrenaline rush.

Besides, Amelia doesn't need to repeat what I already know. I know what I do every night, just like I know what I am to them, just like I know in a few months or so they'll get tired of me and send me to another place with a different home where everything I do will annoy those people, too, and eventually they'll pass me along. It's like clockwork and I don't expect anything more. Expecting only leads to disappointment. I expected things once when I was little—that I'd continue to grow up with my mom and dad, smile, and be happy—but that dream was crushed the day they died.

"Violet," Amelia snaps and I quickly turn my head to her. She and her redheaded friend are staring at me with worry and a hint of fear in their eyes and I wonder just how much her friend knows about me. Does she know about that night? What I saw? What I escaped? What I didn't escape? Does it make her afraid of me? "Are you listening to me?" she asks.

I shake my head. "No."

She crooks her eyebrow at me as she opens the cupboard above her head. "No, what?"

I set the teddy bear on my lap and tell myself to shut off the anger because the last time I released it, I ended up breaking lots of things, then got sent here. "No, ma'am."

Her eyebrow lowers as she selects a few cans of beans out from a top cupboard. "Good, now if you would just listen the first time then we'd be on track."

"I'm listening now," I say to her, which results in her face pinching. "Sorry. I'm listening now, ma'am."

She glares at me coldly as she stacks the cans on the countertop and takes a can opener out from a drawer. "I said would you go into the garage and get me some hamburger meat from the storage freezer."

I nod and hop off the chair, taking the teddy bear with me, relieved to get out of the stuffy kitchen and away from her friend who keeps looking at me like I'm about to stab her. As I head out the door into the garage I hear Amelia saying, "I think we might contact social services to take her back...she just wasn't what we were expecting."

Never expect anything, I want to turn around and tell her, but I continue out into the garage. The lights are on and I trot down the steps and wind around the midsize car toward the freezer in the corner. But I pause when I notice Jennifer in the corner, along with a boy and two girls who are messing around with bikes in the garage.

"Well, well look what the dog dragged in," she sneers as she moves her bike away from the wall. Her bike is pink, just like the dress she's wearing. I used to have a bike once, too, only it was purple, because I hate pink. But I never learned how to ride it and now it's part of my old life, boxed away and sold along with the rest of my childhood. "It's Violet and that stupid bear." She glances at her friends. "She always carries it around with her like a little baby or something."

I keep the bear close and disregard her the best that I can, because it's all I can do. This isn't my house or my family and no one's going to take my side. I'm alone in the world. It's something I learned early on and becoming used to the idea of always being alone has made life a little easier to live over the last several years.

I hurry past her and her friends who laugh when she utters under her breath that I smell like a homeless person. I open the freezer and take out a frozen pound of hamburger meat, then shut the lid and turn back for the door. Jennifer has abandoned her bike to strategically place herself in front of my path back to the door.

"Would you please move?" I ask politely, tucking the hamburger meat under one of my arms and my teddy bear under the other. I dodge to the side, but Jennifer sidesteps with me, her hands out to the side.

"Troll," the boy laughs and it's echoed by the cackling of laughter.

"This is my house," Jennifer says with a smirk. "Not yours, so you don't get to tell me what to do."

I hold up the hamburger meat, fighting to keep my temper under control. "Yeah, but your mom asked me to get this for her."

She puts her hands on her hips and says to me with an attitude, "That's because she thinks of you as our maid. In fact, I overheard her talking to my dad the other day, telling him that's why they're fostering you—because they needed someone to clean up the house."

Don't let her get to you. It doesn't matter. Nothing does. "Get out of my way," I say through gritted teeth.

She shakes her head. "No way. I don't have to listen to you, you loser, smelly, crazy girl."

The other kids laugh and it takes a lot of energy not to clock her in the face. *You were taught to be better than that. Mom and Dad would want me to be better.* I move around to the other side but she matches my step and kicks me in the shin. A throbbing pain ricochets up my leg, but I don't give her the satisfaction of a reaction, remaining calm.

"No wonder you don't have any parents. They probably didn't want you," she snickers. "Oh wait, that's right. They died...you probably even killed them yourself."

"Shut up," I warn, shaking as I step closer to her. I can feel anger blazing inside me, on the brink of exploding.

"Or what?" she says, refusing to back off. The boy on the floor stands up and starts to head toward us with a look on his face that makes me want to bolt. But I won't. I'm sure they'll chase me if I do and in the end I'm going to get blamed for this incident.

"What do you mean, she killed her parents?" he asks, wiping some grime off his forehead with his thumb.

Jennifer grins maliciously and then turns to him. "Haven't you heard the story about her?"

"Shut up." I cut her off as I move so close to her I almost knock her over, then raise my hand up in front of me, like I'm going to shove her. "I'm warning you."

She keeps talking as if I don't exist. "Her parents were murdered." She glances at me with hate and cruelty in her eyes. "I heard my mom saying she was the one who found them, but I'm guessing it's because she did it herself because she's *crazy*."

I see the image of my mom and dad in their bedroom surrounded by blood and I lose it. I quickly shove the image out of my head until all I see is red. Red everywhere. Blood. Red. Blood. Death. And a stupid little girl who won't walk away from it.

I throw the hamburger meat down on the ground, not concerned about what happens to me, and grab a handful of her long blond hair and yank on it. "Take it back!" I shout, pulling harder as I circle around to the front of the car, away from the boy, dragging Jennifer with me.

She starts to cry, her head tipped back, tears spilling out of her eyes. "You evil bitch!"

"Let her go!" the boy yells, running around the car at us. "You crazy psycho." He turns to the other girls and tells them to go get someone and then they take off running, looking at me like I'm crazy, too.

I know it'll be just moments before Amelia comes out and then not too long after she'll call social services to come take me away. I'm trembling with anger and hate all directed toward Jennifer, because she's the one here in front of me. No one else. My vision blurs along with my head and my heart and it feels like I'm back at my childhood home walking into the room again, seeing the blood...hearing the voices...

I'm trembling so much my fingers have no strength left to hold on to Jennifer and I release her. She immediately stumbles forward into the front of the car. Regaining her balance, she spins around and shoves me so hard I fall to the ground and my head bangs against the wall.

"You psycho!" she shouts, her face bright red, tears streaming out of her eyes. "My mom and dad are so going to send you away."

I stare at the space on the floor in front of her feet, hugging my teddy bear, motionless.

She lets out a frustrated grunt and then stomps her foot on the floor before running out of the garage.

Moments later, Amelia comes rushing in, shouting before she even reaches me. "You're done here! Do you understand?"

"Yes." I don't have a single drop of emotion left and my voice sounds hollow.

"Yes, what?" She waits for me to answer her with her arms crossed.

I don't reply because I don't have to anymore. I'm finished with this home. There's no erasing what just happened. I can't change the past just as much as I can't control my future.

She gets livid, her face tinting pink as she tries to contain her fury. She tells me I'm worthless. She tells me that no one will want me. She tells me I'm leaving. She tells me everything I already know.

"Are you even listening to me?!" she shouts and I shake my head. Fuming, she snatches the bear from my hands.

That snaps me out of my motionless trance. "Hey, that's mine!" I cry, jumping to my feet and lunging for the bear. My shoulder bumps into her arm as she moves it out of my reach.

She moves back and tucks her arm behind her back. "Consider it a punishment for hurting my daughter."

"Your daughter deserved it." I panic. If she does anything to that bear I won't be able to take it. I need that bear or else I can't survive—don't want to. *Why did I survive?*

"Well, when you're ready to apologize to Jennifer, you can have it back." She heads toward the door to the house where Jennifer is standing with a smile on her face, expecting an apology.

"Sorry," I practically growl, wanting the damn bear back enough that I'll do whatever she asks at the moment. "Please, don't take it away." Desperation burns in my voice. "It's all I have left of my mom and dad—it's all I have of them." I'm begging, weak, pathetic. I hate it. I hate myself. But I need that bear.

Jennifer grins at me as she crosses her arms and leans against the doorway, her cheeks stained red from the drying tears. "Mom, I don't think she's really sorry."

Amelia studies me for a moment. "I don't think she is either." She frowns disappointedly, like she's finally seeing that she can't fix me, then turns for the door with my bear in her hand. "You can have it back when I see a real apology come out of that mouth of yours. And you better make it quick because you won't be here for very much longer."

"I said I was sorry," I yell out with my hands balled into fists at my side. "What the hell else do you want me to say?"

She doesn't answer me and goes into the house with my bear. Jennifer smirks at me before turning for the house, shutting the lights off and then closing the door on her way inside.

I'm suffocated by the dark. But it's nothing I can't handle. Seeing things is much harder than seeing nothing but the dark. I like the dark.

I slide down to the ground and lean back against the wall, hugging my knees to my chest as I let the darkness settle over me. A few tears slip out and drip down my cheeks and I let more stream out, telling myself it's okay, because I'm in the dark, and nothing can be seen in the dark.

But after a while I can't get the tears to stop as what

Jennifer and the other kids said plays on repeat inside my head. I think about the last time I saw my parents lying in their coffins and how they got there. The blood. I'll never forget the blood. On the floor. On me.

More tears spill out and soon my whole face is drenched with them. My heart thrashes against my chest and I tug at my hair as I scream through clenched teeth, kicking my feet against the floor. Invisible razors and needles stab underneath my skin. I can't turn off the emotions. I can't think straight. My lungs need air. I hurt. I ache. I can't take it anymore. I need it out. I need to breathe.

I stumble to my feet and through the dark, until I find the door that leads to the driveway. I shove the door open, sprint outside into the sunlight and race past the cars parked in the driveway and toward the curb. I don't slow down until I'm approaching the highway in front of the house where cars zip up and down the road. With no hesitation, I walk into the middle of the road and stand on the yellow dotted line with my arms held out to the side. Tears pool in my eyes as I blink against the sunlight, my pulse speeding up the longer I stay there and that rush of energy that has become the only familiar thing in my life takes over.

It feels like I'm flying, head-on into something other than being moved around, passed around, given away, tossed aside, forgotten. I have the unknown in front of me and I have no idea what's going to happen. It feels so liberating. So I stay in place, even when I hear the roar of a car's engine. I wait until

I hear the sound of the tires. Until I see the car. Until it's close enough that the driver honks their horn. Until I feel the swish of an adrenaline rush, drenching the sadness and panic out of my body and mind. Until my emotions subside and all I feel is exhilaration. Then I jump to the right where the road meets the grass as the car makes a swerve to the left to go around me. Brakes screech. A horn honks. Someone shouts.

I lie soundless in the grass, feeling twenty times better than I did in the garage. I feel content in a dark hole of numbness; a place where I can feel okay being the child that no one wants. The child that probably would have been better off dying with her parents, instead of being left alive and alone.

Don't miss Jessica's latest, passionate series.

Begin with the first book,

Breaking Nova

Nova Reed used to have dreams of becoming a famous drummer, of marrying her true love. But all of that was taken away in an instant. Now she's getting by as best she can, though sometimes that means doing things the old Nova would never do. Things that are slowly eating away at her spirit. Every day blends into the next, until she meets Quinton Carter.

Quinton once got a second chance at life, but he doesn't want it. The tattoos on his chest are a constant reminder of what he's done, what he's lost. He's sworn to never allow happiness into his life, but then beautiful, sweet Nova makes him smile. He knows he's too damaged to get close to her, yet she's the only one who can make him feel alive again. Quinton will have to decide: does he deserve to start over? Or should he pay for his past forever?

Out now.

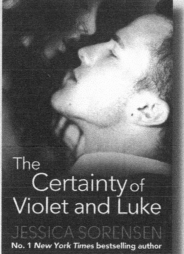